CHRISTOPHER BUSH

THE CASE OF THE THREE LOST LETTERS

With an introduction
by Curtis Evans

DEAN STREET PRESS

INTRODUCTION

RING OUT THE OLD, RING IN THE NEW
CHRISTOPHER BUSH AND MYSTERY FICTION IN THE FIFTIES

"Mr. Bush has an urbane and intelligent way of
dealing with mystery which makes his work much more
attractive than the stampeding sensationalism of some
of his rivals."
—Rupert Crofts-Cooke (acclaimed author of the Leo
Bruce detective novels)

NEW fashions in mystery fiction were decidedly afoot in the
1950s, as authors increasingly turned to sensationalistic tales
of international espionage, hard-boiled sex and violence,
and psychological suspense. Yet there indubitably remained,
seemingly imperishable and eternal, what Anthony Boucher,
dean of American mystery reviewers, dubbed the "conventional
type of British detective story." This more modestly decorous
but still intriguing and enticing mystery fare was most famously
and lucratively embodied by Crime Queen Agatha Christie, who
rang in the new decade and her Golden Jubilee as a published
author with the classic detective novel that was promoted as her
fiftieth mystery: *A Murder Is Announced* (although this was in
fact a misleading claim, as this tally also included her short story
collections). Also representing the traditional British detective
story during the 1950s were such crime fiction stalwarts (all of
them Christie contemporaries and, like the Queen of Crime,
longtime members of the Detection Club) as Edith Caroline
Rivett (E.C.R Lorac and Carol Carnac), E.R. Punshon, Cecil
John Charles Street (John Rhode and Miles Burton) and
Christopher Bush. Punshon and Rivett passed away in the
Fifties, pens still brandished in their hands, if you will, but Street
and Bush, apparently indefatigable, kept at crime throughout
the decade, typically publishing in both the United Kingdom

and the United States two books a year (Street with both of his pseudonyms).

Not to be outdone even by Agatha Christie, Bush would celebrate his own Golden Jubilee with his fiftieth mystery, *The Case of the Russian Cross*, in 1957—and this was done, in contrast with Christie, without his publishers having to resort to any creative accounting. *Cross* is the fiftieth Christopher Bush Ludovic Travers detective novel reprinted by Dean Street Press in this, the Spring of 2020, the hundredth anniversary of the dawning of the Golden Age of detective fiction, following, in this latest installment, *The Case of the Counterfeit Colonel* (1952), *The Case of the Burnt Bohemian* (1953), *The Case of The Silken Petticoat* (1953), *The Case of the Red Brunette* (1954), *The Case of the Three Lost Letters* (1954), *The Case of the Benevolent Bookie* (1955), *The Case of the Amateur Actor* (1955), *The Case of the Extra Man* (1956) and *The Case of the Flowery Corpse* (1956).

Not surprisingly, given its being the occasion of Christopher Bush's Golden Jubilee, *The Case of the Russian Cross* met with a favorable reception from reviewers, who found the author's wry dedication especially ingratiating: "The author, having discovered that this is his fiftieth novel of detection, dedicates it in sheer astonishment to HIMSELF." Writing as Francis Iles, the name under which he reviewed crime fiction, Bush's Detection Club colleague Anthony Berkeley, himself one of the great Golden Age innovators in the genre, commented, "I share Mr. Bush's own surprise that *The Case of the Russian Cross* should be his fiftieth book; not so much at the fact itself as at the freshness both of plot and writing which is still as notable with fifty up as it was in in his opening overs. There must be many readers who still enjoy a straightforward, honest-to-goodness puzzle, and here it is." The late crime writer Anthony Lejeune, who would be admitted to the Detection Club in 1963, for his part cheered, "Hats off to Christopher Bush....[L]ike his detective, [he] is unostentatious but always absolutely reliable." Alan Hunter, who recently had published his first George Gently mystery and at the time was being lauded as the "British Simenon," offered similarly praiseful words, pronouncing of *The*

Case of the Russian Cross that Bush's sleuth Ludovic Travers "continues to be a wholly satisfying creation, the characters are intriguing and the plot full of virility. . . . the only trace of long-service lies in the maturity of the treatment."

The high praise for Bush's fiftieth detective novel only confirmed (if resoundingly) what had become clear from reviews of earlier novels from the decade: that in Britain Christopher Bush, who had turned sixty-five in 1950, had become a Grand Old Man of Mystery, an Elder Statesman of Murder. Bush's *The Case of the Three Lost Letters*, for example, was praised by Anthony Berkeley as "a model detective story on classical lines: an original central idea, with a complicated plot to clothe it, plenty of sound, straightforward detection by a mellowed Ludovic Travers and never a word that is not strictly relevant to the story"; while reviewer "Christopher Pym" (English journalist and author Cyril Rotenberg) found the same novel a "beautifully quiet, close-knit problem in deduction very fairly presented and impeccably solved." Berkeley also highly praised Bush's *The Case of the Burnt Bohemian*, pronouncing it "yet another sound piece of work . . . in that, alas!, almost extinct genre, the real detective story, with Ludovic Travers in his very best form."

In the United States Bush was especially praised in smaller newspapers across the country, where, one suspects, traditional detection most strongly still held sway. "Bush is one of the soundest of the English craftsmen in this field," declared Ben B. Johnston, an editor at the *Richmond Times Dispatch*, in his review of *The Case of the Burnt Bohemian*, while Lucy Templeton, doyenne of the *Knoxville Sentinel* (the first female staffer at that Tennessee newspaper, Templeton, a freshly minted graduate of the University of Tennessee, had been hired as a proofreader back in 1904), enthusiastically avowed, in her review of *The Case of the Flowery Corpse*, that the novel was "the best mystery novel I have read in the last six months." Bush "has always told a good story with interesting backgrounds and rich characterization," she added admiringly. Another southern reviewer, one "M." of the *Montgomery Advertiser*, deemed *The Case of the Amateur Actor* "another Travers mystery to delight the most critical of a reader audience," concluding in inimitable American lingo, "it's a swell story." Even Anthony Boucher, who in the Fifties hardly could be termed an unalloyed admirer of conventional British detection, from his prestigious post at the *New York Times Books Review* afforded words of praise to a number of Christopher Bush mysteries from the decade, including the cases of the *Benevolent Bookie* ("a provocative puzzle"), the *Amateur Actor* ("solid detective interest"), the *Flowery Corpse* ("many small ingenuities of detection") and, but naturally, the *Russian Cross* ("a pretty puzzle"). In his own self-effacing fashion, it seems that Ludovic Travers had entered the pantheon of Great Detectives, as another American commentator suggested in a review of Bush's *The Case of The Silken Petticoat*:

> Although Ludovic Travers does not possess the esoteric learning of Van Dine's Philo Vance, the rough and ready punch of Mickey Spillane's Mike Hammer, the Parisian [sic!] touch of Agatha Christie's Hercule Poirot, the appetite and orchids of Rex Stout's Nero Wolfe, the suave coolness of The Falcon or the eerie laugh and invisibility of The Shadow, he does have good qualities—especially the ability to note and interpret clues and a dogged persistence in remembering and following up an episode he could not understand. These paid off in his solution of *The Case of The Silken Petticoat*.

In some ways Christopher Bush, his traditionalism notwithstanding, attempted with his Fifties Ludovic Travers mysteries to keep up with the tenor of rapidly changing times. As owner of the controlling interest in the Broad Street Detective Agency, Ludovic Travers increasingly comes to resemble an American private investigator rather than the gentleman amateur detective he had been in the 1930s; and the novels in which he appears reflect some of the jaded cynicism of post-World War Two American hard-boiled crime fiction. *The Case of the Red Brunette*, one of my favorite examples from this batch of Bushes, looks at civic corruption in provincial England in a case concerning a town counsellor who dies in an apparent "badger game" or "honey trap" gone fatally wrong ("a web of mystery skillfully spun" noted Pat McDermott of Iowa's *Quad City Times*), while in *The Case of the Three Lost Letters*, Travers finds himself having to explain to his phlegmatic wife Bernice the pink lipstick strains on his collar (incurred strictly in the line of duty, of course). Travers also pays homage to the popular, genre altering Inspector Maigret novels of Georges Simenon in *The Case of Red Brunette*, when he decides that he will "try to get a feel of the city [of Mainford]: make a Maigret-like tour and achieve some kind of background. . . ."

Christopher Bush finally decided that Travers could manage entirely without his longtime partner in crime solving, the wily and calculatingly avuncular Chief Superintendent George Wharton, whom at times Travers, in the tradition of American hard-boiled crime fiction, appears positively to dislike. "I generally admire and respect Wharton, but there are times when he annoys me almost beyond measure," Travers confides in *The Case of the Amateur Actor*. "There are even moments, as when he assumes that cheap and leering superiority, when I can suddenly hate him." George Wharton appropriately makes his final, brief appearance in the Bush oeuvre in *The Case of the Russian Cross*, where Travers allows that despite their differences, the "Old General" is "the man who'd become in most ways my oldest friend."

"Ring out the old, ring in the new" may have been the motto of many when it came to mid-century mystery fiction, but as another saying goes, what once was old eventually becomes sparklingly new again. The truth of the latter adage is proven by this shining new set of Christopher Bush reissues. "Just like old crimes," vintage mystery fans may sigh contentedly, as once again they peruse the pages of a Bush, pursuing murderous malefactors in the ever pleasant company of Ludovic Travers, all the while armed with the happy knowledge that a butcher's dozen of thirteen of Travers' investigations yet remains to be reissued.

Curtis Evans

PART 1

I

HENRY BALDLOW

I KNEW Seahurst well enough but I didn't know Montague Road. I had come my usual way into that famous south-coast resort and parked just short of the second traffic lights and spoken to a policeman. Montague Road was quite near, it seemed. It ran parallel to the sea-front and about a couple of hundred yards behind it, and I turned into it from Montague Square.

The houses were prosperous-looking, each in an ample garden, and in that sun of an early October morning those various gardens looked gay with dahlias and Michaelmas daisies. Number 28 was quite a way along, so I drew the car in at the kerb and had another look at the letter.

> The Croft,
> 28 Montague Road,
> Seahurst.

Dear Sirs,

I regret that a permanent indisposition makes it impossible for me to see you in town, but I should be grateful if a responsible member of your firm could see me here in the very immediate future.

The matter is one of urgency as I should be leaving England in about a fortnight's time. Perhaps you would be so good as to telephone me. The number is Seahurst 922.

I should add that your firm was strongly recommended to me for the kind of work I had in mind.

> Yours truly,
> HENRY BALDLOW

The Broad St. Det. Agency.

On receipt of that letter I had had a brain-wave and had rung Grainger, the Seahurst Chief Constable, whom I knew pretty well.

"This is in strict confidence," I said, "but do you know anything about a Henry Baldlow of 28 Montague Road?"

"Can't say I do," he said. "Wait a minute, though."

I guessed he was referring the matter to his superintendent and chief-inspector, for it was quite five minutes before he was back on the line.

"Nothing about him at all," he said. "He seems to have been there for at least seven years but we've had no contact with him."

"That's fine," I said. "I may be down your way tomorrow, so I may look you up. In the meanwhile I'm much obliged."

A minute or two later I was ringing Henry Baldlow. When I first heard his voice I was rather surprised, for I'd expected to hear that of an invalid. I don't know why, for the letter mentioned an indisposition, which is certainly a wide enough term. It might even have meant he was lame, for instance, or badly arthritic, neither of which would have had an effect on the voice. What I actually heard was a voice that had a kind of high-pitched heartiness. He wouldn't give any indication, by the way, of why he wanted to employ us: he merely repeated that the matter was urgent. I said I would see him myself at eleven o'clock the following morning. He seemed both satisfied and grateful.

Looking at that letter and thinking back to that telephone conversation didn't make me any better equipped to anticipate the needs or character of a probable client, so I moved the car on. But Norris, my manager, has always insisted that it pays to know as much as possible about a client before discussing business, and I've come to agree with him. We have had two unpleasant experiences with people about whom we knew far too little and whom we took at their face value. But, as I said, I moved the car on to the front gate of The Croft and left it there when I got out.

The house has its counterpart in thousands of houses in hundreds of streets in suburban England—red-bricked, modified Edwardian Tudor, crazy paving path to a front door and garage built on at the side; garden sloping slightly down to the road and screened from its neighbours by a none too well stocked herbaceous border backed by a shrubbery at each side. What lay at the back I couldn't see, but a path ran round the garage to what was probably a tradesmen's entrance. Neither house nor garden told me much about Henry Baldlow.

I rang the bell and almost at once the door was opened. The woman who opened it was short and plump and she had on an apron and dust-cap and was holding a duster in her left hand.

"Good morning," I said. "My name's Travers and I have an appointment with Mr. Baldlow for eleven o'clock."

She had been looking at me in a kind of puzzled, questioning way until the last few words and then she gave me a smile that seemed like one of relief.

"Oh yes, sir. Mr. Baldlow's expecting you. Just wait a moment here, sir, will you?"

She was showing me into a dining room, its furniture heavy and depressing and its oil-paintings a waste of a considerable quantity of canvas. Above the large, ornate mantelpiece was a portrait of better quality of an elderly man with a greying beard. I gave my horn-rims a polish and read the inscription at the foot of the garish gilt frame.

JAMES HENRY BALDLOW
presented by the staffs of
JAMES BALDLOW AND SON
on the occasion of his seventieth birthday.

Before I had time to look more closely at the actual portrait the door opened.

"Mr. Baldlow will see you now, sir. This way, please."

In the hall I caught again that smell of mustiness with a touch of boiled cabbage. The woman preceded me up the wide, heavily carpeted stairs. She was about sixty and made rather heavy going of the ascent, and was panting slightly as she went across the wide landing to a door. She didn't announce me. She merely opened the door and I went past her and inside.

The room was a bedroom that had been made a snuggery. A nice fire was burning in the grate and there were easy chairs and books and a side table on which stood a chess board with certain pieces in position. The walls were smothered in prints and photographs. There was a mahogany roll-top desk in the window recess and Baldlow had been seated there with his back to me. I was to learn that he was slightly deaf and, as my feet had made no sound on the thick carpet, it was not until I gave a cough that he turned, and got to his feet and held out a hand.

"Mr. Travers?"

"Yes," I said. "And you're Mr. Baldlow?"

"Yes, sir, and very pleased to see you. Take this chair. I think you'll find it comfortable."

He was smallish, five-foot-six, perhaps, and of spare build. His clean-shaven face had a greyish, unhealthy pallor and his shoulders were slightly bent. I put his age at around seventy, but I was to be six years ahead. But after that reference of his to an indisposition—a curious word in any case—I found him somewhat of a puzzle, for he moved briskly enough. There was in fact no exudation of mortality: what exudation there was had more the nature of a hectic cheerfulness. He was a man, I was deciding, who was uncommonly sure of himself, pleased with most things till that moment in time and confident enough about what was still to come.

"I wonder if I might ask something personal?" I said as soon as I was seated. "You mentioned an indisposition—"

"Ah!" he cut in. He had the gift of the gab. It took no more than a couple of minutes to find out that. Then for a good ten minutes more he was the Ancient Mariner and I was listening to that voice of his, a voice as full of heartiness as a tyre's full of air. Occasionally I got in a word or two by way of question and it was like pressing on the valve and out came the air again. Not that I minded. I was learning quite a lot about Henry Baldlow.

He suffered from emphysema, he said—a legacy from a serious attack of pneumonia some nine years back. I didn't quite know what emphysema was and he explained about the little factories of the lungs and how they could become choked with air. Breathing became difficult, especially in cold weather, and if he were to inhale a blast of really cold air it would double him up. Emphysema wasn't a disease that would kill you, he said, unless too much coughing put a strain on the heart. What one wanted was an equable climate so that the lungs would always inhale air of a reasonable warmth. That was why he had made plans to end his days—except for short and very occasional summer visits to England—in South Africa. It was that emphysema which kept him from London. To breathe October air that was smoke-ridden and petrol-laden might put him in bed for days.

"Was it your father's portrait—"

"You noticed it in the dining-room?" he said, and was off at once on a new tack. James Baldlow and Son—the son being himself—had their own little factory in Birmingham and ran about half-a-dozen high-class shops for the sale of jewellery, gold and silver ware and so on, one of which shops was in Bond Street. He himself had carried on the business for several years after his father's death and then, just before the war—and shrewdly anticipating that war—had sold out to the far larger firm of United Jewellers Limited. He had ultimately settled in Seahurst, which was good, he had been told, for his complaint, not that he had found it particularly so. One reason for his selling had been the death of his wife which had unsettled him very much at the time. He had no children.

I thought I had his background very well so I cut in with the vital question.

"And what is it you wish us to do for you, Mr. Baldlow?"

"Ah, that!" he said, and frowned for a moment. Then his face cleared. It was almost ingratiatingly that he leaned forward from that chair on the other side of the fire.

"Permit me to ask you a personal question, sir. You believe in a God?"

I'd listened to all sorts of cranks in my time. One more made no difference.

"Yes," I said. "At least to the extent that I can't credit the Universe as being self-made."

"But not a personal God?"

There was a kind of alert smugness on his face, and I hated it.

"Never mind it," he was saying quickly, for he must have seen my frown. "You will at least respect my own views as to a personal God. They are, I may say, very strong views."

Had he not been a possible client I think I should have told him that God must be very gratified.

"I'm a fairly wealthy man, Mr. Travers," he was going on. "A business has to be conducted honestly. Lose the confidence of your customers and you might as well shut up shop. Nevertheless there came a time when I had to look back and I saw all sorts of petty dishonesties of which I'd been guilty. They're common enough in business but they wouldn't stand scrutiny in the eyes of God. Not that I was then converted. You believe in conversion?"

"To this extent," I said. "I've known people who've definitely changed the whole course of their lives on account of some personal religious experience."

"Ah!" he said with a quick wave of the hand. He leaned forward again.

"You know the Buchmannites—as they used to call them?"

"I know of them." As a matter of fact mine was a guarded answer. I knew little of them except what I had read years before in a novel by Rose Macaulay.

"Well, I was induced by a Seahurst friend to attend one of their meetings in the town. It was at a time—about a year ago, in fact—when I was somewhat anxious about this complaint of mine. Something moved me at that meeting, Mr. Travers. Other people had stood up and made contributions to the discussion or personal confessions and all at once I found myself on my feet. I couldn't help myself. Something was moving me stronger than myself."

He gave himself a slow shake of the head as if the wonder of that moment was still upon him.

"Since then, Mr. Travers, I've known a personal God, I know that it's my duty to see that my money gets into the right hands. Money is still the root of all evil. Those old sayings will always be true. I have to regard my own money as a sacred trust. There are certain possible heirs, for instance, into whose lives I have had to make guarded enquiries. Before I leave for South Africa I may have to do certain unpleasant things—for the ones concerned, that is. It may involve me in personal danger, not that I fear that. All the same I'd rather avoid that kind of unpleasantness. That's why I wrote to your firm."

"What is it exactly that you want?"

"Well," he said, and frowned, "what I want is for you to provide me with a man who can act as companion and"—he smiled deprecatingly as if ashamed of the word—"as a kind of bodyguard. I'd like him to be someone who could be passed off as the son of an old friend. An educated man, if you know what I mean. If possible I'd like him to be someone who plays chess."

"And for how long would you need him?"

"From at once till the time of my actual sailing."

"Exactly. And pardon what seems a reiteration, but what would be his actual duties?"

"Nothing onerous at all," he told me hastily. "He would live here with me and sleep in an adjoining bedroom. Just so that I'd never be alone."

Before I could get in a word he was doing still more explaining. He lived very simply because he preferred it that way. The Mrs. Carver whom I'd seen, and her daughter—a Mrs. O'Brien—came in each morning, cleaned the far too large house, prepared the midday meal, cleared up after it and left at about 2.30 p.m. Mrs. Carver returned at about six o'clock and saw to the evening meal at seven and went home for good after washing-up. The man we sent down could have his leisure while the women were actually in the house. He would have nothing to do except be on the premises when Baldlow would otherwise have been alone. If he played chess, and liked it, that would be a pleasant relaxation.

"Mind if I use your telephone?"

"Use it by all means," he said, and waved towards the top of the writing desk.

In a few moments I was through to Norris and putting the problem up to him, with a special emphasis on an operative who played chess. Since he had to look something of what one calls a gentleman, I asked about Patrick Nordon. He asked if he might ring me back in about ten minutes.

"Well, there we are," I told Baldlow. "It looks as if we can find a man to suit you. The question now is terms."

"And what would your terms be?"

"Five guineas per day, with full board for the operative. An advance of fifty guineas set against the total charge."

"A lot of money," he told me ruefully.

"I'm sorry," I said, "but those are the terms. And if our man is really to protect you—save your life if you like—then what's five guineas a day? You can't spend an awful lot of money in a morgue."

He forced a chuckle. The telephone bell went.

"Norris here, Mr. Travers. Nordon should be okay. He plays chess but says he's pretty rusty. We can spare him from that present job. It's practically finished and Luke can clear up the rest."

I reported to Baldlow. He said he was pleased.

"You'll like Nordon," I said. "He's a man of excellent education. An ex-Commando and also did good work with Intelligence."

I had two contract forms with me but it took quite a time to draw them up. Finally we agreed to supply a man as long as needed, with no strings attached and no responsibilities. The unwritten agreement ran that Baldlow was to ring us at once if the service we were providing wasn't satisfactory. He signed and I signed: he wrote a cheque for fifty guineas and that was that. He shook hands with me at the door and I assured him that Nordon, plus ration book, would arrive that evening. At the door of that snuggery I should have said, for he had rung for Mrs. Carver and it was she who showed me out.

I didn't call on Grainger after all. I wanted to get back to town to fix things up, but as it was well after midday I had a quick lunch in the town before driving back. As I ate my meal I wasn't feeling too happy. It wasn't a question of the comparative smallness of our share of the fees, for that would neither make nor break us. It was a queer feeling as of shabbiness and furtiveness, born of the long hour in that room at The Croft. I didn't like Henry Baldlow. I didn't like a single thing about him but I hated quite a lot. His smugness, for instance, and parade of religion. I thought him a liar. That God-palaver of his might reasonably be a cover for something remarkably shady: a something that would soon be making him in fear of his life. There was something bodily and spiritually unhealthy about him. He had been too ingratiating and too plausible. The very fluency of his various relatings showed a definite rehearsing. Emphysema he might have—he had had at least one minor bout of coughing while I was with him, and Mrs. Carver had told me in answer to a careful question that sometimes he "coughed something dreadful". But my idea was that he was going to South Africa to escape from more than emphysema. He might not even be going there at all, but to somewhere else.

Still, the man was now a client, and, since I could put my finger on nothing definitely wrong about him, he had to be accepted as such. But I made up my mind to do a pretty thorough job of briefing before Nordon left for Seahurst. If he left. Maybe I had suggested his name too quickly to Norris and I was beginning to wonder if after all he was the right man for the job.

You get all sorts in a high-class agency like ours: men of different kinds of intelligence and with different backgrounds and interests. You have your hewers of wood and drawers of water, and you have your specialists—a specialist in arson, for instance, if you work for one of the big insurance companies. Occasionally you work in with other agencies whom you know and respect, and they work, when they need it, with you. Sometimes we employ a free-lance, like Luke Layman who had been working with Nordon on a blackmail case. Nordon himself was a specialist. He was the man-about-town: an operative who was at home in the best circles, and I don't necessarily mean criminal ones.

He was Public School and Oxford and, up to the war, had been the grievously spoilt darling of a widowed mother, who was French, by the way, and reasonably well off. It was because French was practically his mother tongue that he was hauled out of the Commandos, where he had done remarkably well, and was transferred to Intelligence. There he did quite a good job and when he was finally demobilized in 1947 his mother died. It was the worst thing that could have happened. The war had made a man of him, or so I gathered from old Arthur Nordon, his uncle, who happens to be a member of my club. Now he proceeded to be one of the luxuriously unemployed and in four years he managed to run through an inheritance of some thirty thousand pounds. It was Arthur Nordon who button-holed me one afternoon and finally suggested I might find him a job. He said his nephew had come to his senses now the money had gone and was quite prepared to get down to some sort of work.

I interviewed Patrick Nordon myself. He seemed perfectly frank. When I asked him where his money had gone, he gave me virtually a list of accounts: loss on the sale of a Bentley, losses on two wild-cat schemes into which he had been inveigled by so-called friends, and what he admitted was a really good standard of living.

"No pretty ladies?"

"No, sir—not to excess," he told me with his infectious grin. "Honestly, I'm not all that interested. My idea of using money is to live well, if you get me, and have really good stuff—clothes and that sort of thing."

"Even if I can use you," I warned him, "you won't get that kind of money."

"I'm not all that worried," he told me. "I think I'd like this kind of work and that's half the battle. After all, I simply loved Intelligence."

"Between that and a detective agency there's a great gulf fixed," I said. "With us you'd be on your own: no authority and often precious little backing. You'd have to hold down a job by results."

"Fair enough, sir," he said. "If I can hold the job down, my uncle's making me an allowance so we needn't argue too much about money."

To cut the story short, I put things up to Norris and we took Pat Nordon on. He was in double harness for a time and then began to do well enough in solo jobs. At the end of three months I interviewed him again. He said he loved the work. He seemed modest about it too: owned up he was far from an expert but hoped to go on learning.

I confess I'd come to like him, even if I wasn't too sure that one day or other he wouldn't land us in the soup with that swash-buckling Commando approach of his, tempered though it might be with that somewhat blasé indifference which Intelligence, in my experience, uses as its principal cloak and camouflage. But, as I said, I liked him, at least in the sense that he was a nice person to have around. He was tallish and lithely built, and his clean-shaven face reminded me of a famous actor of my youth. His manners, as you may suppose, were charming and unforced. And he definitely had brains, if by that term you mean he was quick to apprehend and ingenious to suggest.

I had a half-hour with Norris as soon as I got to Broad Street and he was telling me about that blackmail case and how it had come out. From what I've told you, you're probably thinking that as a managing director Norris was an excellent figure-head. But there you'd be wrong. I lend a hand at the agency when Norris needs me and I'm willing to do anything to help out. There are plenty of jobs that Norris directs, about which I know precious little, and that blackmail job was one.

It was the old story of a big conference in a certain city and the visiting husbands largely free of their wives. One such husband had been a victim of that hackneyed but always prof-itable scheme of being found in a bedroom by the supposed husband of the bed-fellow. Victims of that sort of blackmail fear publicity and rarely go to the police. This particular victim had come to us. Nordon had suggested that he himself should get in touch with the same woman and allow himself to become a victim. Norris had thought the idea a good one and, as we were short of men, had brought in Luke Layman to act as witness in trapping the tricksters. Everything had come off fine, according to Norris. Our client ought to be extraordinarily satisfied.

I saw Nordon that early afternoon, and in the presence of Norris I told him everything it seemed needful for him to know, though I didn't tell him bluntly that it was hardly his kind of job.

"You're going to have a pretty restful time," I told him, "but there's a good few strings attached. You must be perfectly honest if he talks religion, which he's bound to do. It'll be what I'd call a bourgeois household but you've got to accept it as if you've known nothing else. Don't be obsequious but on the other hand don't disagree too much with anything he has to say or views he may put forward."

"I get you, sir."

"But there's one other thing," I went on. "Your job's not only to protect him but also, and always, to protect the agency. You'll find him a kind of bantam-cock: pleased as Punch about something, and it's a something which he kept to himself. There was about him a curious aura of enjoying some sort of power, or it might have been the anticipation of playing some sort of trick. So keep your eyes open and your ear discreetly to the ground. Don't telephone reports. Write and post them each morning when you have your free time. If there's nothing to report, simply say so."

That, briefly, was that. Nordon had his own little car which he'd picked up in connection with the sale of the Bentley, and he'd merely to pack after he left the office and then run down to Seahurst. Baldlow's garage was empty: Mrs. Carver had told me that.

I was thinking of going home when Luke Layman turned up and Norris thought it might be as well if I gave him a pat on the back. Luke used to have his own agency—quite a small business just off Charing Cross Road. Then he lost his wife in a blitz and started lifting his elbow and the business went. But everyone liked him. He was a smallish man of about fifty, quiet, well-spoken and unobtrusive even in his cups, and he was first-class at most kinds of jobs. He could get plenty of work and most of the agencies had used him at one time and another. He told me once he was doing better than when he was his own boss. Spending it a bit quicker, he admitted ruefully, not that he was drinking as much as after his wife's death.

So I gave him a pat on the back and all he said was that he was glad to have helped and, if we needed him again, we knew where he was. I liked Luke. He had that touch of the forlorn. He looked as if he'd had a lifetime of being henpecked and trampled on and had come to accept it as part of the daily round and common course. But, as I said, he knew his job, and that forlornness of his was the finest possible camouflage a man could have in his line of work. I say again that I liked him. When I heard of his death I was quite upset.

II
DAMP DEATH

WHAT was happening at The Croft, Seahurst, cannot be seen through my eyes. All I can do is draw on the reports sent by Nordon and take extracts from them and edit them generally and pass them on. I was certainly anxious to see those reports. I'd rarely been so distrustful of a client as I was of Baldlow and, though I'd seen to it that we were protected by the terms of the contract, I was very far from happy. Here then since they were to be vitally important, are the extracts.

FIRST REPORT (written on the Friday, the morning after arrival, as instructed).

Arrived just after six o'clock. Took precaution of ringing from Tunbridge Wells to state probable time. Mrs. Carver had garage key ready for me. Saw B. at once. No mention of anything but myself. I'm to be the son of an old Birmingham friend and he seemed to think that'd be enough. No drinks in the house and no smoking for me except downstairs.

A nice bedroom with a connecting door—left open—to his. Good evening meal. B. isn't stingy about food. Mrs. C. told me he kept a very good table: didn't mind buying fowls and game and so on to supplement rations. After meal he suggested chess. In spite of being rusty I could have mated him inside twenty moves but knew it better to let him win. He was very cock-ahoop. Halted during game to hear nine o'clock news. He went to bed about ten, so I thought it as well to turn in at same time. We have cups of cocoa (!) which I make and I'm almost sure he takes sleeping pills. If so they're in his bedroom. No sign of any in the bathroom. He must have knelt for quite five minutes in prayer at his bedside, though whether that was for my benefit or even if he was actually praying I can't say.

This morning an excellent breakfast. He has all his meals brought up to his room now that colder weather has set in. I have mine downstairs, which gives me a chance to talk to Mrs. C. The daughter, Mrs. O'Brien, seems extraordinarily shy or scary: I don't know why. I didn't like to ask her mother.

Learned little of importance except that B. has a few friends. A parson, Canon Orifice of St. Martin's, calls occasionally, but usually of mornings when I'm out. It's my chance for some fresh air and to read my paper in peace in a pub over a pint. B.'s papers are *The Times* and *Financial Times*. In politics he's a solid Conservative. Certain relatives used to call or stay but haven't done so since what—according to my working out—must have been the time of his supposed conversion. His emphysema is now supposed to make visits impossible. Am going to ask Mrs. C. much more about those relatives. They may be important.

Prefer not to give general impressions of B. till next report at the earliest.

SECOND REPORT (Saturday)

Principal additional facts learned about relatives are these. He has a niece—a very nice lady according to Mrs. C.—who's married to a man called Howell, a farmer or landowner in a big way in Sussex. Hunts and all that. I gather she's about thirty and has a son aged three. B. also has a nephew who's still connected with that goldsmiths' and silversmiths' business or the company that bought it.

During the summer, if it was warm and fine, B. apparently lived a fairly normal life. It was only when the autumn came on that he reorganised himself and his habits. As he can't get out to church, he listens on his wireless to all talks concerning religion and I gather that on Sundays there'll be a regular orgy. It's only since his conversion that he's given up having a drink. Funny how converts are always the bigots.

I'm in agreement about what I was told as to his characteristics. He *is* pleased with himself—when he can forget all about that complaint of his—and he does strike me as having something up his sleeve. The strange thing is that he hasn't yet mentioned to me the bodyguard side of things. I'm left to infer it. Or does he assume you mentioned it to me? If so, he hasn't given even a hint as to what the danger is or where it's coming from.

He talks a lot. It's a kind of mania as if he considers he owes a duty to mankind to talk, so that it may profit by listening. He monopolises conversations and resents being interrupted, so I wait till I'm spoken to, so to speak. He's remarkably well-informed about a great number of things—I will say that—and many of his anecdotes are quite amusing. I even faintly like him when he's in a reminiscent mood. The rest of the time, as far as I'm concerned, he stinks. Even as a bantam-cock, he's an unpleasant one.

THIRD REPORT (Sunday)

Last night I absentmindedly allowed myself to beat him at chess. He wasn't too pleased about it since he was mated too soon and too drastically, but he cheered up when I showed him what a complete fluke it was. He asked me about my war experiences but couldn't bear to hear me speak for more than a minute or so, and then was off again on his own. Brought in religion at last. I tried to be very modest and very ill-informed about everything. I feel in my bones that he's going to try to convert me. If so I'll demand a raise from the firm.

Am trying to compile a sort of Baldlow family tree.

FOURTH REPORT (Monday)

Yesterday was pretty trying. Mrs. C. doesn't come in after a quick clear-away of lunch, so we had a cold supper. I took up his tray. Wireless services going full blast whenever available.

Have done some work on the family tree with the help, unsuspected, of Mrs. C. who's been here about four years. I've filled in gaps but think it's reasonably correct.

James B. was married twice. Of the first marriage he had a son—our client—and a daughter, much younger, who married a man called Tinley. This Sarah Tinley had two children, the niece and nephew I mentioned in a previous report. The Tinleys, I gather, were reasonably well off. They were killed during the war in that big raid on Exeter.

A few years after the death of his first wife, J.B. married a widow named Lorde who had a son, much younger than his two children. There were no children of that second marriage. Those are all the relatives or family connections I can trace through talk with Mrs. C. B. obviously did a lot of talking to her for want of a better audience.

No chess on Sundays. Fortunately B. belongs to a lending library and reads a lot when there's no one to talk to. He always has a nap, by the way, from after his hearty lunch till about half-past two. I bring him up a cup of tea after my lunch downstairs and then he goes to sleep. Since I've seen a small round pill or capsule box at hand, I shouldn't be surprised if he takes one—pill or just a sedative—in his tea.

FIFTH REPORT (Tuesday)

Something very much in the wind. This morning all the locks to doors, except garage, are being replaced with Yales or new Yales. The two men doing the job arrived early. B. told me when I saw him after his usual nine o'clock breakfast, that there'd been several burglaries in the town and he was taking precautions.

Yesterday morning, Monday, I got back rather early from my usual constitutional and met a man coming down the path from the house. He turned out to be the doctor, Krane, who'd just been paying a routine visit. He gave me a smile and halted.

"You're Mr. Nordon?"

"Yes, sir."

"I'm Dr. Krane. Mr. Baldlow's been talking to me about you and how much you're cheering him up. What an excellent fellow he is!"

The interlude herewith is something unknown to Nordon. Baldlow rang the office at about eleven o'clock when I happened to be there. It would be, incidentally, when Nordon was out. Norris introduced himself, then passed the receiver to me.

"Ah, Mr. Travers, how are you?" came that high-pitched yet somehow unctuous voice.

"Very well indeed," I said. "And you? The emphysema isn't any worse?"

"It's being kept in check, thanks to suitable precautions," he said. "But I really rang to tell you in his temporary absence what a very nice young fellow it was that you sent down here. I'm remarkably pleased with him and it's only fair to all concerned to tell you so."

I said we were very gratified to hear it.

"While I *am* talking," he went on, "I think I ought to tell you that I'm now pretty sure that my affairs can't be settled up as soon as I thought. It may still be another fortnight before I'm able to leave. If you therefore want another cheque, you must let me know."

"We're not worrying about that," I said. "It's all covered by the contract. But thanks for letting us know."

That was about all. We resume with the reports.

SIXTH REPORT (Thursday)

I rather guess the balloon of some sort is going up in the very near future. B. must have spent yesterday morning writing letters and I was home in time to overhear him as I came out of the bathroom giving them to Mrs. O'Brien to post at once at the pillar-box at the end of the road. He told her not to mention them to her mother! I peeped out and saw that she had at least three letters.

Two things happened that morning which I think should be reported. I saw in the town notices of a meeting in connection with the Oxford Group (Moral Re-armament?) to be held next Wednesday in the Parish Hall of St. Martin's at seven o'clock.

The other thing was that as I was letting myself in at about twelve-thirty with one of the new Yale keys, Mrs. C. was showing someone out. We had quite a chat on the doorstep, so to speak.

He was the rector of St. Martin's, a short, red-faced man with a very blue jowl, all hot air and heartiness. I thought it'd do no harm to mention the forthcoming meeting and at once he was asking me if I was coming to it. I said it might be my duty to stay with my host, but he just waved that aside. I managed to get away before he could start digging into my own ideas and beliefs.

B. telephoning quite a lot recently when I'm not apparently in earshot. Maybe he's keeping in touch with his friends. One thing quite remarkable happened after lunch when I brought up his tea. I generally lie on the bed and read a thriller or something likeable I've bought in the town, and so when there was the sound of him gently opening my door after he'd drunk his tea, I whipped quickly over to face the wall and made as if asleep. I thought he'd come in for a chat for some reason or other, and that was the last thing I wanted. I heard the door gently shut again and in a second or two I could hear him at the telephone. I heard only one thing distinctly, and that was because he said it urgently and raised his voice.

"No, Maurice, I tell you no! You're *not* to come here!" *Maurice* might have been *Morris*. I naturally couldn't tell from the sound.

He lowered his voice after that and rang off almost at once. When I later brought up the tea he seemed rather worried about something, but after the evening meal he was full of beans. He said he would be having callers in the course of a day or so and he'd be needing my assistance. Just how or why he didn't say and I thought it as well not to ask any questions.

The above report, as you will have noticed, was written on the Thursday morning and reached our office by the last post that same day. It was the last report from Nordon that I was to read or have read to me over the telephone. The following morning I was busy about something else. The office was rung by Mrs. Prince—Luke Layman's landlady and the widow of a former operative of his—speaking from 17 Miller's Lane, Southwark, and using, of course, Luke's telephone. She asked if we knew anything about him. He'd gone off the previous afternoon in that old Standard Nine of his that he garaged locally and had said he'd be in well before ten. But he hadn't turned up at all. There'd been no news of him or from him that morning and she was getting worried. Luke had only to telephone, and she hadn't left the house for even a minute. She had rung us because we were the ones who had last employed him. I said I'd be round at about two o'clock to see if I could be of any help.

Miller's Lane has not deteriorated like much of Southwark property. It's still a rather nice little backwater that escaped the bombing by no more than a few yards. Its terraced houses are small but neat and tidy almost to smartness. Mrs. Prince I'd met before—a thin, tallish woman, who always appeared to have her hands at her chest, not that she seemed consumptive, for she didn't as much as cough while I was in the house.

"Tell me just what happened," I told her when she'd said there was still no news of Luke.

She said she was in the kitchen making a nice cup of tea at about a quarter to four. It was extra to the usual tea at five o'clock, she was careful to explain. While in the kitchen she just heard Luke talking to someone on the telephone, so she waited till he'd finished.

"Sorry, Ma"—that's what he always called her—"but I've got to get off at once."

"But you must drink your tea? Look, I'll bring you some more milk."

She came back with the milk and he was taking something from his desk and putting it into his breast pocket.

"Just a minute," I said. "What sort of thing was it?"

She couldn't say. His back had been towards her.

"When're you going to be back?" she asked him.

"Can't say, Ma. Oughtn't to be late, though. By bedtime probably." He turned round, the something in his pocket, and lifted back the flap of the desk. It was a desk which he never locked, she said. Then he poured enough milk in the cup to drown it, as she put it, and a couple of swallows saw the cup empty.

"Just going round for the car. Cheerio, Ma."

That was the last she heard or saw of him. She stayed up till long after the wireless had closed down and it must have been two o'clock when she went to bed. She left a note saying his supper was in the oven.

She slept fitfully, heard no sound of him, and was up early. After that, as far as concerned Luke, nothing but silence.

"Can I have a look in his room?"

She took me through at once. I'd been in it before and it hadn't altered a bit, except that the fire wasn't on but was laid ready. It was a small room but snug and well cluttered up. The desk was Luke's own, a small oak one at least a hundred and fifty years old.

"Mind if I have a look through the drawers?"

"No, sir," she said. "I'm sure Luke wouldn't mind."

I found in the drawers not the slightest clue to his absence. I didn't even find a clue to his jobs over the last few months.

"He kept a sort of diary book, sir," she told me. "Isn't it there?"

I said it wasn't. Also there wasn't a cheque-book.

"He didn't have an account," she told me. "He did once but then he stopped it. He kept everything in cash."

I fiddled about with the small drawers of the part beneath the flap and, sure enough, there was a secret drawer. Practically every desk of that type and age has one, so it wasn't any feat on my part: just a try at the likely places. In that drawer was over seventy pounds in notes, many of them in fivers. I counted them in her presence and put them back. I tried for a second secret drawer but had no luck.

"Tell me something, just between ourselves," I said. "We gave Luke quite a useful cheque a week or two back which he probably got cashed by a friend or at a bank that knew him. But did he do a job after it? Last week, for instance?"

"No, sir." Her thin lips stretched to a smile. "He told me it was about time he had a holiday."

"Did he do any drinking?"

"No," she said. "Not more than his usual. When he came in at night he'd always be in control of himself. He'd had a drink or two, you could tell that, but that was nothing. He was never the worse for drink, if that's what you mean."

"Good," I said, and what more was there to say? Only that she was to ring the office as soon as she had any news. She was to ring us in the morning if there was *no* news. Meanwhile if there was anything we could do, we'd do it.

"He's never been away like this before?"

"Never," she said. "He was most considerate."

"Well, don't worry," I told her as she showed me out. "Probably there'll be a perfectly simple explanation when we hear from Luke. One thing's sure. If any accident had happened to him, you'd have heard long ago. He had business cards on him and you'd have been rung up."

I was trying to be plausibly helpful but I don't think she believed those verbal sedatives. I was pretty worried myself. I was fond of Luke and I'd have hated anything serious to have happened to him. But there it was. All I could do was hope for the best and wait.

For the rest of the afternoon it kept popping in and out of my mind as a kind of recurrent worry. I had no responsibilities where Luke was concerned and yet somehow I felt a responsibility. In any case I'd promised Mrs. Prince to do what I could. Then there was the mystery of the whole business, and a mystery with me is like a touch of neuritis that won't let you rest or forget it. Why *should* Luke disappear into thin air even for twenty-four hours? Wherever he was, he couldn't be wholly out of reach of some telephone or other, and Mrs. Prince had spoken of him as considerate. I could well believe it. I couldn't see Luke ever giving trouble to a soul. Quiet, reticent, unobtrusive and yet friendly—that was Luke.

It would be about seven o'clock when the telephone went at my flat. Norris was speaking.

"A pretty bad business about Luke. Mrs. Prince just rang us to say the police at Maverton have Luke's body. He was drowned. His car for some reason or other pitched over a cliff."

"Dreadful!" I said. "I just can't believe it. How the devil did it happen?"

"Don't know," he said. "What I've just told you is all I know. All I can conjecture is that he was tight."

For a moment or two I thought things over.

"Do this for me, there's a good fellow. Don't ring but slip round to Miller's Lane and see Mrs. Prince yourself. Tell her I'll do the identification and all that. First thing in the morning I'll go down there and do anything there is to do. She'll have to attend the inquest, of course, but you needn't worry her about that now. We'll help her out when the time comes."

"What the devil was he doing down there?" Norris was asking. "Only about eight miles west of Seahurst, by the way."

"I don't see how Seahurst has anything to do with it," I told him. "Mrs. Prince said he had a telephone call at about four o'clock, and off he went. Probably on some new case or other."

I got away that Saturday morning to an early start, and it was about eleven o'clock when I got to Maverton. It's only a small place. I found the police-station, saw the sergeant in charge and explained why I was there. He could tell me nothing except that the car had not been noticed just above water till the tide went out soon after lunch. Then he had got in touch with Seahurst.

I knew that the police jurisdiction of Seahurst extended over a pretty big area, but it had never occurred to me that it might include Maverton.

"I know Mr. Grainger very well," I said, "and I'll see him at once, but would you mind telling me anything you can?"

All he could tell me was that Luke was in the semi-submerged car. In his wallet was his business card, with, of course, his address and telephone number. His body, and his car, had been taken to Seahurst.

"Like to show me just where it happened?"

He went with me at once. The place was some four hundred yards short of the first bungalow of the little resort. The none too wide road merged into the close sea grass at each side. On the near side the cliff—it was a pretentious name for it—was about thirty feet high. There was no protecting rail and no need of any, provided a car had reasonable lights.

"Which way was he coming?"

"Towards Maverton," he said. "There are faint tyre marks and the car fell with its bonnet that way."

"Then he was probably coming from Seahurst?"

"Not necessarily," he told me. "A mile along there's the road that connects up with the London Road. There're all sorts of side roads."

"You get any sea mist here on Thursday night? There was a slight fog in town."

"Yes," he said. "There was quite a bit of mist. Patchy, of course. You always get it this time of year after a fine day."

I drove him back to the police-station and asked him to ring Seahurst and tell the Chief Constable that I'd be with him in under half an hour. As I came to that spot where Luke's car had left the road for the thirty-yard detour to cliff and sea, I got out and had another look round. The grass was close and firm. I doubted if a Luke who was under the influence of a good many drinks would have noticed the transition from road to grass. If he had suddenly come into a patch of fog, then the tragedy was explained—drink or not. As for the tyre marks, my eyes weren't good enough to discern them.

I moved my car on towards Seahurst, and kept an eye on my near side for the side roads and lanes. It was about midday when I got to police headquarters. Grainger, I was told, was expecting me.

III
DRY DEATH

It's queer, that attitude of the police towards detective agencies. I hate snobbery and I hate snobs: I hate them more than the devil's said to hate holy water. And yet I put it to you. Why should I, with what the world would regard as good enough breeding, background and upbringing, and with a clean sheet, concern myself with anything tawdry or shady? And yet you get that implied superiority and the faint suggestion that your job is just a bit beyond the pale.

My father used to quote something, from Job, I think, and I've probably got it wrong. *"You are the wise ones and wisdom shall die with you."* One might say that a considerable number of police regard themselves as the only wise ones. They would tell you they have the experience and the machinery to cope with crime, which automatically suggests that you haven't. The infinite complexities of human behaviour are apparently to them an open book. We private enquiry agents are not only inexperienced amateurs but nuisances and positive dangers to the rightful traffic of the law.

I know Grainger well, as I've said. I did him a good turn not so long ago when one of his departments had made a curious error, and I kept the fact under my hat. That's why I expected him to regard me, if not as an equal, at least as a person with honest intentions. But he seemed to be doing neither. He annoyed me.

"Look," I said. "I don't give a damn what you believe or don't believe. If you don't want to tell me all you know about Luke Layman—well, that's your affair. I shall hear most of it at the inquest."

He began hedging.

"It isn't that at all. I'm grateful for what you've told me about Layman, but it's an open and shut case of accidental death. The man had been drinking heavily. There was a quartern bottle of Scotch—empty—in the car with his prints on it. He died with some of it in his belly and sea water in his lungs."

"Well, I'm grateful for that much information," I told him a bit wryly. "What did you find on him?"

"The usual," he said. "Nothing you wouldn't expect. His wallet had some notes in it and his driving licence and some business cards."

"What about his diary book?"

"Diary book?"

"Ah!" I said provocatively. "Still things you don't know. His landlady mentioned it to me yesterday and I rang her about it before I left this morning. It'd be a fairly old book, red-covered, and about seven inches by four. I think he'd used it ever since he left off doing business for himself. He kept in it a brief record of his jobs: whom he worked for and what on and where, and probably what happened. He wouldn't keep any other notes of his various jobs. His reports would be handed to the firm who employed him. I'm quite prepared to show you, in strict confidence, for instance, his report to us on the job he ended for us less than a fortnight ago. He had that book in his pocket. The landlady as good as saw him put it there."

He frowned.

"All the same, I don't see how that affects things. He might have lost that book anywhere between town and Maverton."

"Agreed," I said. "But let me ask another question. Was there any trace of dope in the whisky?"

"Look," he said, and the smile was irritatingly superior. "Didn't you and I argue that out over that drowning case of last year. You can't have it both ways. If someone had slipped a Mickey into that bottle, there'd be no trace left."

"Must do like the politicians—explore every avenue," I said. "All the same I don't like the sequence. Luke hadn't been drinking heavily lately even though he had the money. He even had money saved. He got a telephone call, which can't be traced probably, and it took him out at once to his car and Maverton. Why should he drink neat whisky on the way? And to that extent? If he was going on a case he'd need a clear head."

"You can't conjecture like that," he told me with an exaggerated patience. "Who knows if he was going on a case?"

"An enquiry among all the known agencies would answer that," I reminded him.

He shrugged his shoulders.

"Why shouldn't it have been bad news? The man had some sort of private life, didn't he? And I think I can explode your theory of a job. If it was an agency ringing him up, it'd have asked him to come round and get his orders. He didn't go round to anywhere. We know when he took his car out of the garage and we reckon he'd just about have made it to Maverton soon after six o'clock. That was somewhere about the time of his death."

"You still haven't covered everything," I said, and got to my feet. "The Agency might have told him, or asked him if he was prepared, to go down to Maverton or somewhere near it and meet someone who'd pass on instructions. It's the sort of thing we've had to do dozens of times."

He shrugged his shoulders and rose too.

"Might I have a look at him?" I said.

"Glad for you to. I'll take you down."

It was a fine mortuary, as I've said elsewhere. We picked up the sergeant in charge as we passed his cubby-hole and we went along the passage to the morgue itself and the operating room. The sergeant pulled out a long rack and drew back a sheet.

"Yes," I said slowly. "That's Luke."

There he was, quiet and peaceful as ever and with a forlorn-ness that now had in it something of the pathetic. I let out a breath and turned away.

"Well, that seems to be all," I said. "I take it you'll be expecting a verdict of accidental death. Will you bring in the whisky?"

"You mean you wish I wouldn't?" he said as we went through to the entrance hall.

"No," I said slowly. "God forbid that I should try to tell you your job. All the same, would you let me tell you what some people might do if they had even the faintest doubts about the manner of his death?"

"And what *would* they do?"

"If the Broad Street Detective Agency were commissioned to make an independent enquiry—something which can't possibly happen—then it'd find out where that bottle of whisky came from. He didn't take it from anywhere in his lodgings. It'd check every London agency and its operatives and so find out the full list of the agencies who'd ever employed him. It'd discover whether or not they'd telephoned him that afternoon. It'd try to follow him along his route from town that afternoon: find out if he'd stopped anywhere for tea or pulled up at a filling station or to buy the whisky. It would enquire about the missing diary book. If all that produced nothing, then it'd go into his past cases and see if he'd made any enemies. In fact, it'd cost a client a whole lot of money if we enquired into Luke's death. But believe me when I say we'd do it thoroughly."

I expected him to rear up, but he didn't. There was a little ironic quirk at the corners of his mouth.

"And you're expecting us to do all that when a known soak runs off the road and gets himself drowned? Ah, well!" He shook his head as if in pity. "It's tax-payers' money we use, not clients'."

"True enough," I said, and held out a hand. "Sorry to have been such a nuisance to you. Let me know the inquest date. You'll want his landlady here and we've rather promised to do what we can."

"We'll see to everything," he told me; and rather more friendly: "She'll be well looked after."

"Good," I said. "Like to have lunch with me?"

"Sorry," he said, "but I've got an appointment. Good of you all the same. I'd have been glad to."

I gave him a cheerful wave of the hand and was actually half way through the door when I heard him calling. I turned back.

"Sorry," he said, "but something I forgot to ask you. That old boy in Montague Road you enquired about. Is he a client of yours?"

I had to smile.

"My dear fellow, you surely know that if he were, then I'd be betraying a confidence by telling you so. But why'd you ask?"

"Just wondered," he said. Then he frowned slightly. "Tell me. If you people ever had an idea that a client of yours was up to something—about to commit a felony, for instance—what would you do?"

"A tricky question. I think any reputable agency would confront the client first and then, if its suspicions looked well founded, inform the authorities." My own look was meant to be a bit quizzical. "Don't tell me you've been making enquiries into our friend of Montague Road merely on the strength of that confidential telephone enquiry?"

"Not a bit of it," he told me largely. "Naturally I was interested but that's as far as it went."

He too waved a hand, said he might be seeing me, and I went out and down the steps to my car.

It was well after one o'clock so I drove to the front and had lunch at a hotel that I knew. There weren't many people there and I was entitled to take my time in any case, and over my coffee I was trying to get to grips with the vague uneasiness that had begun seeping through me as soon as I'd left Grainger. Was what he had said strictly the truth? Had he been keeping an eye on Montague Road immediately after that telephoned enquiry of mine? And if so, was that question about a client's committing a felony supported by something that he already knew?

In a minute or two I was convincing myself that I was wrong in suspecting Grainger of duplicity. Baldlow was a man of means. He might be a hypocrite and smug as hypocrites usually are, but what felony could he possibly be thinking of committing? Or was I wrong? Was there something in his past that had to be at all costs concealed?

Let me confess that I have a far too active and imaginative brain. To prove it, let me tell you what I went on thinking. Suppose that Baldlow, I told myself, had been guilty of something mighty serious but that some partner or accomplice had taken the rap and was just due to come out of jail. Wouldn't that make Baldlow in fear of his life? Mightn't that be why he was proposing to leave the country almost at once? If so, South Africa was a blind, and heaven knew where he would skip to.

I recover quickly from such imaginative bouts, even though the things envisaged remain at the back of my mind. But out of all the thinking there emerged one thing—the knowledge that I shouldn't do any harm if I took advantage of my presence in Seahurst to make another call on Baldlow. So I paid my bill and went out to the car. I had only a rough idea how to get into Montague Square, so I went along the front for a couple of hundred yards and then took a turn which would bring me at least to the main shopping centre. I had to wait at the traffic lights and a man told me to go first right and then first left.

On went the green and I swung right into the main street. I looked out for the first left and took it and found myself in Montague Square. And just ahead of me was someone I seemed to know, walking at a considerable pace towards Montague Road. I drew the car up.

"Hallo, Nordon! Out for a constitutional?"

"My God, sir, you gave me a shock!" He let out a breath. "Thought it was the police caught up with me at last."

"Going to 28? If so, hop in."

He got in beside me and I turned into Montague Road.

"You seen my report, sir? But of course you haven't. This morning's, I mean."

I drew the car in by the kerb.

"Why'd you ask? Something important, was there?"

"Well, I wouldn't call it that," he said. "But he's having visitors this afternoon and he told me I could take the time off till six o'clock. Mrs. Carver's going to be there to handle them. What I've been out for, though, is something that *is* peculiar."

He took something out of a plain, unsealed envelope. It was a Last Will and Testament form: the sort you can buy at any good-class stationer's.

"Uh-huh," I went. "Must obviously have something to do with the callers. Perhaps they're witnesses."

He gave a little clearing of the throat.

"Excuse me, sir, but why're you down this way? Or is it a rude question?"

"Not at all," I told him. "Luke Layman was drowned by running his car over a cliff about eight miles from here on Thursday night. I promised—"

"Luke drowned!"

"That's what I said. Trapped in his car and drowned."

"Oh my God, no!" He sat limp for a moment. "He couldn't have been drinking."

"Why not?"

"Well, because he was as good as off it. I knew that, sir, when I was working with him a fortnight ago. He'd take a drink or two but he was never anything even remotely resembling tight."

"There was considerable mist that night. He could easily have gone off the road. But tell me this. Did Luke ever mention to you any friends or relatives down this way?"

"No," he said slowly. "He rarely talked about himself. But surely he must have been on another case? A few inquiries and you'll know why he was down there, wherever it was."

"At Maverton. His landlady was worried so we knew we had to do what we could."

"It's damnable," he said. "I liked old Luke. He was a damn fine character."

"Most of us knew it," I told him dryly.

My hand went to the starter and then I saw someone approaching No. 28.

"Isn't that your Mrs. Carver?"

"That'll be her," he said. "She had to go home to change into her best black. The old man rather sprang it on her this morning, so I gathered."

I moved the car on. I was stopping it in front of the garage.

"If you're staying for any time, sir, just draw along a bit. I'd like to run out to that Maverton place and hear more about what happened to Luke."

I did draw on although, as I told him, I wanted a word with Baldlow as a matter of courtesy and no more. Nordon let us in at the front door. The hall looked spotlessly clean and yet it had the same look of frowstiness.

Mrs. Carver heard us and peeped out. She gave me that same apprehensive look that she'd given me before. Nordon called to her.

"It's only my uncle, Mrs. Carver. He's just having a word with Mr. Baldlow. Slip up, will you, and tell him Mr. Travers is here and would like to see him for a minute?"

She went up the stairs. She looked very Sundayish in her black with the cameo brooch at the neck. Her shoes weren't so good, though, as I watched them up the stairs.

"Damn!" Nordon said. "I forgot this. I might as well give it to him and then come down and wait for you, sir."

It was that Will form that he'd forgotten. He too went up the stairs. But he didn't get very far. Mrs. Carver was looking down from the landing, eyes staring and her tongue at her lips.

"Him!" she said, and made a faint gesture back. "Him. I think he's dead!"

He was dead as mutton. He lay on his side beneath the eider-down of his four-foot bed, and on top of the clothes. Only his coat was off and it hung on the back of the bedside chair with his tie. His collar was loosened. I didn't turn the head or touch him at all, but there seemed something peculiar about his face.

"Ring Doctor Krane," I told Nordon. "Tell him to get here at the double."

Mrs. Carver had gone downstairs. I sprinted down to see how she was feeling. I found my way to the kitchen where she was putting on the kettle. She looked quite startled although she must have heard my steps.

"That's right," I said. "Make yourself a good strong cup of tea. It must have been quite a shock to you."

"It was, sir," she said. "You could never dream of him going off sudden like that. Ate his lunch too, he did. Cleared up every bit of it."

"Well, it's a fine way to die," I told her fatuously. "But what about the visitors this afternoon? What time are they due?"

"The first at three o'clock, so Mr. Baldlow told me."

"That's another quarter of an hour. You'd better show them into one of the rooms and don't tell them what's happened. I'll probably do that myself. You understand?"

I heard the ring at the front door.

"That'll be the doctor," I said. "He lives quite close?"

"Just around the corner, sir."

I heard that as I was making for the corridor and the front door. Krane looked surprised, as well he might, at the sight of me. As we went up the stairs, I explained that I was an old friend and happened to be in the town.

Nordon and I stood back while Krane made his examination. He was a short man, very dark, and with an alert, almost jerky manner. His back hid the body from us but I could see the movements of his arms as he turned the head this way and that. Once or twice he bent right over for a close look. He straightened himself and turned.

"I'm afraid I'll have to call the police. You two gentlemen had better stay here."

"The police?" Nordon said.

"Yes," Krane told him curtly. "I'm not satisfied with the cause of death."

There was a gasp from the door. Mrs. Carver had been standing there, but, as we turned, she turned too and we could hear her making a sobbing sound as she went down the stairs.

"Bit of a shock," Krane said. "You two gentlemen had better come in with me."

He went through the connecting door to the room where I'd first seen Baldlow and made for the telephone. I noticed the chess men on the board and it might have been the same problem that Baldlow had been working out that first morning. Krane was asking for Grainger.

"Where's the tea-cup?" I whispered to Nordon. "The one he had before his nap?"

"Mrs. C. collects it after he's gone to the bedroom," he whispered back.

"You'd better come along," Krane was saying. "Yes, I'll be here. You can bring your own man later. . . . Yes, I'm pretty sure."

I glanced at my watch. It was three minutes to three.

"Some people should be calling here at three o'clock and that's almost at once," I told Krane. "Don't you think you'd better see if Mrs. Carver's in a fit state to let them in?"

"They shouldn't be let in," he told me aggressively.

"Someone's got to tell them as much. If you're not going down, then I shall go down myself."

He looked out of the side window that overlooked Montague Road. I guessed he was looking for my car.

"I'm not trying to make a getaway," I told him amusedly. "I'm more anxious than you could ever imagine to find out what's really happened. I happen to be the head of a detective agency and Mr. Nordon here is one of our operatives. I was here to see Mr. Baldlow on business. Now, with your permission I'll go downstairs."

From where I stood I could hear the front bell. Whoever it was was well on time.

At the foot of the stairs I listened for Mrs. Carver, but there was no sound of her. I opened the front door. A woman stood there. She was a handsome woman of about thirty and was wearing quite an expensive fur coat. There was a faint but mannered surprise when she saw me. She stepped forward at once as if she'd a right to walk into the house.

"You've come to see Mr. Baldlow?" I was asking her.

"I'm Jane Howell," she said. She had a clear, cultured voice. "Mr. Baldlow's my uncle, or did you know that? He asked me to see him at three o'clock."

"My name's Travers," I said. "I'm here to see your uncle too. I wonder if you'd mind waiting in here for just a moment."

I showed her into the dining-room and for a moment she stood looking about her. Then as I glanced towards the far window I noticed something. I turned my eyes quickly back to her.

I gave her a little friendly smile as I went out. She was a class well above Baldlow I was thinking as I made for the kitchen. Mrs. Carver wasn't there. Maybe she was upstairs, I thought, and went up myself, and into Baldlow's den. There was no one there but the door to the bedroom was open. Krane was standing as if on static sentry duty by the bed. Nordon was sitting by the window.

"Mrs. Howell, his niece, is down in the dining-room," I told Nordon. "I couldn't find Mrs. Carver. You go down and talk to Mrs. Howell. The police ought to be here at any moment. See Mrs. Howell stays where she is. Say there's been a burglary—anything you like, but see she stays there."

There was the sound of a car and another car. I went through and saw Grainger getting out of the first car.

"I'll let Mr. Grainger in," I told Krane through the door. "I was with him only a couple of hours ago."

Grainger's eyes nearly popped out of his head at the sight of me. I raised a finger, shushed him to silence and nodded at the dining-room door.

"Let your people come up quietly," I whispered. "I'll explain it all later."

I went ahead of him up the stairs. I heard him giving instructions to this one and that on the landing, then he came in, and a tall, sandy-haired man with him. He had the usual black bag.

"Now what's all this?" Grainger was asking. "Krane, you know Calvadge. He's come to have a look."

He looked at the opened door to Baldlow's snuggery. He peeped through, then motioned me across. The two doctors were already huddled over Baldlow's body.

"Now what's all this?" Grainger was asking me as soon as we were inside the room. It seemed a favourite opening gambit.

"All what?" I asked him naively.

"Mean to say you don't know?"

"I know nothing except that Baldlow's dead. I came here to pay him a courtesy visit. His cook or housekeeper or daily woman—call her what you like—went to announce me and found him dead. The only other thing I know is that Krane didn't seem satisfied about the cause of death and promptly rang you."

He grunted non-committally.

"And what was all the hocus-pocus downstairs?"

"The hocus-pocus, as you call it," I told him evenly, "was because a niece of his had been requested by him to see him at three o'clock this afternoon. I showed her personally into the dining-room and told her nothing. Simply asked her to wait. A man of mine is with her now."

He fairly gaped.

"A man of yours? What d'you mean? A detective?"

"Yes," I said bluntly.

"Then Baldlow *was*—"

He hardly got the first word out. Calvadge was calling him from the bedroom. Grainger gave a vicious shake of the head and moved off. I moved slightly later, and unobtrusively. Grainger went over to the two by the bed. I stayed just inside the door.

"No doubt about it in my judgment," Calvadge was saying. "Death by suffocation. Probably with this very pillow."

"How long ago?"

"Don't know. That electric fire's probably been going full blast all the time. The stomach content ought to tell us once we know the exact time of his lunch. Who can tell us that?"

"One of two people," I said quietly. "Mrs. Carver, the woman here whom Dr. Krane probably knows. Failing her there's Mr. Nordon, whom I believe Dr. Krane also knows, if only by sight."

Grainger gave me a scowl: a sort of keep-your-damn-nose-out-of-it sort of scowl. But he went out to the landing for all that. I heard him telling someone to bring up Mrs. Carver.

"Something else you ought to know," I told him when he came back. "There were to be other callers this afternoon besides his niece. When they're coming I don't know but Mrs. Carver was instructed to stay here—and it's her free afternoon—till six o'clock to let them in and so on."

"You seem to know a devil of a lot?"

"All capable of explanation," I told him.

I was going on with something else when his man came in. "No sign of Mrs. Carver, sir. I looked in the dining-room and a man there told me he'd seen her go out."

I said it'd be Mr. Nordon in the dining-room. Grainger did some more scowling, to himself.

"Bring Mr. Nordon up here," he said. "Show the lady into the room through there. You can't mistake the door." The silence was pretty heavy. Not a word was said till Nordon was shown in.

"Your name's Nordon?" Grainger snapped at him.

"Why, yes," Nordon told him, and very mildly.

"You can tell us when Mr. Baldlow had his lunch or dinner or whatever he called it?"

"I think so," Nordon said. "His tray was taken up at exactly one o'clock, as it always is. I then had my own lunch in the dining-room with the electric fire on. At as near half-past as makes no difference I took him up his usual cup of tea and came down again for a cup of my own and a smoke. As soon as he'd gone into this room for his nap, Mrs. Carver came up and collected the tray and the tea-cup."

"Clear enough," Calvadge said, and looked up from his note-book. "What did Mr. Baldlow have for lunch?"

"Toad-in-the-hole. Two sausages, I think, and mashed potatoes and cauliflower with white sauce. Plum tart afterwards, with cream. Top of the milk, if you know what I mean."

IV

THE CALLERS

THERE was an interruption. Two men came in. One was Inspector Padman, Grainger's C.I.D. man, and the other was Padman's sergeant. From what was said I gathered they'd been away on a case—that of Luke Layman for my guess—and had been recalled.

"Anywhere else we can talk besides that other room?" Grainger asked generally.

"There's my bedroom," Nordon said. "The room through there."

"Right," Grainger said. "If you gentlemen will go through I'll be with you in a couple of minutes."

So Nordon and I went to the bedroom and the door was closed behind us.

"What's the idea, sir?" Nordon asked indignantly. "From the way they're treating us we might be a couple of suspects."

"Take it easy," I told him. "Grainger's telling his Inspector what it's all about. You're a young hand at all this. Everyone'll calm down. After all, we do hold most of the trumps. They know very little about Baldlow. We know quite a lot."

I passed my cigarette-case. We still had plenty to draw on when Grainger came in. Padman came with him. He looked a decent sort of chap. He actually shook hands with us at the formal introduction.

"Now," Grainger said, and sat on the bed. "Just what was your position here, Mr. Nordon?"

Nordon looked at me. I gave an indication for him to carry on.

"My instructions were to report here and act as a kind of companion to Mr. Baldlow. He was kept to the house by that lung complaint of his and he didn't like being alone."

Grainger was staring. He looked round at me.

"You really expect me to believe that? That you supply baby-sitters?"

"There's more to it than that," I said. "Let Nordon carry on."

"Also I was a kind of bodyguard," Nordon told him. "The old man had a mania about his life being in danger. And he was afraid of burglars. Perhaps you noticed all the locks in the house are new. Only changed this week."

Grainger thought that over. He turned to me again. "What's your version, Travers?"

"I don't want to be awkward in any way," I said. "In fact I want to co-operate, but I rather object to that word *version*. Or do I take it you want to know the truth?"

Grainger had flushed slightly.

"Yes, that's what I mean."

"Fine," I said. "Then I've nothing to add to Nordon's account. I saw Baldlow here and he told me what you've heard. He wanted a man to spend the night in this room with the connecting door open. A night bodyguard, one might say. He wouldn't tell me what his fears were and, frankly, I didn't care for the proposition. I quoted stiff terms and he agreed to them. That rather stymied me so I drew up the contract in a way that put no onus on us. You're quite welcome to see it."

"Yes," he said, and gave a little grunt. "But there seems to have been reason on his side. After all, he *was* murdered. And at about two o'clock this afternoon, as a first guess. But about that change of locks. Surely he told you why they were changed?"

"He did," Nordon said. "It was because of a spate of burglaries in the town."

Grainger stared. He looked at Padman. Padman shrugged his broad shoulders.

"You're not pulling my leg by any chance?"

"No," Nordon told him curtly. "That's what he told me. It's in a report I sent to the office."

"The man must have been balmy," Padman told us. "We've been practically free of burglaries for months."

"Well, we'll take that much as read," Grainger said. "But who saw him last?"

"Probably I did," Nordon said, and explained about the after-lunch cup of tea. "He asked me to run down to the town and buy him this."

He passed that Will form over. Grainger looked at it and stared. He was having quite an afternoon of surprises and more were to come.

"What'd he want it for?"

"Don't ask me," Nordon said. "He merely wanted me to go down to a stationer's and buy it. But about who saw him last. There's just the possibility that he wasn't asleep when Mrs. Carver came up for the tray and cup."

"Mrs. Carver. She's the woman who went out."

"Yes," Nordon said, "and she shouldn't have gone out. Her instructions for this afternoon were to be ready at three to receive any callers, and to stay till six o'clock, when she would go for the night. I was to have the afternoon off till six o'clock."

He expanded a bit. Mrs. Carver had gone home to change, since Baldlow had rather sprung the job on her. She had returned when we two had arrived.

"Who went out first?"

"I'm pretty sure I did," Nordon told him.

"At what time?"

"Well, about ten to two."

"And you got back at?"

"After half-past two. Mr. Travers overtook me in his car and we came together."

Grainger pounced at once.

"Forty minutes to go down to a stationer's!"

"Oh, no," he was imperturbably told. "I had a beer at the Dog and Partridge. Baldlow never got really awake till half-past two, so I'd plenty of time. This house is teetotal, by the way. And I was only allowed to smoke downstairs."

Grainger looked at Padman. Padman had no questions.

"Why should Mrs. Carver suddenly go home?" Grainger asked.

Nordon shrugged his shoulders.

"I expect she'll tell you if she comes back."

"Where's she live?"

"No idea. I've never heard her mention it. I do have a vague idea it isn't too far away."

There was a moment of silence. I managed to cut in.

"There's something which might be urgent that I'd like to point out. When I showed Mrs. Howell into the dining-room I noticed a window was open at the bottom. It might have been the way by which the murderer came in."

"Why on earth didn't you say so before?"

Grainger was at the door. We followed him down the stairs and into the room. The window was still open. Grainger looked pretty hard at Nordon.

"You were in here with Mrs. Howell. You saw the window?"

"As a matter of fact I didn't. It wasn't cold in here, for one thing, and I sat in this chair. She was facing the window. If she'd felt a draught she'd have mentioned it." He shrugged his shoulders. "It may sound unobservant but that's the way it was. I was seeing to Mrs. Howell. I wasn't concerned with windows. And I had my back to it."

"Put a man outside and get it printed and look for footprints," Padman was told. Then Grainger was cocking an ear. He nipped across to the door. Mrs. Carver was just letting herself in. Padman was blocking my way and I couldn't see what was happening. I could only hear Grainger's voice.

"Mrs. Carver?"

"Yes"—somewhat tremulously—"that's me."

"We're the police, Mrs. Carver. I believe you found Mr. Baldlow dead."

"Yes, sir, and I never was so taken aback. I just couldn't—"

"You would be. But where've you been? We've been looking everywhere to ask you some questions."

"But I don't know anything. I went up to the poor gentleman—"

"All right, all right," Grainger's voice was very soothing. "Don't worry about that now. Just tell me why you left the house. I'm asking you because I'm given to understand you were to be here till six."

"It was my nerves, sir. I was all scared. If I stayed a minute longer I knew I was going to faint. I went out for a bit of fresh air, and when I was out I began to feel better so I came back."

"That's all right," Grainger told her. "But you stay on now and carry out your instructions just as if Mr. Baldlow was still alive. What's this room?"

"The drawing-room, sir. It isn't used much now."

Padman moved. I went forward in the queue and Nordon was behind me. Grainger and Mrs. Carver were in the second of the two front rooms. All I could see of it was a fawn carpet, a table with a pot plant in the bay window recess and a handsome corner cupboard packed with silver—good stuff by the look of it at that range. Then Grainger drew back. Nordon and I backed towards the front door.

"Good," Grainger said. "Light that electric fire and show any visitors in here. Then let me know who they are. Tell anybody you see.

"Just one question before I leave you," he was going on. "What time was it when you went home to dress?"

"About two, sir."

"Mr. Nordon had gone?"

"Yes, sir. I saw him go."

"And when you went up for Mr. Baldlow's lunch tray and tea-cup, did he speak to you?"

"Why no, sir! The bedroom door was shut and he was having his nap."

The sergeant came tentatively down the stairs.

"The lady upstairs is getting impatient, sir. She has an urgent appointment for four o'clock."

As we went up the stairs I was thinking pretty hard about Mrs. Carver. That excuse of hers seemed very much of a concoction. She'd been reasonably all right when I'd left her making herself a cup of tea in the kitchen. Why then had she suddenly left the house? Where had she been? And how did it fit in with that apprehensive look she'd given me each time she'd seen me? And hadn't Nordon reported that the daughter had looked scary at times?

There wasn't time for more conjecture. Grainger was entering the snuggery and we came behind him. Why he didn't keep out Nordon and myself I didn't know but we halted unobtrusively just inside the door. Mrs. Howell was kneeling by the fireplace, using a pair of bellows. She laid the bellows down and got to her feet. She was perfectly poised—just an enquiring look and the shadow of a polite smile.

Grainger introduced himself and Padman. Nordon and I—he had to explain us somehow since we were there—were two gentlemen who might be able to help. She looked faintly puzzled.

"Your uncle's died very suddenly," Grainger said, "and naturally it has to be enquired into. You're here to see him?"

There'd been never a tremor at that mention of death. On her face was only a kind of polite interest.

"He's dead, you say?"

"Yes. Mrs. Howell, isn't it?"

She gave a little nod.

"Do I understand you were asked to come here today?"

"I was," she said. "I had a letter from him on Thursday. It asked me to see him most urgently at three o'clock precisely."

"May I see his letter?"

"The letter?" The poise went for the merest moment. Her face flushed slightly. "The letter's probably at home."

"Then perhaps you'll bring it or send it on. Where do you actually live, Mrs. Howell?"

"At Liverdale. Grange Farm."

"That'd only be about thirty miles away. You came straight here?"

"No," she said. "We thought we'd have lunch here and we did have it here, at the Metropole. Just after half-past one. I left my husband to do some shopping"—she smiled—"window-shopping, mostly, and we agreed to meet at the Metropole again at four o'clock."

Grainger glanced at his watch.

"You still ought to make it. But your husband wasn't invited, then, to see your uncle?"

"He wasn't."

Grainger gave what was probably his nicest smile.

"That wouldn't mean that your uncle and he were on bad terms?"

Her eyes narrowed.

"It wouldn't," she told him curtly. It was like a slap in the face but Grainger was pretty resilient.

"Just a passing question," he told her. "But may I ask you to do something, Mrs. Howell? Go to the Metropole and have tea or do whatever you were going to do—except go home, of course—and then bring your husband here. Shall we say about five o'clock? I promise not to keep you more than a minute or two. You'll do that for me?"

"Certainly." The voice still had a certain frigidity. "If you think it necessary."

"Believe me I do. That's all, then, Mrs. Howell, and thank you for your co-operation. The Inspector here will see you down. It's still only a quarter to four."

The two went out. Grainger had a look at the fire which showed only a pin-point or two of red. He began tinkering with it and puffing with the bellows. He went through to Baldlow's bedroom and I followed. The body had gone and the doctors with it. A couple of finger-print men were at work. Grainger began telling one of them to see Mrs. Carver about the fire. I nipped back to the snuggery. I looked out of the window at Montague Road and the Corporation tennis courts that lay beyond. Mrs. Howell had gone. It was then that I heard the front-door bell.

Padman was just entering and he heard it too.

"Maybe another caller," I remarked to no one in particular.

Grainger must have heard that bell too, for he was looking down from the landing. I heard a man's voice—a youngish man's—and the voice, now absolutely different, of Mrs. Carver. She seemed to be greeting the caller with almost an enthusiasm.

Grainger must have beckoned to Padman. The two had a moment's conference and Padman fairly sprinted down the stairs. I drew back again. The finger-print man came in with some kindling. Grainger came in and took it from him and began rebuilding the fire. A few puffs with the bellows and there was a cheerful flame. Grainger began building the fire up with knobs of coal from the scuttle.

"You need us any longer?" I asked him quietly.

"Nordon certainly," he said. "You, I don't know. Depends on what you know."

"And that's a whole lot," I said. "I haven't even begun to talk."

There were voices on the stairs. A moment or two and Padman was ushering in a man of about thirty-five. He was about five-foot-nine, somewhat thin-faced, very well dressed and with rather a public-school look about him.

"Mr. Charles Tinley, sir."

Grainger came forward and shook hands as he introduced himself. Nordon and I were ignored in the background.

"You've come to see your uncle?" Grainger asked.

"Yes," Tinley said, and he had a pleasant baritone. "And perfectly staggered I was to hear from the Inspector here that he was dead." He gave Grainger a shrewd look and let it rove round the room to include Nordon and me, rather like one of those revolving cameras that take pictures of school groups. "I didn't mention it to the Inspector, but must I assume there was something wrong about the manner of his death?"

"Any sudden death, sir, necessitates enquiry," Padman told him.

"But not by the police, surely!"

Grainger scrubbed round that one.

"Did your uncle telephone you, Mr. Tinley, to see him this afternoon?"

"No," he said. "I had a letter from him on Thursday and it asked me to see him on urgent business at a quarter to four today. It mentioned a quarter to four *precisely*, and don't ask me why."

"May I see the letter?"

"The letter?" There was the same quick blankness that had been on the face of his sister. But he remembered to smile.

"Yes, the letter. It's at my flat. No reason, is there, why I should have it with me?"

"None whatever," Grainger told him suavely. "He didn't give any reasons for the urgency?"

"None at all. But I thought I'd better humour the old boy."

"You came from where?"

"From town, actually. I'm in business there and I live there. A flat at Friar's Court, Hendon."

"You got here, when?"

Tinley looked a bit puzzled but he answered the question.

"I had lunch at the Splendide and that'd be from about half-past twelve till half-past one."

"And then?"

"Oh, I just had a look round—the antique shops mostly. I knew where to find them. Used to be here quite often before my uncle got that damn complaint of his—got it badly, I mean."

"Ah, well," Grainger said almost resignedly; and then, as an afterthought: "You didn't run across your sister in the town?"

Tinley's eyes narrowed.

"My sister?"

"Yes. She had a letter too. Her appointment was for three o'clock, precisely."

At that moment there was an unexpected interlude—a kind of kick at the door, and, when Padman opened it, the entry of Mrs. Carver with a huge tea-tray.

"The master said anyone who called was to have tea," she announced, "so I'm doing as he said, even if he isn't here."

The flap of the desk was down and she put the tray there.

"How thoughtful of you, Emma," Tinley said. "Just what I can do with—a nice cup of tea."

She gave him a smile, then had a look round.

"Not enough cups. I'll bring two more, and some more hot water."

"Don't bother, Mrs. Carver," Grainger told her. "We'll manage."

"No trouble at all, sir," she told him. "A cup of tea does nobody any harm. I know Mr. Nordon likes his little cup."

She bustled out. Grainger shrugged despairing shoulders.

"Help yourself to tea, Mr. Tinley. But we were mentioning your sister. You didn't see her?"

"Hadn't the foggiest notion she was in the town."

"Your uncle was fond of you both, I take it?"

"Hard to tell," he said. "Between ourselves he was a selfish, self-centred old boy. Ever since I was of an age to appreciate the fact I've known that with him it was self first, and second and then a good helping of what was left over."

Emma Carver came in with two more cups and a jug of hot water. A word or two and she was out again. I was thinking how remarkably she had picked up. It was almost as if that little surreptitious trip of hers had taken quite a load off her mind.

"You knew your uncle had got religious?" I said to Tinley in the brief silence after the door closed.

Tinley, Grainger, Padman—the three were staring at me. Tinley was looking a bit confused. If I'd done nothing else I'd at least forced Grainger into introducing me. But I knew at once that I *had* done something else. I'd verified the fact that I did know a whole lot more than I'd told. That could be the only reason why he was introducing me handsomely. Mr. Ludovic Travers, often associated with the Yard, and head of the Broad Street Detective Agency.

"Religion, you say?" That was Tinley, after he'd said a how-d'you-do.

"Yes," I said. "He had it rather badly. But Mr. Grainger will tell you about it in his own good time."

Quite a masterstroke that, even though I say it. Grainger, from the mantelpiece where he'd set his cup, cut in at once.

"If it's important—yes. But may I suggest something to you, Mr. Tinley? Your sister and her husband are coming here at about five. I don't want to hurry you but could you come back here too?"

"Why not?" he said, and hastily gulped down the rest of his tea. "You say Tom Howell's here?"

"So your sister told me."

"You don't know where they are?"

"Can't say I do," prevaricated Grainger. "But you'll be seeing them at five."

The door closed on Tinley. Grainger waited a moment and then slightly opened it.

"Might be more visitors," he told us. "If they follow the pattern, then they're due at half-past four, and that's another quarter of an hour. Draw a chair up, Travers, and you too, Nordon. Sorry if I've seemed a bit abrupt but you know how it is and we don't expect murder cases down here. Tell us about that religion business you mentioned to Tinley just now."

I gave a strictly edited account of my first interview with Baldlow. I didn't mention his references to callers and to the last disposal of his money as being a sacred trust. I didn't think, for one thing, that I could have got across with the almost nauseating smugness and, for another, I still wanted to keep things up my sleeve. I wanted to be in at that enquiry, and for Grainger to have to lean on me. I didn't want bad publicity for the agency—that's what most of the reticence amounted to.

Nordon added his bit, chiefly atmosphere: teetotalism, long prayers, Sunday broadcasts and so on.

"Tell us something," Grainger said, and shrewdly. "That Last Will and Testament form you were sent to buy at the last moment. Was he going to change his will?"

"If so it would have to be a very quickly written one," he pointed out. "And there wouldn't be two witnesses tonight. I was due in just when Mrs. Carver was due out—at six o'clock."

"One thing seems certain," Padman said. "Mrs. Carver would be downstairs all the time, so she didn't count. But that letting Mr. Nordon off for the afternoon shows that things were going to be said that Baldlow wouldn't want him to hear. If that isn't tied up with the will, then I've lost my judgment."

We had helped ourselves to second cups and the cake plate had long been cleared. For quite a minute each of us was busy with his thoughts. Grainger spoke first, and to me.

"Think you can stay on till latish tonight?"

I said I could, provided I could ring the office. When I went to the telephone Grainger wanted to know if he should clear out, but I told him there was no need. I did get the office. Norris wasn't there but the operative in charge took a message. My wife was to be told I might be home quite late and Norris was to tell Mrs. Prince that the inquest was to be on—

I cupped the receiver and looked towards Grainger.

"Monday," he said. "We'll see to everything, if it's the Layman affair."

I passed that on, had the message spoken back and rang off. At that very moment there was the sound of the front-door bell. Padman was up like a streak and making for the landing and stairs.

"Might be a gentleman of the name of Lorde," I said casually.

V

THE VITAL QUESTION

I FELT a bit ashamed of that rather cheap display of omniscience, but Grainger had given me only a quick look as he went out. In any case I was lucky to be right. The man who came up with Padman did happen to be Francis Lorde, stepbrother of the dead man. When Grainger made the introductions this time, they were quite formal: just a, "Mr. Travers; Mr. Nordon."

Lorde was a tallish, heavily built man whose age was probably in the late fifties. His hair was greying and he had about the bushiest eyebrows I've ever seen. A pair of dark and what I'd call highly intelligent eyes looked out from under them.

"Mr. Lorde is Mr. Baldlow's step-brother," Grainger told me, and he couldn't help adding ironically: "Or did you know that?"

"I'd heard *of* Mr. Lorde but I hadn't had the pleasure of meeting him," I said.

"You're a solicitor, Mr. Lorde?" Grainger asked.

"Yes," Lorde said. "But about Henry—Mr. Baldlow. I understand he's died suddenly. May I be told just why it is that the police are here?"

He had spoken rather precisely, like a man accustomed to choosing words with care.

"With you I'll be frank," Grainger said. "We're not satisfied as to the cause of death. But to get back to yourself. Don't say that you had a letter telling you to see your step-brother on a matter of urgency and at four-thirty precisely?"

Lorde was quiet. I can only put it like that. It was as if the whole mechanism of the man halted for a good few seconds.

"You saw a copy of the letter?"

It was a queer question.

"Oh, no," Grainger said. "We haven't had time to look through any of his papers. But you're the third caller this afternoon. The first had had a letter to come at three o'clock precisely, and the second to come at a quarter to four precisely. You arrived at four-thirty and the rest seems obvious."

"May I ask who those callers were?"

"You mean you have no idea?"

A quick flush that might have been anger came to Lorde's face. A moment, and he had controlled himself.

"I'm afraid I haven't."

"Well, one was Mrs. Howell and the other her brother, Mr. Tinley."

"That's strange," he said. "I was spending the night with the Howells. I told her I had business this way and—"

"You didn't mention Seahurst by name?" I ventured to ask.

"I didn't." He gave me a not too successful smile. "We legal people have to be circumspect, you know. It's a natural instinct not to commit one's self, even over trivialities."

"May I see the letter from your step-brother?" Grainger asked.

"The letter?" Curious, wasn't it: the same hesitation or gaining time. "But the letter wasn't important. What I did with it I don't know. Probably threw it in the waste-paper basket."

"But it was important enough to bring you here?"

"Let's not get involved," Lorde said. "A letter asks me to come here on urgent business at a certain time. Why keep so simple a letter?"

"You replied to it?"

"There was no need. Henry and I understood each other. Besides, now I come to think of it, there was the usual addendum about expecting me unless he heard to the contrary."

"I understand. You've had tea, Mr. Lorde?"

"Thank you, yes."

"I asked partly because the Howells and Mr. Tinley are coming here at five o'clock," Grainger said. "But just for the records, when did you get to Seahurst?"

"When you say *records*, do you mean you want my alibi for some time or other?"

"I mean what I say," Grainger told him evenly. "I have to know the whereabouts of everybody concerned in any way with the dead man at a particular time."

The telephone went. Grainger took the call. His grunts and monosyllables told us nothing. In just over two minutes he was hanging up. He made a note in his book.

"You were saying, Mr. Lorde?"

"As a matter of fact I was saying nothing," Lorde told him dryly. "What I'm going to tell you will be, I hope, fully comprehensive. I'm the now senior member of French, Son and Lorde, of Dunland. You know it?"

"In Essex, isn't it?"

"Yes. A thriving market town. A letter reached me there by the afternoon post on Thursday last to the effect which I've already told you. The next day I rang the Howells—I'm very fond of them both—and told Tom Howell, who answered me, that I'd be down this way, etc. etc. He said Jane was out but he knew they'd be delighted to have me. I said I'd be along in time for the evening meal."

"That's indeed comprehensive," Grainger said. "And you got to Seahurst—when?"

"Earlier than I thought, but I didn't mind that. I've spent two holidays here, though I haven't been here for a couple of years now, and it was rather nice to look round again. I came by Tilbury-Gravesend and I think it was about midday when I got here. I had lunch straightaway at the Sussex, where I stayed before, and then I had a look round the town. I think it was about a quarter to two when I left the hotel. I got back again just after three o'clock and sat in the lounge talking to some people and had tea at just short of four o'clock. Then I came here."

"That's all very clear and we're most grateful to you." Grainger got to his feet. "If you'll excuse me a moment, I have to do something. Perhaps you'll come with me, Mr. Travers, and you too, Mr. Nordon."

We went through to Baldlow's bedroom. Grainger's suavity fell from him quicker than a rotten apple from a shaken bough. "Well, what else do you know?"

"I can't say," I told him mildly. "It's only when things begin to happen that one begins to remember. Lorde, for instance. Nordon was told about him by Mrs. Carver. He was the only relative left. Therefore he had to be the one who rang the door-bell at half-past four."

He frowned for a moment.

"Get this under your hat," I went on. "We're not here to obstruct. We're here, as long as you need us, to help."

"That's good of you," he said, if a bit grudgingly. Then he was looking at Nordon. "But we're getting all cluttered up. You prepared to go down to headquarters and dictate a full statement of all that happened while you've been here?"

Nordon looked at me. I said he'd be delighted. I asked if Grainger had got the exact time of death.

"From about two o'clock to a quarter-past," he said. "Judging by how far digestion had proceeded. One other thing. He'd taken a sleeping tablet after the meal."

Nordon gave me a look.

"I reported on that," he said. "I saw what looked a biggish flat pill-box by his bedside one day."

"Nothing particularly mysterious about that. The box was in that room of his. That complaint of his rather bothered him and Dr. Krane supplied him with the usual pink pills. But what I don't get is this. He had people coming to see him on what he'd called urgent business. I'd have thought he'd have wanted either to stay awake or else to wake up before what you, Mr. Nordon, called his usual half-past two."

Nordon shrugged his shoulders. All he could suggest was that the whole thing had become routine.

"You've found the box?"

"It was in his room," Grainger said. "The remaining pills were counted and Krane thinks all's in order."

There was the sound of the front-door bell. Grainger told Nordon to get along to police headquarters and then went out quickly to the stairs.

I went as quickly to the door and listened, and I was also trying to think. Perhaps it was that attempt at concentrating on two things at once that made the thinking muddled, but about the case as I so far saw it, there were things that were contradictory and highly suspicious, and the queer thing was that Grainger didn't seem aware of them. Maybe he too had been trying to do too many things at the same time.

I heard people coming up the stairs, so I went back to the snuggery. The fire was burning nicely and Lorde and Padman faced each other across it. Both got up as the main party came in. There were handshakes and smiles among the relatives and it was a minute or two before Grainger got everyone seated. All I'd noticed was the almost horrified look of surprise on Jane Howell's face when she saw Francis Lorde. I think, too, he must have given her some sign to keep quiet or else to be careful.

"There's no point in concealing the fact any longer," Grainger began, and as he bluntly gave them the facts about the murder, I was watching the newcomer, Tom Howell. He was a man of about five-foot-ten, his quite good-looking face tanned by the open air. He looked about forty and was wearing a cropped moustache, just a bit heavier than my own. There was quite a lot of the sahib about him. His clothes were good and he carried them well.

"There it is and there's the problem," Grainger was saying. "Correct me by all means if any of you think I'm wrong, but surely it can't be a coincidence that the murder took place on this of all days. We know that Mr. Baldlow led a quite uneventful life until today, but this one day he was doing something we're entitled to call eventful. He had all his relatives here to see him about matters which he termed urgent. Anybody like to suggest what the urgency was?"

"Nothing was mentioned in *my* letter." That was Tinley. The others echoed it.

"Well, something else. Just before he took his fatal nap, Mr. Baldlow sent for a Last Will and Testament form. Does that strike a chord?"

"As far as my wife and I are concerned, we didn't give a damn what he did with his money," Howell said brusquely.

"I think that applies to me too." That was Tinley.

"Money's a useful commodity," Lorde said, "but I could survive without any legacy from Henry Baldlow."

"Well, you're all lucky to be in that position," Grainger told them. "But a very blunt question and I want blunt answers. No statements are being taken, as you see. The question is this. You, Mr. Lorde. What was your frank opinion of Henry Baldlow?"

Lorde pursed his lips and frowned.

"Strictly between ourselves he grew up into a man impossible to like or to—how shall I put it—to see through. I knew him to be selfish and dictatorial. That's as far as I'm prepared to go at the moment, unless I add that when I was here I didn't stay with him but at the Sussex. Outwardly we were quite good friends."

"You, Mr. Tinley?"

"I neither liked him nor disliked him. I could do without him, if you know what I mean. I agree he was dictatorial. Even aggressive. He liked his own way. A kind of miniature Hitler. Well, not so bad as that, of course, but you gather what I mean. I stayed in this house with him for one holiday but I took damn good care not to repeat the dose."

"And you, Mrs. Howell?"

"Well, he was a business man," she said. "That explains a lot. Also he liked to interfere and he expected you to be excessively grateful for the smallest thing. I felt I had a niece's duty to him and that's all. Frankly, I didn't like him."

Grainger looked round at them.

"Well, I promised not to keep any of you. I must modify that to this extent. I'd like you to have dinner together, shall we say, at an hotel. Which hotel?"

They looked round at each other. Lorde suggested the Sussex.

"Very well, the Sussex. Not later than half-past eight. I'll ring Mr. Lorde there to say if any of you will be wanted any further tonight." He switched on the light, for the room was getting very near dark. "I think you can practically rely on my not wanting you. If I do want you later, then I know where to find you. Just to check, you might write down your private addresses and telephone numbers. You'll probably be needed in any case for the inquest."

*

The house seemed very quiet. Mrs. Carver had been sent home. Padman had gone I didn't know where. The curtains had been drawn in the snuggery, and a snuggery it looked, with the fire stirred to a hearty blaze. Grainger had just told me there were no prints except Mrs. Carver's on that dining-room window. We'd agreed that it was a mystery how it came to be unlatched, even if he'd found one of the kitchen windows unlatched too. It was curious. But for the impeccability of Nordon and Mrs. Carver and her daughter, it might have been an inside job. Refitting the whole house with fresh locks and then not to have the windows properly checked was merely lunacy according to Grainger. There were faint marks of feet outside that window, by the way, though nothing capable of being used for a cast.

"It was as good a window to try as any," I said. "Hidden from next door by that horrible shrubbery and nothing to overlook the house from the front. But it doesn't look like a woman's job. Those high heels Mrs. Howell was wearing must have made marks."

"I doubt it," he said. "No flower-beds under that window. The grass is almost like concrete. Feel like giving me a hand with his papers? Better take your prints first."

We went methodically through the desk and found nothing that seemed to have the least bearing on things.

"This seems to prove something," I said, and pointed to the pile of receipted bills. "I wondered if Mrs. Carver had got alarmed—as she certainly did—at the mention of the police, because she'd been cooking the accounts. But this shows Baldlow paid all bills. She merely did some of the ordering."

"I think she just got the wind up generally," he said. "I don't think she's anything but an inoffensive old soul. Wonder if Baldlow had a safe?"

That going off at a tangent put me off my mental balance for a moment. And Grainger had begun looking behind pictures. I was about to suggest ringing Nordon when he took a bunch of keys out of his pocket—Baldlow's keys that had been in the dead man's trousers pocket. He made for the little square mahogany cupboard on which stood the wireless set. I'd seen it but had taken it for a record cabinet. It had twin doors. Grainger tried a key or two and a door opened. He unlatched the other and opened it too and there was the safe: not too massive an affair of about fifteen inches high and a foot each way. It was an old-fashioned type opening with a key.

Grainger dusted for prints. One or two of Baldlow's came up, but no others. He gently opened the door and inside were quite a lot of papers. It took us half an hour to go through them thoroughly. They were practically all to do with investments or his former business and had again no apparent bearing on the case. There was no will.

But we had the name of his solicitors whom he'd apparently acquired since coming to Seahurst. Probably they'd been the vendors' solicitors in the purchase of the house, Grainger said, and Baldlow had taken them on. They were an excellent firm. He himself knew George Bowchett well, through the Rotary Club.

"Wonder if he might happen to be at home," Grainger said, and looked up his number. He began to flick the pages of the directory when something caught his eye. He called me over. It was that Page 1 that he was pointing out—the one with the spaces for writing down the names and numbers of friends, tradesmen and so on.

"Bowchett's here. Look, under the A to D."

He made a mental note of the number and gave the directory to me.

"Look through those people he's written, will you, and see if there's anything that strikes a bell."

I found no more than half a dozen: the Howells, Charles Tinley, Francis Lorde, United Jewellers, Canon Orifice and Dr. Krane. Several were just initials, and not one of those had an S for Seahurst before the number, so heaven knew where they were actually located.

"Bowchett won't talk over the telephone," Grainger reported. "He's only a couple of hundred yards away so he'll slip along at once. I had the devil of a job convincing him it was urgent. You found anything?"

I told him what I'd found and drew his attention to the numbers with only initials or a single letter for names. And the curious thing was that two of those initials were on the stubs of his cheque-book.

"Probably old friends. I'll slip down and meet Bowchett. Your car, by the way, has been put in the garage way."

When I heard him downstairs I switched off the light, drew the blind slightly and had a look out. A street lamp made things reasonably bright and I saw Grainger speak to the uniformed constable on duty at the gate. He turned back and then halted. Someone—Nordon, it looked like—was at the gate. Grainger had a couple of minutes' talk with him. Nordon moved on. I replaced the curtain and switched on the light. I heard Grainger coming quickly up the stairs.

"Bowchett'll come right up," he told me. "I've left the door open. Your man just turned up, by the way. He said he'd made a complete statement. I told him to get himself a meal at my expense. He may have to stay here all night. Almost certainly will. I'll have to go into that statement of his for one thing. That all right with you?"

"Most certainly," I said. "Didn't I assure you we'd do all we could to help?" I almost added that Nordon couldn't protest in any case. Murder's a mighty serious business.

Grainger was warming his hands at the fire. Steps were heard and in a minute Bowchett was coming in. He was a somewhat untidy man of about sixty: rather short, plump almost to fatness and wearing horn-rims almost as big as my own. Grainger introduced me.

"A dreadful business about Baldlow," Bowchett said. "Am I to gather he was murdered?"

Grainger told him so much and no more. What he wanted to hear about was the will.

"There is none," he said. "Unless he made one of his own or someone else drew it up."

He explained. There had been a will which Baldlow cancelled when he came to Seahurst. Bowchett's managing clerk had drawn up a new will, after an interview in which Bowchett had noted the provisions.

"Strictly between ourselves I think Baldlow got alarmed when that first symptom of emphysema hit him," he said. "He was a bit of an old woman: very careful about his health and all that, but at any rate he made this new will."

"Remember the main provisions?" There was a little chuckle as Grainger put the question. "You'll have to tell us sooner or later so you might as well tell us now."

"Yes," Bowchett said reflectively. "I suppose we shall. The estate then might have come to about six figures gross but it'll be much less now. His investments were practically all industrials and they've depreciated heavily the last three years as you know. After duties I'd say there might be forty or fifty thousand."

"And who got it?"

"Very briefly, and as far as I remember, Lorde, his step-brother, got ten thousand and there was something for Lorde's two sons. Mrs. Howell got ten thousand; his nephew got a hundred pounds. There were various small legacies and the remainder was to be in trust for any Howell children. That's very roughly, of course, but I don't think you'll find it so far out."

"Charles Tinley only a hundred pounds," Grainger said. "Almost like a legacy of spite. Did he say anything to you about it?"

"I don't think he did, except perhaps that he was well provided for."

"So are the Howells, apparently. So is Lorde, or ought to be. But let's leave it. What happened to that Will?"

"About a year or so ago he cancelled it and said he'd have another drawn up. As far as we're concerned, he made no other."

"Any reasons?"

"None—really. He said circumstances had arisen. You know the kind of thing."

"Did you deduce anything?"

"It isn't our business to. We merely awaited his instructions. But I did happen to meet him on the front one day—in August, I think it was—and ventured to remind him that he was at that moment intestate. He told me quite genially that he was perfectly well aware of it."

*

The downstair door that opened for Bowchett must have admitted Padman. I wondered where he'd been. Grainger was good enough to let him tell me.

He'd been at headquarters and had had a look, for one thing, through Nordon's statement. He'd also been making enquiries about Mrs. Carver. And he'd come across something that might be important. Mrs. Carver hadn't taken a walk to steady her nerves or sat in a shelter on the front. She'd apparently gone straight from Montague Road to her home. A nosey character across the way at Albert Road had happened to see her and had been interested because she had seemed in such a hurry.

She stayed in the house for best part of half an hour, and was in the same hurry when she left. But the interesting thing that was gleaned was that her son-in-law—O'Brien—used to look after the garden of The Croft in his spare time. He was a garage-hand, employed by the Wayside Garage, a smallish concern at the corner of Albert and Halpin Roads.

"What are the gardens here?" I asked him. "I haven't had a look at the back."

"Just grass and another shrubbery at the end," he said. "I've checked it myself. All O'Brien would have to do would be to cut grass and keep things tidy. Three or four hours a week'd see to the whole thing."

"O'Brien hasn't bolted?"

"Can't say yet, sir. A man's on the lookout. I'll know pretty soon if he has."

By the time we'd exhausted the strange case of Emma Carver, Nordon was back. It was eight o'clock.

"You didn't have much of a meal?" Grainger said.

"Didn't feel like one. Had a couple of sandwiches and a beer."

It was I who told him he'd be staying all night at the least. Grainger added he might as well get along to headquarters with Padman and he'd be there himself in a few minutes. Nordon tipped me a wink. What it meant I didn't know, unless it was that he'd been highly circumspect about that report of his.

"I may as well be pushing off myself," I said when the other two had gone.

"Why not," he said. "I know where to get in touch with you."

Then he gave a rather queer smile.

"It's curious, in a way. Suppose we can't get to the bottom of this business—haven't all the facilities and so on—and have to call in the Yard, there's just the chance that you might be co-opted, so to speak, yourself."

"That's a faint chance," I said. "But you'll get to the bottom of it. So far there seems a very limited circle of suspects."

"But tell me," he said. "Imagine you were in my shoes. What's the sort of focal point? Someone who knew Baldlow was about to make a new will?"

"In that case it was someone who knew he'd destroyed the old."

"Yes," he said heavily. "And everything points to the fact that he hadn't made a new one. So what *is* the focal point, if you know what I mean."

"I know what you mean," I said. "It's another expression for motive. But shall I tell you what to my mind is the one outstanding clue? Not clue, perhaps, but a question you've got to answer?"

"Just what I'm waiting for."

"The question's this," I said. "Why did Baldlow intend to see those three relatives at carefully spaced intervals? God knows I'm not claiming any kind of mental superiority, but that's a question that wants answering. When you have the answer I'm prepared to bet you'll finish the case."

He went down with me to my car and gave me the road while I backed out. He looked in the window for a last word. I had it, or at least the first.

"Sending those relatives home?"

"Probably," he said. "I've still a few minutes in which to decide."

He drew back and I moved the car on. I had to smile to myself as I rounded the bend into London Road. It would indeed be strange if I did happen, as Grainger had put it, to be co-opted to that case. For many years I had been acting as what the Yard calls an unofficial expert but only when Chief-Superintendent George Wharton took over a murder case. It was in such a capacity that I had first run across Grainger, but the ironically amusing thing was that he had envisaged the possibility of his own failure to find who'd killed Baldlow, and he'd looked sufficiently far ahead to come off his high horse and let me in on those beginnings of his enquiry.

I didn't know then what was to happen in the morning.

PART II

VI
NEW ASSIGNMENT

BERNICE, my wife, asked me why on earth I was scowling. It was about half-past nine that Sunday morning. We'd eaten a service breakfast and she was running a quick duster over the lounge where I was cosily in front of the electric fire and ostensibly doing a crossword.

I said mildly that I wasn't actually aware that I had been scowling and I was sorry if I'd terrified her. She said indignantly that she hadn't been terrified. There might have been one of those fatuous but not unfriendly domestic arguments if the telephone hadn't rung.

It was Nordon. He said Grainger had just given him the all clear and he was coming back to town. What he wanted was any instructions. I said he'd better see me at the office at nine-thirty in the morning. Bernice had departed to the bedroom. I hung up and went back to my crossword. And still ostensibly.

I like crosswords: they might have been invented for my kind of brain. I look forward to doing my one each weekday, and two, or even three, on a Sunday. But that morning I was obsessed with a different kind of crossword and I had questions to ask myself that differed vastly from those on the printed page. There was that vital one I'd mentioned to Grainger. There was the unsolved mystery of Emma Carver's hasty and surreptitious visit to her home. There was the look I'd seen on her face and the same apprehensive look that Nordon had seen on the face of her daughter. Floating around, like nebulae among these comparative planets, were things like the look on the face of Jane Howell when she'd seen Lorde, and Baldlow's mention of money as a sacred trust, and a forthcoming Oxford Movement and the purchase of a Will form which a man in Baldlow's position would never be likely to use. I think I was just about at those three (?) letters which Baldlow had surreptitiously given to Mrs. O'Brien to post when the telephone went again. It was Norris this time, ringing from his private address.

We had a talk about business generally and he wanted to know if I'd found out anything more about Luke Layman. I realised then that Norris must have assumed I'd been tied up all day on the Layman affair, for that was what had taken me to Maverton and Seahurst. I didn't feel like going into things over the telephone so I said everything could keep until the morning. I did add that it looked as if Luke had had an accident in the fog and that later I'd got my own self mixed up with something at Seahurst which had kept me late.

"I'd have rung you down there if I'd known where to get you," he said. "There was a new development with Mrs. Prince. She's a bit scatterbrained at times and she was all upset when you saw her. But Luke didn't get that telephone message by chance. I wondered about that myself and that's why I asked her. Luke'd have been at the pictures or somewhere, if he wasn't working. He wouldn't, have stayed in that room doing nothing. He was there because a call had come for him in the morning when he was out. A man had asked to speak to him and hadn't given any name. He said Luke'd know. She said Luke was out and he said he'd ring again at about a quarter to four. She told Luke that when he came in to dinner."

"Does she remember the kind of voice?"

"An old man," she said. "A bit quivery-quavery."

I said we'd go into it in the morning. So much for Norris. I went back to my crossword, and this time I couldn't keep my mind away from Luke. I turned to the book page and looked at the new announcements of masterpieces and knew that from past experience both Bernice and I would probably find them unreadable or even nauseating. Then that telephone went for the third time. It was the man on duty at the office.

A Mr. Howell had asked for me and had been told, quite rightly, that the agency was only open, as it were, for the running of work in hand. Howell, however, insisted that his was a matter of extreme urgency. Had it been right to give him my private number?

Howell rang me about ten minutes after that.

"I'd like to see you today," he said. "It's something I consider really urgent."

I was interested. I asked him where and when. He suggested a half-way house, a very nice private hotel just off the main road through Bromley. He'd see me there at noon and would arrange for lunch. I said I'd be there. Bernice and I always had a service lunch on a Sunday and she in any case was going to a symphony concert.

I got to the hotel just before time but he was there already. The first time I saw him I'd thought there was an air of money about him, and there was definitely a look of money about that car of his—a Jaguar that was almost new. He was on the watch for me and was holding out his hand as soon as I got out of my own car.

"Come and have a drink," he said. "Lunch is at twelve-thirty."

We had our drinks in front of a fire in a deserted lounge. He got down to business after the first gulp.

"Mind if I tackle this in my own way?"

"Why not?"

"Well, then, you'll want to know how I got on to you. Your people acted for Harley-Grear and he's a friend of mine. He was rather struck by you yourself, I gather, and when I saw you down there yesterday I began to get ideas. Like to tell me why you were there?"

"That's confidential," I told him. "I will tell you that I personally blundered into things. I just happened to be there."

"You know everything that happened last night?"

"Up to a quarter-past eight—yes."

"You didn't know that Grainger came to the Sussex and gave us all a grilling?"

"I didn't. Between ourselves, what did he grill you about?"

"We had best part of an hour of it. None of us had a perfectly good alibi for one thing."

"Tell me something, still in the strictest confidence. I shan't turn you in if the answer's yes, and, of course, you could deny it. But did you kill Baldlow?"

He gave me a rather dry look.

"You're the sort of chap I like dealing with. But, no. I didn't kill him. I didn't like him: he just wasn't my sort. We'd nothing in common. He stayed at our place once and I found him a frightful old bore. One had to be decent to him and all that, but there you are."

"You know how he was killed?"

"Oh, yes," he told me unconcernedly. "Grainger tried to spring it on us but we were all a bit too sated at the time. Like expecting you to be terrified of the last jump after you've got round the course. But what I didn't like was this." He lowered his voice and leaned forward. "He said the crime was just as easy for a woman as a man. I didn't like that. My wife had been upset enough already."

"Did he emphasise anything else?"

"Yes—the letters. Each of them, so I gathered—I didn't actually see my wife's—said no need to answer if coming, if you follow me. What *he* kept hammering at was why three people who'd owned up they didn't like him should have come running at the double when he wanted them to."

"And the answer was?"

He shrugged his shoulders.

"Well, blood's thicker than water, for one thing, and he did say it was urgent. And money's money. As Lorde said, it's useful. Why antagonise the old boy?"

"Three very sound reasons," I said. "And now a question of my own. What do you want us—I mean the Broad Street Detective Agency—to do about it?"

"I want you to look after my wife's interests."

I didn't see it. I asked him to be more explicit. Did he mean that he wanted us to undertake an independent enquiry into the murder of Henry Baldlow?

"Yes," he said. "That about covers it."

"Then it's only fair to tell you that you're likely to waste a whole lot of money. The Seahurst police will do their damnedest to solve the case: if they can't they'll almost certainly call in Scotland Yard. If your wife is innocent, and you're sure enough about that, why employ us? Frankly, it doesn't make sense."

"I thought you'd say that. All the same it'd relieve my mind. All this is off the record?"

"Strictly so."

He leaned forward again.

"I'm worried about Jane—that's my wife. There was something wrong about her when she got the letter. I didn't know about it till lunch and she told me about it a bit too casually."

He was a man, I'd say, who rarely indulged in gestures, but now he lifted his hands and let them fall.

"You're married?"

"Yes."

"Then you'll know," he said. "That letter upset her somehow. She'd been crying but I didn't let on that I knew. I actually saw her crying on the Saturday morning before we left for Seahurst, and she isn't a one to do that sort of thing. She's got all the pluck in the world. Now she's a bit better, only worried a bit over that letter which Grainger wants. She thinks she must have burnt it."

The gong went for lunch. Howell reckoned our table would be fairly secluded and we could go on talking over the meal. That was how it turned out. There was no one within a couple of tables of us.

"Your wife knows about your coming here this morning?" was the first question I asked him.

"No," he said. "Lorde had to leave soon after nine and she seemed much more cheerful. I had to see a man not far from here about a horse, and I'm busy tomorrow, so I made it an excuse. She didn't suspect anything, I'm sure of that. And I don't want her to. This business is strictly between you and me."

I thought it tactful to say his wife might have read into her uncle's letter some resentment or annoyance that might have prejudiced, say, any bequests to her or the boy.

"She has money of her own," he said. "That wouldn't worry her. I'm not a millionaire but I've plenty, even in these times. Mind you, there *is* another baby on the way. I only knew it a fortnight ago, but that wouldn't have worried her. She was delighted about it. We'd always intended to have about three. And she had no trouble at all when the boy was born."

"Don't think me ultra-cautious," I said, "but conducting an independent enquiry into a murder is a mighty tricky business. I've got to know every angle. This business of your wife's being upset, for instance. Would you like to give me her history, as you know it? How you met her? What her background was?"

He made no bones about it. Her people were well enough off and she had been to a very expensive school. During the war she was an officer in the W.R.N.S. He met her at the house of mutual friends in town in 1947 and they had been married the following year. She had about fifteen thousand pounds from her parents' estate. They'd been killed—he wasn't aware that I knew it—in a raid on Exeter.

"Everything simple enough, as you see," he said. "We've been most happy. She likes the things I like and—well, I guess we're lucky people. Or were, till this came along."

There'd been something of the schizophrenic about me during that long talk. To undertake such an enquiry was something that I normally would never have dreamed of considering, but there were things to set on the other side. Our name seemed bound to crop up at the inquest on Baldlow, and the fact that we'd supplied protection that hadn't protected was a something that might do the agency considerable harm. And if I did accept Howell's proposition, then I could keep it to myself, to this extent, that I could convince Grainger that I had a legitimate interest in the case because of Nordon. I could even tactfully throw myself in his way and hope that he'd find a private use for me, and for what he'd think his own ends.

"Let's say I'll undertake this enquiry," I told Howell. "It's going to cost a lot of money. If I employ another man or two besides myself, it'd cost you twenty-five pounds a day and expenses. We'd work for a fortnight and then, if nothing had happened, you'd have the option of calling us off."

"As you wish," he said. "I'm prepared to start off with a thousand pounds and what you quote is well inside it. My wife is to know nothing. I'm not going to have her badgered by anyone."

That was virtually the end of it. He agreed to come to the office on the Tuesday and sign a contract and give an advance cheque. I shouldn't be waiting for that. I was getting to work the very next morning.

I didn't drive straight back but rang Norris at his house to make sure he'd be in and then drove round that way. We had a very long talk. The job was worth a lot of money and it would be a tricky one. Our last item for discussion was who was to work with me. Nordon couldn't be the man. He couldn't show his face in Seahurst without giving the game away: besides, I had another job for him. I suggested Hallows. Norris thought certain readjustments would make him available.

Hallows had been with the agency since long before my time. He was an operative for whom I'd always had a great regard, and he and I had worked together more than once on jobs which might be called out of the rut. He was about forty. In appearance he was unobtrusive, and that's a good thing in his job. He was a man at whom you'd never look back if you passed him even in a lonely street. Even if you glanced at him he'd have gone at once out of your mind. And he had the right sort of brains.

Norris wasn't too happy about this new case of ours: it wasn't hard to see that. It wasn't the unusualness of it all that was worrying him but the method of tackling it. He didn't see how we could work under cover. Sooner or later Grainger's lines of enquiry would cross our own and then we'd have to come out into the open. There might arise a question of our concealing evidence.

"That won't arise just yet," I told him. "What I have in mind hasn't yet occurred to Grainger, or at least I'm pretty sure it hasn't. I'm proposing not an enquiry into the actual murder to begin with, that is—but into Mrs. Howell."

He stared.

"But that isn't the assignment! It's the very thing her husband doesn't want done."

"You're a little ahead," I told him. "Her husband won't have her badgered and she's not to know what he's done. She won't be badgered, and she won't know. But she's our main clue. That letter she got from Baldlow upset her badly. I've got to know why. She didn't show it to her husband. Now she says she burnt it. And now Baldlow's dead—still according to her husband— she's chipping up a bit. And something else about that letter. Baldlow had it posted more or less surreptitiously by Mrs. O'Brien. He didn't ask Nordon to post it. He wanted Nordon out of the house when Jane Howell and the others arrived."

"But there were three letters, one to each of the relatives."

"I know," I said. "But we start with Jane Howell's. We find out all we can about her. If we get the right answers, then we'll have the answers to the other two people and their letters. If we don't, then we shift the enquiry to either Tinley or Lorde."

"But suppose they produce their letters."

"Lorde's already said he threw his into the wastepaper basket. It's almost a certainty that Tinley will claim something of the sort. Grainger let ail those people get together at the Sussex Hotel for an hour or two. Even though Tom Howell was there, you can bet there was a fusing of ideas, deliberately or by chance. By half-past eight last night they'd all decided that their letters had said there was no need to reply unless they weren't coming. Those letters, Norris. *That's where the answer is.*"

"I'm beginning to see that," he said. "There *was* something in them that made them all come running. But about the enquiry. Would it be possible to glean things from Grainger? Have him work for us without knowing it?"

I said I'd be seeing him in the morning and was going to try to use him through a piece of information. Then I remembered Nordon. We'd be seeing *him* in the morning. He might tell us quite a lot more about Grainger's ideas, especially if Grainger had questioned him closely.

We did learn a thing or two from Nordon. About that opened window, for instance. Mrs. Carver had been seen by one of Padman's men and had admitted that she always opened that particular window after lunch, so as to clear the room of tobacco smoke. It was the nearest window and the natural one to open, but she couldn't swear to fastening the catch. She had been all of a fluster, she said, after Baldlow had sprung that afternoon job on her. Grainger was wondering if she'd forgotten the window altogether and had left it open.

"I'd been worrying about something," Nordon said, "but I think I've got the answer. It was why did Baldlow spring that afternoon job on Mrs. Carver so late. I think the answer's this. On Saturdays there's a final delivery of letters at between midday and one o'clock, according to district. Baldlow saw the postman go by, which meant that none of the people he'd written to were calling off. If they had been, then he might have had to change his plans."

That seemed an excellent piece of deduction, and yet it gave me a glimpse of a further mystery. Everyone was on the telephone. Inability to come might have been telephoned—with the courage and immunity of distance—asking what the urgency was. Apparently no one had done so. The letters must have been peremptory and backed by some authority. Those who received them *had* to come, and Jane Howell—level-eyed and superbly poised—had been brought to tears at the prospect.

I didn't mention those thoughts to Norris or Nordon. For one thing the ideas merely flashed through my mind, and I had to take in what Nordon was saying about Mrs. Carver. The Carver ménage, according to Nordon, was Grainger's hope. The man O'Brien, hadn't yet been questioned, as far as Nordon knew, but he was certainly going to be.

"Grainger question you a lot?" I asked.

"No," he said. "Only asked me to elucidate a point or two, or add to something. He didn't seem interested in that religious business."

"Just what report did you give him?" Norris wanted to know.

"Well, I hadn't a chance to confer with anyone here, and I don't know the law on such matters, so I told practically everything I knew. I thought it might be awkward for the agency if they saw my original reports and things didn't tally."

"You were right," I said. "As my old nurse used to say—tell the truth and shame the devil."

In any case I wasn't worrying. When I'd briefed Nordon I hadn't told him everything that had transpired between me and Baldlow that morning at Montague Road. What I told him now was that Norris had a new job for him, and that he'd better report again at two o'clock for briefing. I did add we were very satisfied with how he'd handled everything at Seahurst.

Even before Nordon had arrived, Bertha Munney—the secretary-receptionist—had been ringing the various agencies in town, beginning with those who, we knew, had employed Luke Layman. Just after midday those enquiries had ended in the air. No one had rung Luke about an assignment that fatal day. In connection with that, I had to point something out to Nordon when he arrived for briefing. He was pretty surprised to know he was going to put in a couple of days on the matter of Luke's death, that is, until he learned of certain suspicions.

"That diary book of his," I said. "Mrs. Prince will swear he took it with him. It was a record of his various assignments. Why take it with him that afternoon if an agency wasn't employing him?"

Nordon had no idea.

"Of course it might have been some out-of-town agency," I said. "Now you knew him fairly well—"

"Not so well as you'd think," he said. "Luke wasn't a talker. I doubt if I knew any more about his private affairs after that job we did together than I did at the start. As for that book, I never saw it. What was it like?"

I told him. I said he was to start from Luke's garage and work his way down to the scene of the presumed accident, leaving the London Road for that side road that came out just a mile or so short of Maverton. The pubs wouldn't have been open, so it'd be no use enquiring there, but somewhere Luke had acquired a quartern bottle of whisky. Garages might be questioned in case he'd pulled up for anything, and, if so, had they found that diary book. Wine and spirit stores should be questioned.

"It sounds a vague assignment," I told him finally, "and, frankly, I'm not too hopeful. But I think we owe it to Luke to be absolutely satisfied his death was due to no outside cause. If you don't find anything, don't report till you're satisfied you've done all you can. And do the job thoroughly. It's the firm's time you're using, not your own."

Nordon left. Bertha rang through to say Hallows was waiting.

VII

ON THE JOB

HALLOWS left for Exeter by a late afternoon train. I left at about four o'clock for Seahurst by car, and I shouldn't get there till well after dark. The previous day we'd had to put the clocks back and it'd be dusk soon after half-past four. I'd booked a room by telephone at the Sussex.

It was six o'clock when I drew up outside police headquarters at Seahurst. Neither Grainger nor Padman was there, but they got Grainger on the telephone and he asked me to come round to his house. It was only three minutes' walk away, so I left the car in the police garage.

I'd never somehow thought of Grainger as a married man with three children. The youngest, a girl of sixteen, was quite charming, and I liked the wife. She said I must be frozen after a drive on such a raw night and insisted on making me a cup of tea. After it came in, Grainger and I were left to ourselves. I'd told him, perfectly truthfully, that I'd a new case in Devonshire and that I'd intended to leave for it the next morning, but I'd thought of something to do with the Baldlow case, so I'd booked a room at a hotel in Seahurst and had decided to look him up.

"Anything new yourself?" I said. "Just in case it should happen to overlap?"

There was nothing, he said, except that O'Brien had been questioned. He'd been working on his allotment, which was on the waste ground at the back of his house, from about half-past one till nearly three o'clock. He'd just been clearing up generally, he said, and anyone might have seen him. But he couldn't quote anyone whom he'd seen. His wife said he'd been indoors from at least three o'clock onwards. As for working at The Croft, he hadn't been there since the beginning of October. The grass hadn't looked like growing any more and he'd left everything tidy.

"Doesn't get us much further forward," he said. "But what's this idea of your own?"

"It's just a bit involved," I said, "but I think you ought to see Canon Orifice of St. Martin's. I believe he's a strong supporter of the Oxford Movement, or Moral Re-armament or whatever they're now calling it."

"Mind explaining? You're getting me out of my depth."

I explained. Baldlow had got religion through the Oxford Movement, or Moral Re-armament or whatever they preferred to call themselves. I'd seen him only the once and it had struck me that he'd become slightly off his balance—religiously, that is. He'd told me, for instance, that he'd come to regard his money as a sacred trust. Mightn't that connect up with some religious mania whereby or where-through he was intending to leave that money only to people minded like himself? Had he, in other words, called the original beneficiaries to an interview—carefully timing things so that each should be unaware of the visits of the others—in which he intended to make sure if they were the right sort of people, from his new point of view, to be left money?

"It's possible," he said. Then he frowned. "Something I haven't told you. Mrs. Howell rang yesterday to say she must have inadvertently destroyed her letter. Tinley wrote this morning to say much the same thing. Lorde had already admitted destroying his. Funny, isn't it?"

"It certainly is," I said. "And if those letters contained something by which the recipient knew he was likely to be cut out of the will, then you have a motive for murder."

"I've thought so all along, but not from the same angle."

"So why not see Orifice?" I said. "It's quite likely that Baldlow may have made him a confidant."

He went to the telephone at once. Five minutes later we were on our way. The rectory was less than a five minutes' walk.

I recognised Orifice from Nordon's description. He was the hearty, chatty sort too: one whose harp was never likely to be hung on the willows. And he might have made quite a reasonably good character actor. There was his solemnity at what he called the tragedy of Baldlow's death in contrast to his gradual burgeoning into full and enthusiastic bloom in the matter of the Oxford Movement.

"That's one of the tragedies," he said. "It was he and I together who had organised that meeting for Wednesday next. You knew about it?"

I'd primed Grainger about it on the way.

"I saw a notice of it," he said. "But any special reason for next Wednesday?"

"Well, yes," Orifice said. "He was very shortly going to South Africa—his complaint, you know. There wasn't a lot of time left, and as it was at one such meeting here that his outlook changed, he wanted another as a sort of parting—what shall I say?—well, remembrance or benediction."

"What are such meetings like? Just ordinary religious services?"

"They vary very much," Orifice told him. "I must confess that it was shaped very much to suit myself. We opened with a prayer and a hymn and a short Bible reading and then there was a speaker: after that the meeting was open for anyone to mention personal experiences or difficulties. It was two members of my old college who actually arranged that first meeting here."

"And it was at that meeting that Mr. Baldlow changed his point of view as far as religion was concerned?"

"Undoubtedly. Three or four people had spoken and then he spoke—"

"Pardon me," I said, "but it was you who asked him to be there?"

The Canon smiled. His dentures were an appalling fit. "Not asked—suggested."

"And what did he actually say when he spoke at that meeting?"

Orifice frowned.

"That's rather like revealing the secrets of the confessional."

"We're trustworthy people," Grainger told him. "We're talking in the strictest confidence."

"Well"—he pursed his lips as he hesitated—"I can only say he alluded to himself as one who had been a business man and had been guilty, perhaps, of what one calls sharp practice. He told me afterwards that something had impelled him to get on his feet. The speaker's subject, by the way, had been honesty in business."

"Would I be right in saying he underwent a kind of conversion?"

"Quite right."

"He was absolutely sincere?"

"Absolutely. I was his friend as well as his pastor and I knew."

Then something struck him. I wondered why it hadn't before.

"But may I ask where all this is leading?"

"Nowhere," Grainger said bluntly. "Baldlow was murdered. It's up to us to find out everything about his life and habits and even his friends. Something might emerge to give us a clue to who killed him."

He went right on, cutting off the Canon's attempt to speak.

"You, for instance, were his close friend. Did he ever mention any enemies to you?"

"None. None at all. I couldn't conceive of him having enemies."

"No trouble with anyone at all?"

"None."

He hesitated again, made as if to speak, and then gave a quick shake of the head.

"Yes?" Grainger said. "You've thought of something?"

"Nothing of importance, I assure you."

"Won't you let us judge that? Everything's in confidence, you know."

"Well, it was only that spare-time gardener."

"O'Brien?"

"Yes. That's right—O'Brien. He'd been charging for time when he wasn't there and for petrol for the motor-mower that he hadn't actually had. And there was some question or other about repairs to the mower. Henry merely told him he wouldn't be wanted again. I believe he was intending to give him another chance if he'd owned up but O'Brien persisted in lying. There was never any intention of making a charge against the man. I was told all that in confidence."

"That clears that up," Grainger said. "You anything else to ask, Travers?"

"His money," I said. "He used a phrase to me that I've remembered. He called it a sacred trust. Did he ever discuss that with you?"

"Let me think," he said. "After all, we did discuss so many things. Money a sacred trust. Yes, I think he did say something of the sort but it must have been some time ago."

"Did he mention any of his relatives in that connection?" He didn't follow.

"I mean, mention them as not fit or proper persons to be left his money."

"Never," he said, and seemed quite shocked. "I've met his niece once or twice, for instance, and she's a most charming woman. She has a brother who must be quite well off."

"Ever mention making a new will?" Grainger asked him.

"No," he said slowly. "But I did gather something of the kind. He did say that we at St. Martin's would have a most pleasant surprise if anything ever happened to him. And I know he was leaving something to Moral Re-armament."

He was looking hopefully as if Grainger might give him some news. But Grainger was getting to his feet. Three minutes later we were closing the rectory gate behind us. Our ways would part if he were going home and I to the hotel.

"Have dinner with me," I said. "I'm staying the night at the Sussex."

He thought it over and said he would. He could ring his wife from the hotel. My car could be brought to the hotel garage.

"Well, we certainly picked up something about O'Brien," he said as we turned my way.

"Not enough for a murder motive," I said. "Besides, I'll wager O'Brien never said a word about that dismissal to his wife or mother-in-law, and apparently Baldlow didn't intend to make it in any way public. So why did Mrs. Carver hurry home that afternoon? That isn't explained yet."

"First thing in the morning I'll have her in," he said. "You got any ideas yourself?"

I admitted I'd been wrong about Baldlow. I'd rather thought of him as a man who'd attended that meeting and found himself at the centre of things and who simply had to use his gift of the gab. Now I was inclined to believe he'd been sincere, even if that emphysema of his had scared him a bit and made him receptive, so to speak.

"I can never credit any of it as being sincere," Grainger said. "These open confessions—well there's something about them that turns my stomach. And I don't like any of these short cuts to heaven."

I didn't care a lot for our twentieth-century flagellants myself. But, as I said, we British like to think of ourselves as strong, silent men. In quite a lot of circles, the sin against reticence is one of the unforgivable—deadly.

We talked a whole lot more during that dinner and got nowhere in particular. What I gathered was that the two strings to his bow were O'Brien first and then the relatives. Not Jane Howell and her husband. He'd known or learnt enough about them to be sure the loss of a legacy would be no concern. But Lorde might be hard up.

"He'd have known the provisions of that earlier will," Grainger said. "Baldlow, according to everybody, couldn't keep his mouth shut. He'd have loved people to regard him as a future benefactor. Look at what he said to Canon Orifice about a legacy for his church. As for Tinley, I've got to find out why he was cut off with a mere hundred."

There was just one other matter he put to me. What was my idea of the significance of that staggering of the times of the visits of the relatives on that Saturday.

What could I say except that the significance lay in the staggering itself. Clearly he had wanted to tell each of the three a something that wasn't to be known by the other two. One might go on to deduce that the first visitor, Jane Howell, would not have been told of the coming of the others, and therefore she'd go straight home. In any case Seahurst was a large place and there wasn't all that risk of her running across the other two. And the same might have applied to the second caller—Tinley.

"Any significance in the fact that Lorde was the last?"

"There's just this," I said, "for what it's worth. Lorde's a solicitor. He might have been asked to draw up a will for Baldlow after Baldlow had interviewed the other two and come to certain decisions about them. Whether they were after all the right people to handle that sacred trust of his."

"That's a good idea," he said. "The trouble is we'll never be able to prove it. According to Lorde there was never a hint of any such thing in the letter. And there's another extraordinary thing—those three letters. Sorry to keep coming back to it, but not one of them kept. If that isn't fishy, then I don't know what is."

That was about all that was said. Grainger left soon after nine o'clock and I thought I'd take a short walk. There was a moon and the night was dry and cold.

I made my way to Montague Road. The Croft was darkness itself and no one seemed on duty. When I was sure the road was deserted I went through the garage gate and round past the back door. There was a largish brick outbuilding and, slightly along another crazy-paving path that led back, a wooden building with a padlocked door. That, I guessed, would be the one that housed the motor-mower and garden tools. As for the back garden, it was just as I'd been told—nothing but lawn with an old-fashioned shrubbery of principally evergreens all round and with trees in addition at the far end to make an additional privacy screen against the garden that backed on.

I was out of that garden within three minutes of entering it, and went back to the hotel. I had breakfast at seven-thirty and an hour later I was on my way to Exeter.

The morning was cold but dry and I got to Exeter at one o'clock and went straight to Hallows's hotel. He'd had a reasonably good morning. He had seen the site of the Tinley house and as a result of certain enquiries had found some people with whom the Tinleys had been friendly. He was leaving it to me to call on them.

But it wasn't so easy as all that. If these people—Habbord by name—were still in touch with the Howells, it'd be dangerous to bring in their names. But something had to be done. Hallows had the telephone number, so I rang immediately after lunch.

It was Mrs. Habbord who spoke.

"You wouldn't know me, Mrs. Habbord," I said, "but I'm connected with a firm of solicitors. Just a matter to do with a will, and we understand that you used to know people named Tinley, who were killed in the blitz."

"Oh, yes," she said, quite animatedly. "We knew them very well. My daughter was at the same school with their daughter. We were very good friends."

"Ah!" I said. "Their daughter Jane. Have you kept in touch with her?"

"No," she said. "That's quite a mystery. Phyllis, my daughter, hasn't heard of her for years. The last time I saw her we were wondering about her."

"I wonder if I might give myself the pleasure of a brief call on you," I said. "My name's Travers. I shouldn't keep you for more than a few moments."

"I think that will be all right," she said. "At what time?"

"Any time this afternoon to suit your convenience. The earlier the better. I have to get back to town."

Half-past two found me at Holmbury, the Habbord house. Mrs. Habbord, a well-preserved woman of about sixty, opened the door to me. No maid, she said: only a daily woman. Not that she particularly needed a maid now that her husband was dead. I had a word or two about the maid problem and we were on quite good terms when we settled down in the drawing-room.

She was an intelligent woman who spoke briskly and to the point. She had always been very fond of Jane, she said, and Phyllis simply adored her. As small children they had gone to the same preparatory school together, and then on to that expensive school whose name I won't mention. They were both just over eighteen when war broke out. Phyllis was going to be a doctor but Jane joined the W.R.N.S. The two had always kept in touch.

"Jane always came to see us when she was on leave, and I knew she and Phyllis always corresponded. Then suddenly she seemed to drop out. I know her home had been destroyed and her parents were dead, but you'd have thought she'd have at least kept in touch."

"And your daughter?" I said. "Where is she practising?"

She smiled.

"Oh, she isn't a doctor. She completed her finals and then she met a man. She's married now and has two children."

"She was your only child?"

"The only one. But I'm very happy about the grandchildren."

"Grandmothers always are," I said. "But I wonder if I might call on your daughter? It's Jane Tinley we're trying to trace."

"I'm sure Phyllis would be delighted," she told me. "Her name's Cavendall. Her husband's an estate agent at Dorchester. He was a Major in the army when she met him."

"If I pay for the telephone call, will you tell her about my visit and say I would like to call on her in the morning?"

"No need whatever to pay," she said. "I'm constantly ringing Phyllis up."

I told her where I was staying and said I'd now remain till the morning. Unless I heard to the contrary I'd call at Dorchester on my way to town.

I didn't like to mention Baldlow, whom she'd probably met, for the murder had been news in the previous day's papers.

"One thing I would like," she said, "and that's for you to let me know if you do get in touch with Jane. I can only think that she must be dead. Nothing else would make me believe she would have dropped Phyllis like that. They simply idolised each other and she was such a charming girl. Absolutely incapable of any duplicity. And always most affectionate."

I said I'd certainly give her what news there might be, and that was about all. I did leave a private card in case she should remember anything important and might wish to get into touch with me. I went back to the hotel. Hallows was to stay on in Exeter for at least another whole day, trying to get more of the Tinley background. We agreed when I left the next morning that I'd be ringing him from Dorchester at one o'clock.

It was not a long way to Dorchester and I timed my arrival for about eleven o'clock. Mrs. Habbord had assumed that the facts she'd given me would be enough for me to locate her daughter, and they were. The telephone directory gave me the Cavendall private address, and one enquiry told me the whereabouts of the house. It turned out to be just another example of Edwardian Gothic. The gardens were good and well kept. A nurse girl was sitting in the spacious porch, knitting and keeping an eye on a pram. Everything seemed to say the Cavendalls weren't pinched for money.

I glanced at the baby.

"Boy or girl?"

"Girl," the young nurse said, and looked as pleased as if she were responsible.

I gave her a smile, rang the bell, and almost at once an elderly maid was opening the door. I was shown into a kind of morning room, warm enough from one of those stay-in fires. Phyllis Cavendall came in before I'd even time to look round.

"Mr. Travers?"

"Yes," I said, "and you'll be Mrs. Cavendall. Your mother told you to expect me?"

"She rang yesterday evening. Do sit down, won't you. You'd like some coffee?"

"Not if it's going to give you any trouble."

"It's practically ready. I always have some myself about this time."

She left me to myself for no more than a couple of minutes. I wouldn't have called her handsome but she had a most attractive face: a nose slightly snub, a widish mouth, really beautiful brown eyes: a face, in fact, that was full of character. A man's woman would have been my description of her. She was tallish, like Jane Howell, but even more slim. She had very little colour and wore no make-up, and yet she contrived to look chic in a plain skirt and an old-gold jumper. There was something of her mother's vivacity about her and she had an air of extreme competence.

She brought the tray herself. It was good coffee and there were home-made buns.

"Mother said you were enquiring about Jane Tinley," she began. "Didn't she tell you everything?"

I explained. I'd promised to trespass no more than a few minutes on the mother's time and, as soon as she mentioned the daughter as a very close friend I thought it better to see that daughter.

"By the way, Mrs. Cavendall, you've a delightful little daughter outside there."

"She is rather sweet," she said. "There's also a boy. He's four. You have children yourself?"

"Unhappily, no. But I do imagine daughters are—well, almost a questionable asset. Take your own case. Hundreds of pounds must have been spent on your medical training and then you get married, and down the drain it's gone."

"It isn't all wasted," she said. "It's constantly coming in handy. But about Jane. I gathered you're looking for her in connection with a legacy."

"Yes," I said. "When did you actually see her last?"

I don't know why that should have been an awkward question, but it seemed to be. That palish face of hers flushed quite a lot.

"I hardly remember," she said. "I think it was about a month after the Normandy landing."

"And then she dropped completely out?"

"Completely. What happened to her I never knew."

"You made enquiries?"

"No," she said. "I suppose I had too much pride. I did write to her but the letter wasn't answered, and then I was informed that she'd been demobilised, if that's the word. Then I didn't know where to find her. Her parents were dead, as you know. But she could always have found me. I'm permanent. Through mother and Exeter, I mean."

"And you've never heard a word of her from that day to this?"

"Nothing whatever. Some more coffee?"

I had a second cup. She was frowning slightly as she passed it to me.

"This legacy. Who's it from?"

"Just from a friend." I'd had to think quickly.

"The name wouldn't by any chance be . . . McLeod?"

"No," I said. "Not McLeod. But why did you suggest that name?"

"Oh, she was rather friendly once with a man of that name. I met the two of them in town. I forget his regiment but he was an army captain."

"Too difficult a lead," I said. "Heaven knows how many McLeods were in the army."

"Yes," she said, "but what about Charles, her brother?"

"She has a brother?"

"Oh, yes. He was about two years older. I didn't meet him a lot. Used to see him at her house during holidays sometimes. He was in the navy during the war. The Tinleys had naval connections, you know. If anyone knows where she is, he should."

"But he's got to be found first."

"But surely," she said. "A simple advertisement. Or why not one for her? Then there's the uncle and aunt. No, not an aunt. I think she died early in the war or just before. The uncle was quite fond of Jane, I believe. I never actually met him. I think there was rather bad blood between him and the Tinleys. They seemed to think he'd—well, it's hard to put. Shall we say acted not too fairly about the family property when the grandfather died."

"Do you know the uncle's name?"

"I don't," she said. "But surely he might be a clue of sorts."

My forehead wrinkled in thought. I looked up to see her eyes queerly on me. Then her head went sideways as if she was listening.

"Excuse me a moment, I must go to baby."

VIII

A NEW TACK

SHE was in again in about three minutes. She didn't say a word about the baby. She just smiled as she asked if she might take the tray.

This time she was away longer. I had a good look round the room and out of the french windows at a lawn swept clear of leaves, and some polyanthus roses in their final bloom.

Almost five minutes had gone and then I thought I heard a car. I couldn't see the short circular drive from the windows but about a couple of minutes later I heard steps. Then the door opened. She was introducing her husband.

He was a burly chap, florid, about thirty-five, and wearing one of those desert rat moustaches that gave him a peppery sort of look. She sat down. He remained standing.

"Mr. Travers?" He should have known that from the introduction.

"Yes," I said.

"Sit down, will you? My wife's a bit puzzled about all this."

So it had been the telephone, and not the baby. I was having an idea that my thinking wouldn't be quick enough.

"All what?" I said.

"This legacy business. May I see your card?"

I gave him a private one. I said if he had a London directory, he'd find me in it.

"Not that," he said, but kept the card. "Your firm. You're a solicitor, you say?"

"I'm not," I said, and let him try to stare me down. "But it's something that can be explained. I'm a private enquiry agent."

There was the faintest of sounds from his wife. His back was towards her and he didn't apparently hear it. What little colour there was left her face, and I thought she was going to faint. She leaned back in the chair.

"You mean a detective?"

"Yes," I said, and found a business card. "I'm actually the proprietor. We were commissioned to find Jane Tinley in connection with a legacy."

He looked at the card. Phyllis Cavendall leaned forward again in the chair. Her face still had that intensity of pallor.

"First a solicitor and now a detective." He gave a contemptuous little grunt. "Which is true—if either?"

I passed him the card that's carried by all our operatives, including myself. It had fingerprints and a photograph and a signature.

"My car's outside," I said. "In it you'll find my registration book, insurance certificate and so on."

He was just a bit uneasy. He grunted as he handed back the card.

"You said you could explain."

"I have explained," I said. "Jane Tinley seems to have vanished. We accepted the job of finding her."

"But why the lies?"

"Saying I was a solicitor?" I made the smile an ironic one. "For some reason or other a solicitor's more respectable. Anyone will talk to a solicitor. A private detective's quite a different proposition."

"Well, I still think it's unnecessary," he told me virtuously. "And you look a reasonable decent chap."

"Halstead and Cambridge," I told him. "Not that that matters. All I'm claiming to be is a detective."

"I see. But we just don't happen to think you're a very good one."

"Granted," I said. "We're short of operatives and the boss is always a stop-gap. But just where did I go wrong?"

"Well, Mrs. Habbord would have told you about Charles Tinley. And about the uncle. And why come all this way to make enquiries when you've only to put advertisements in the papers?"

"You're sure we haven't?"

"Not in either *The Times* or *The Daily Telegraph*. We'd have been sure to notice them."

"Good," I said. "I'm learning, as you see. But why not ring our office—reverse the charges—and speak to my managing director?"

"I don't think that will be necessary," he told me. I could see he was showing off: rather like a motorbike rider who goes at speed to thrill his pillion passenger. "I think I'm a pretty good judge of men."

I got to my feet.

"You'd like to do some more checking up at my car?"

"Don't think so. But I will see you off."

"I'm going to have lunch here," I said. "I've agreed to telephone at one o'clock to an operative of mine who's still at Exeter. Where do you recommend?"

He shrugged his broad shoulders.

"The Antelope, perhaps."

"Thanks. I'll be there till just after one o'clock. If you or Mrs. Cavendall should think of anything that might help, I'll be more than grateful."

She had risen too, and now she was looking quite normal. I thanked her, and I trust most charmingly, for the coffee and her help. I added that if we unearthed Jane Tinley I'd let her know.

He gave me a taciturn good-day at the car. I slipped along pretty quickly to the hotel, ordered lunch for twelve-thirty and rang Norris. The line was clear. When I'd finished talking I knew that Cavendall would be reassured if he decided after all to ring.

Over my meal I tried to assess the value of what I'd learned and all the time I kept coming out in almost a cold sweat when I thought of those minutes with Cavendall in his morning-room. I also felt a bit resentful. I think I look reasonably presentable and I dress well enough and speak the Queen's English; things that should have been assurances enough. Phyllis Cavendall was certainly a remarkably astute woman. But why had she been a frightened one? Why had the word *detective* drained all the colour from her face?

Naturally I could find no reasons. As for what I'd learned, it was only that the break between the two life-long and closest of friends had dated from just after the Normandy landing, and that it had been both arbitrary and definite. That mention of a Captain McLeod might or might not be of help. But of one thing I was certain. If Phyllis Cavendall should happen to remember the name of the uncle and connect him with the murdered Baldlow, then the fat might be in the fire. Somehow the thought made me want to shake the dust of Dorchester off my feet.

At one o'clock I rang Hallows. He said he had a little more news but it could keep, so I told him to take the first train back to town. He said there was one at two o'clock, which meant that he'd be at the office sooner than I. I'd rather thought of going the forty miles or so out of my way and seeing Grainger again, but now it seemed just a bit too obvious. At a quarter-past one my car was heading for town, and it was dark well before I got there.

Bertha Munney made me some tea and over it I had a good talk with Norris. Hallows came in just before seven. He had unearthed a girl who had been in the W.R.N.S. with Jane Tinley at Portsmouth, though not as an officer. She said Jane had been transferred from Portsmouth at about the Normandy landing time and she hadn't heard of her since. She hadn't been directly under her but she knew her, even if she couldn't recall anything in connection with her outside the range of normal duties.

I told Hallows I'd have to think about the next move, and he could report in the morning. Then I went home. Bernice hadn't expected me and was out. I was having a service dinner when the telephone went. Norris said Nordon had just reported in and would I like to see him. I said I would, so I hurriedly finished my meal, left a note for Bernice just in case, and went out again.

Nordon's face told me he'd had no luck. He'd made a diary report, hour to hour, which I would see later, but the whole thing amounted to much effort and no success. Never a trace of where the whisky had been bought or of Luke himself, except at one garage not far short of that turning off the main road that ultimately emerged near Maverton. There he had had his tyres seen to—one apparently had a slow puncture—and three gallons put in the tank. Never a trace, either, of that diary book. Nordon had even risked contact with Padman and had been told that no one in Maverton had been on the road and seen or met a car like Luke's.

"Well, that's that," I said. "We've done the best we can and Luke's ghost shouldn't be haunting us. What about the inquest, by the way?"

Norris said the verdict had been Accidental Death. Evidence had been given about the mist, and the whisky bottle.

Mrs. Prince hadn't had too much of an ordeal and Luke's good name hadn't been badly smirched.

That was about all. Nordon would report in the morning for another assignment, or so I was thinking. Norris said there'd be the Baldlow inquest and Nordon would have to be there. I said it was their pigeon and went back to the flat.

By the time I'd finished breakfast in the morning I'd done more than my share of thinking and reluctantly I was deciding that the Jane Howell approach would have to be reckoned as time lost. It hurt to think so, for it had been pregnant with possibilities. But there it was. All we knew was that she'd been an officer in the W.R.N.S., had been stationed at Portsmouth at the time of the Normandy landing, and had had a boy-friend called McLeod. From Portsmouth she had gone to another station and from then on she had dropped completely out of the life of what could only be called a very close friend. Her reappearance was in London where she'd met Tom Howell. If there was anything in that to explain the tears shed surreptitiously over Baldlow's letter, then I was too dense to see it. Nor was I going to throw good money after bad by trying further to find out.

The rush of things had pushed Tom Howell out of my mind the previous night. Norris said he'd been in and signed the contract and paid an advance of two hundred pounds.

"A nice gentleman," he said. "Nice to deal with. The real genuine sort. Not that that sort hasn't ever committed a murder."

"That's a queer rider to add," I told him. "Any particular reasons for it?"

"No," he said. "It just occurred to me. He might be working a pretty big bluff in coming to us."

I didn't think Howell was the smothering kind. Conceivable, of course, that he'd gone to the house for a private interview with Baldlow—to ascertain before Baldlow saw her the reason for his wife's distress—and found the house apparently empty and had walked round and seen an open window. If he had found himself in the bedroom and Baldlow sound asleep, he might have yielded to some sudden hatred of the man and jammed the pillow over his mouth. But somehow I still didn't find it in keeping, and I told Norris so.

"He's a client," I said, "and what we're being paid for is to protect his wife's interests by finding a murderer. There were no strings attached. He's under no misapprehension about the money he's paying us. It isn't and never will be a bribe."

Hallows and I went to a nearby restaurant and had our conference in peace. He came up with an idea.

"Those timings," he said. "I've been wondering if Baldlow was going to pump the first caller, and then the second and the third in order to get information about one of them. To collate the individual items he thought he might pick up, and then to make the new will accordingly."

"It doesn't cover everything," I said. "Unless the piece of information he was after was sufficiently damning for one of the three to have stopped his mouth. But it brings us to the same point. Someone did kill him so as to shut his mouth. We have to find why. What the damning thing was. I'd hoped we'd get something from Mrs. Howell's past history, but that seems innocuous enough."

He asked me to give it to him again, so I did. Family life apparently a happy one. Preparatory school and high-class boarding school with Phyllis, daughter of those good friends, the Habbords. Charles Tinley in the navy, Jane in the Wrens and Phyllis a medical student. The Tinleys killed and Jane—say a year later—had fifteen thousand pounds from her parents' estate. Presumably Charles had the larger rest. Jane stationed at Portsmouth. Had a boy-friend named McLeod, an army captain. Just after the Normandy landing Jane transferred to another station. From then she ceased to write to Phyllis, who never saw her again.

That sudden dropping out, as he said, was the only mystery, even if it was capable of a good many explanations. I told him about the other mystery: that Phyllis Cavendall had had a tremendous shock when I announced that I was a private enquiry agent.

"Maybe it's her we ought to investigate," he said.

"As a last hope—yes. I think the next move is Jane's brother, Charles Tinley. The man who was left only a hundred pounds."

I did some more explaining. He too had had a letter and had professed to have burnt it, since there was no reason for it to be kept.

"But this is the point," I said. "Brother in one place and sister in another, but both on the telephone. Each gets a letter, claimed to be merely an urgent request to see an uncle, at the same approximate time. What would you expect one or the other of them to do?"

"Why, ring, of course."

"Exactly. One rings the other. 'I've had a letter from Uncle Henry, etc. etc. . . .' But did they ring? They certainly didn't. Jane had no idea Charles was in Seahurst. Both had no idea that Francis Lorde was there. So what follows? That Jane's letter, and Charles's, each contained something which neither of them dare mention to another living soul. Jane didn't even mention that something to her husband. And where's that bring us? Back to the letters every time."

He couldn't but agree. The hope that something at Exeter might reveal or give a clue as to what had been in Jane Howell's letter, hadn't been realised. So why not a shift to Charles? With him we might have better luck. If not, then there was always Lorde, though he'd be a remarkably difficult nut to crack.

"I'll see Charles personally," I said. "I'd like you to get into touch with one of the staff. But first we'll reconnoitre that Bond Street shop."

We looked up the exact number in the telephone directory, and checked with United Jewellers, Ltd., and what emerged was that the London head office of the firm had the same Bond Street address. There was also a list of United Jewellers' shops: one in Knightsbridge, one in Hampstead and a third in the Strand. Almost certainly there'd also be some in the provinces.

I drove round by the flat and collected a solid-gold cigar case that had belonged to my father. Bernice had often urged me to sell it but I'd kept it for sentimental reasons. It was about half-past eleven when we drew up just short of the Bond Street shop; an unpretentious two-windowed place with two storeys above and a drive in from the side street. JAMES BALDLOW AND SON was still the name. United Jewellers had apparently bought a profitable goodwill which it had paid to keep.

Hallows went off to park the car and he had the cigar case with him. I went in by the side door and up a flight of stairs to a landing. I asked at Enquiries for Mr. Tinley and had my private card sent in. A wait of about five minutes and I was shown into his room.

There had been the sound of typewriters and people had been coming and going. That office too looked like that of a busy man. Tinley rose from the flat-topped desk when I came in and held out a hand across it.

"How are you, Mr. Travers? What brings you here?"

"You can spare me a minute or two?"

"Maybe five or ten," he said. "It all depends. Bring up a chair. Cigarette?"

He held his gold lighter for me.

"Some nice stuff you have on display down there," I said.

"Displays vary from location to location. You know what Bond Street expects. Not too much and good."

"Well, I'm not an expert," I told him. "I take it you know what I am?"

"I think so," he said. "I made various enquiries. You're a very reputable person."

"Thanks," I said. "Good to hear that."

About thirty-five to thirty-eight, I was thinking, but a businessman to the absolute life. Maybe it was some trick of the light but his thinnish face had something Mephistophelian about it.

"But I still don't know why you've come," he said, and he wasn't looking in the least perturbed.

When I told him about Nordon there was quite a different look. It had surprise in it, and wariness.

"A body-guard companion," he said. Then his lip drooped. "In a way I'm not all that surprised. You wouldn't have thought it to look at my dear uncle, but he'd been pretty unprincipled in his time, and mighty clever. Somebody was bound to have caught up with him sooner or later. There was some mighty shady business over his father's estate. I was too young to know the ins and outs but my people guessed it."

"You know he'd got religion?"

"Well, yes," he said slowly. "There was something that chap Grainger said when he was questioning us at the Sussex. I didn't quite get the hang of it then. He'd got religion, had he? Couldn't have been seriously."

"It certainly was. I had it on the best authority. Whether he was scared or not I couldn't say. That illness of his, I mean. But about my visit this morning, I'm involved, naturally, through that operative of mine. I wanted to ask you in the strictest confidence to tell me any ideas you might have about the whole thing."

"I've only one important one," he said, and waited.

"And that is?"

"That I didn't kill him. That's why I don't give a damn, no matter what the police may or may not do. Innocence gives you a cocksureness, you know."

"It certainly does," I said, "even if innocent men have got into trouble in their time. But to be personal. How'd you get into this jewellery business?"

"Well, it was really intended that I should go into the navy but my own mind wasn't made up. Strange though it may seem, I had a hankering after business. More money in it. Both my sister and I—you remember my sister?"

"Mrs. Howell."

"That's right. Well, our parents never wished us to cut ourselves off from Uncle Henry and Aunt Maria, whatever their own feelings were, and we'd meet one or other of them occasionally in town. I told him—that was just after I'd left my school—that I'd like to go into business, and he suggested his own. My people weren't too pleased about it but I did go in on the ground floor. I had six months in an actual factory. I had—still, that's neither here nor there. When war broke out I'd had quite a lot of experience. But it did break out. He sold the business after my aunt died. My own parents were killed and I came in for quite a bit of money. I literally bought a directorship of United Jewellers and here I am. I did it behind his back, just as he'd sold the business, in a way, behind my back. He tried to take it in good part when he knew, but he didn't like it. Thought he should have been consulted and been the intermediary. He was like that. Always hogging the limelight."

So there was the reason, I thought, for what Grainger had called a legacy of spite.

"Ostensibly you were on uncle and nephew terms?"

"Yes. Rather a hollow mockery on both sides. I was not at all sorry when he let us know he wouldn't be seeing any of us this year because of illness. Jane and I wrote the usual letters of commiseration and that was that."

"And then you got that letter, asking you to see him on urgent business."

"Yes." Strictly monosyllable, and the eyes were watchful. "Neither of you knew the other was going?"

"No. We each took it as something personal. So did Francis Lorde."

"And is it in order to ask what you think now?"

"Certainly. I think he was going to change his will and he wanted to give each of us the experience of being told why we were being cut out. You got a better idea?"

"No," I said. "There was that Will form he went out for."

"That'd be just to flourish in our faces. He'd have had to have a proper affair drawn up by some firm or other. He was a vindictive old devil, you know. Never forgot what he supposed were injuries. And don't forget something. He was off to South Africa. See it?"

"Perhaps, yes," I said. "You think he wanted to get his own back on all of you before he left?"

"That's it. On Jane and me for our parents, and me especially for manipulating myself into where I am now."

"And Mr. Lorde?"

"They never really liked each other. Friendly enough on the face of it but Lorde especially mistrusted him. I know Henry got himself down for a holiday at Lorde's place a year or two ago, but that meant very little."

"Well, the last laugh appears to be on you three," I said. "If he died intestate you'll inherit. But hardly Lorde, though. He wasn't a blood relation. The trouble about that good news is that the police must work a motive into it."

"I'm not worrying," he said, and stubbed out his second cigarette in the handsome ash-tray. He glanced up at the clock. I took the hint and got to my feet.

"Sorry I've been so little use to you." He rose too. "You're not a naval man yourself by any chance?"

"No," I said. "My father was army. I'm a Suffolk man myself."

"Suffolk," he said. "I was at Harwich for a spell during the war. A pal of mine had a nice little craft on the Deben. We used to have quite a lot of fun. A tricky river, the Deben."

"I've been on it several times," I said.

"You're fond of the sport."

"Yes," I said. "It's very exhilarating."

"Look," he said. "I've got a smallish yacht—motor auxiliary and all that—near Littleton. Why not have a day or two down there in the summer?"

"It might be fun," I said. "I'd have to park my wife. You married?"

"Yes and no," he said. "My wife and I have separated, as a matter of fact. She won't give me a divorce and there we are."

"Sorry," I said. "I didn't mean to butt into any private affairs. But I'll probably take you up on that yachting offer."

"Do," he told me. "My manager here, a very nice chap named Rawley, was in the navy too. He gets down when he can."

We shook hands and he wished me luck about keeping the firm's name out of the papers. As he'd said it rather amusedly, I wished him luck in keeping out of the hands of the police. And that was that, though the funny thing was that as I walked down the stairs it seemed to me as if he'd given me information, almost airily and contemptuously, and that no special cunning on my part had been necessary to elicit it. It was a thought that made me rather uneasy, and added to it was the belated remembering of certain things which I'd previously intended asking him and which had somehow been side-tracked in the spate of information which he'd handed out to me.

The car had gone and Hallows with it, so I took a bus. I went on top and smoked a pipe and tried to assess the value of what I'd learned. What it amounted to was really information about the dead Baldlow who had always seemed to be an unwelcome intrusion into the lives of his relations—Lorde included. As for Charles Tinley, he was either an excellent actor or he had indeed had the cocksureness of the utterly innocent. Then I wondered why he had told me about his wife. Could she be another string to our bow? And could anything be learned about Charles Tinley from the place he'd vaguely described as near Littleton. The river there would be the Arun, far from a suitable one for yachting, so he'd always take to the open sea.

I looked at my watch and I saw I had plenty of time for something else that had come into my mind—a look at Charles Tinley's Hendon flat—so I got off near a Tube station and went out to Hendon. It was a fairish walk to Friar's Court, but it was worth it. Those flats looked of the highest class. The building and its surroundings fairly reeked of money.

Charles Tinley, I was telling myself as I walked back, ought to be making about two to three thousand a year, and there'd be the interest on his inheritance. Against that he had a wife to keep—or did he?—and an expensive flat, and a small yacht. Suddenly I began to have ideas.

IX

TEMPTATION FLAT

IT WAS after one o'clock when I got back to the office. Norris said Nordon might be in at any time. He'd rung to say that he wouldn't be needed after all. The inquest was going to be formal with an immediate adjournment. But he was proposing to hang on down there and hear what there was to hear. Norris had told him it was a good idea.

Hallows hadn't rung so I went to lunch. Hallows was in when I returned. He hadn't discovered much, he said, and was rather apologetic. I thought he'd done quite well. He'd been ingenious, if nothing else.

He'd gone into the actual shop where there was only one assistant on view, and had asked if they bought such things as gold cigar cases. Anything gold, the assistant said, so the case was produced. The assistant pursed his lips over it and said he'd enquire about an offer. He must have pressed a bell, for another assistant came in to take his place while he was out.

"They weren't taking any chances on me being a crook," he said. "This other assistant didn't speak to me: he was just there. The first one came back and said the offer was twenty-five pounds. I looked staggered and said I'd thought it was worth at least fifty. Eighteen-carat gold and quite heavy. He asked me to wait a minute and came back with the manager, a very dapper, good-looking chap of about forty or just under. He said the monogram was heavily incised and couldn't be tooled out. In other words the case couldn't be sold as a case. All it was worth was its value as gold. He said it was fifteen carat, not eighteen. I took the case back and said I'd think it over. He said I wouldn't get more anywhere else, but I think he parted with it rather regretfully."

"I know for a certainty it's worth at least forty," I said. "But what happened then?"

He'd gone back to the car and waited. Just after twelve o'clock the second assistant came out. It looked as if lunch times were staggered: at any rate the assistant hopped a bus and got off at Piccadilly. Hallows had followed in the car. He saw the man go into a little restaurant just off Shaftesbury Avenue so he parked the car and went in too. It was a cheap little place and already almost full. While he was going along the tables looking for a place, the assistant caught sight of him. He told Hallows the seat opposite his own was free. Hallows thanked him and took it, and went on reading his paper while waiting for someone to take an order. It was the man opposite who spoke first.

"Excuse me but haven't I seen you before this morning?"

Hallows gave him a look, and remembered.

"Yes," he said. "You were in that shop where I was this morning. Funny, us coming in here!"

The cigar case was examined and Hallows advised to take a good offer. The assistant said his firm gave the highest prices in London. Hallows allowed himself to be convinced. He said he'd be that way again in the morning. After that the meal was a chatty affair.

"But all I learned was that the manager, name of Rawley, by the way, was a bit of a martinet, and probably because the director responsible for the London area had his offices upstairs. Not that he ever poked his nose in. There had been a Mrs. Tinley who was said to be a bit of a shrew. Rumour had it that Tinley was out for a divorce. That was about all. I had to contribute a lot of lurid details about my own life to get that much."

I said it was quite enough. Mrs. Tinley might be in the mood to give us some information.

"Here's the number of Tinley's flat at Friar's Court, Hendon. You get along there and do a couple of things. Find out what his flat costs him—any other gossip if you can get it—and also where Mrs. Tinley's living. I shall probably be going home, so come along there at any time you like and let me know what you've got."

Hallows left. Nordon was waiting so Norris and I saw him at once. He hadn't much to tell us. The inquest had been adjourned. He'd had quite a gossip with Padman.

"The funny thing was, he was trying to pump me and didn't know I wanted to pump him. Mrs. Carver's prints were all over that window, by the way."

"We knew that," Norris said. "But they had to be if she'd regularly opened and shut it to let out the tobacco smoke."

"Well, no other prints were on it. And Mrs. Carver's story now is that when she left the house that afternoon to get some air and still her beating heart, she suddenly found she'd unknowingly got near her own house, so she slipped in for a minute. The police haven't let on they know she was there for best part of half an hour. My guess is they still think O'Brien's involved."

"Well, thank God for one thing," Norris said. "Our name hasn't come out yet. That gives us a breathing space."

Nordon gave me a look but I didn't enlighten him.

"You got another assignment for Nordon?" I asked Norris.

"There might be later. I haven't finished with the Hallows adjustments yet."

I said I'd asked only because I might have a job for Nordon myself in the morning, but I'd let Norris know later. It mightn't be till the evening.

Hallows turned up at half-past four and found us at tea. Bernice lacks all curiosity about my work, an excellent trait for the wife of a man in my position, but she knew Hallows well. She saw he had tea and then we adjourned to my den. I switched on the fire.

"Well, any luck?"

He hoped so. Bakhshish to a commissionaire had produced the likely rent of Tinley's flat—seven hundred and fifty pounds. There'd been a Mrs. Tinley there, but no children.

"Any lady friends now?" Hallows had asked.

The commissionaire had shrugged his shoulders. Who was to know? People could walk in and walk out.

But previous to approaching him, Hallows had been to the desk, asking for Mrs. Tinley. He had made the matter urgent and had been given her address—Flat 21, Anstead Gardens, Kensington.

"That's fine," I said, "but this is going to be tricky. I'd very much like a word with her straightaway. I wonder if she's sufficiently hostile to her husband not to give me away."

"You needn't worry about anyone at the flat bureau connecting me with the one who had a cigar case to sell, that is if they mention to Tinley someone was asking for Mrs. T.," he told me. "I had a complete transformation before I went to Friar's Court. That's what kept me so long."

I had to risk it, so I rang the Kensington flats. I was put through. The voice that reached me over the line wasn't off the top shelf, as I was soon to discover.

"Who is it speaking?" There was a burst of coughing as if she'd swallowed some cigarette smoke. I waited a moment. She repeated the question. No "Sorry about that", or "Excuse me".

"It's to do with your late uncle by marriage, Mrs. Tinley."

"Him," she said, and gave a little snort.

"My name's Travers," I said. "I have a personal interest in the case and I'd be most grateful if you could spare me a minute or two of your time."

"Well, go ahead," she told me, and the words were slurred.

"Too confidential," I said. "Might I come and see you? I'd be most grateful."

"When?"

"Well, in half an hour?"

There was quite a silence. The question emerged from it with a suddenness.

"You're the police?"

"Most decidedly I'm not."

I gave her my telephone number and repeated my name. I was trying to be most ingratiating.

"In half an hour, then?"

"All right," she said, "but don't make it too long. I'm going out."

So far, so good, as I told Hallows. A bit of personal tidying up, and even decoration, and we went to the garage. The flats took some finding, but they had a small car park. Hallows stayed with the car and I went in. Those flats were no cheap affairs. I walked through the entrance hall and made for the stairs as if I owned the place.

Her flat was on the second floor. I pushed the bell and was about to ring it a second time when the door opened. We gave each other quite a look.

"I'm Travers, Mrs. Tinley."

Her eyes hadn't finished running me over.

"May I come in?"

She drew back and moved into the room. A cosy room, luscious with easy things to sit on and heaps of cushions. She was a blonde of about five-foot-eight who'd run rather to seed. The yellowish velvet frock showed bulges under the arms and in spite of the make-up her cheeks and forehead were flushed. I guessed she'd been doing some drinking.

"Take your coat off, won't you?"

She stood there, back to the electric fire, watching me as I took it off and draped it over a chair. I've been told more than once that I can make myself quite—well, I almost said seductive. In any case I piled on what charm the years had left.

"What a delightful room you have here!"

"You think so?"

The trite remark seemed to please her. Maybe she'd not been used lately to being complimented on anything. But not ten years ago, or even five. Then she must have been a fine looker, and with trimmings to match.

She offered the cigarette box, a large silver one, and probably once from James Baldlow and Son. I held my lighter for hers. She had a very attractive scent. The room was somehow pervaded with it, and a faint mixture of scented cigarettes and something else I couldn't place. I helped myself to an easy chair and seemed to sink up to the armpits.

"A hell of a day you've chosen," she told me. The slurring had almost gone but the speech was deliberate.

"I'm sorry about that."

"It's my birthday." She gave a little snort.

"Don't tell me," I said. "I know. They come too fast."

"You're not all that old."

"Too old for my liking. But you: you shouldn't be pessimistic. You're not even in the prime of life."

"You're telling me. Know who that is?"

She was pointing to a medium-sized portrait in oils above the mantelpiece. I hadn't really noticed it. I'd seen the big radiogram and what looked like a cocktail cabinet, and the low table with patience cards and another table almost smothered in magazines, but I'd not looked at the portrait.

"It's you," I said. "An excellent likeness too. You've hardly changed a bit."

Her lip drooped with the cigarette hanging from a corner of her mouth.

"You've got quite a good line of talk," she told me, and she said it rather banteringly. "Have a drink? A cocktail?"

"Delighted to," I said.

Her back was towards me as she poured it and those bulges of hers were more noticeable as she stooped. I got up to take the glass from her. Her own was to be a stiff whisky. That was the elusive odour that had been mixed with scent and smoke.

"Heaps more birthdays and all happy ones."

"No harm in hoping," she told me, and she actually smiled. It made the face suddenly almost youthful and very definitely attractive.

"What's your job?"

I took another sip of the cocktail. The question had been a bit sudden.

"I'm the head of a firm of private enquiry agents. We've been commissioned by an interested party to enquire into Henry Baldlow's death."

The face hardened.

"A detective, eh? This isn't some trick of my husband's?"

"Most certainly not," I assured her. "I'm telling you the absolute truth, Mrs. Tinley. Here's my business card."

She had a look at it, turning it about as if her eyes weren't focusing too well.

"You look too much of a gentleman to me for that sort of game."

I explained that it took all sorts to make a private detective world. We weren't the divorce-case sort.

"You wouldn't think I was a clergyman's daughter?"

"Why not? It doesn't surprise me in the least."

"Well, I am," she said. "He had a parish in Bromley and was killed in the blitz. Elderton was the name. His brother was Hubert Elderton, the actor."

There seemed to be more pride in the brother than in the father. I'd never heard the name.

"Really?" I said, and risked it.

"Yes, and that's how I came to go on the stage. Well, not the stage, really. Musical comedy was my ambition and I was with the Whirligigs. I'll show you."

I had to look at photographs. The Whirligigs were a concert party in fancy dress adorned with black rings on a pale background. Five men and four women.

"That's how I came to meet my husband," she was telling me. "We were at Portsmouth, giving a show for the boys. A couple of months later we were married. Didn't see much of him, though, till the end of the war. Just shows what a fool I was. Do you know I had a good cry when I got these old photographs out this afternoon?"

"Who's this man not in fancy dress?"

"Oh, him. That's Billy Morris. Pinky we always call him."

Morris! The word struck a bell. Nordon's report about Bald-low stealthily telephoning to a Morris: telling him he was on no account to come to The Croft.

"He was the manager?"

"He owned the show, and two others. He's still a friend of mine. Have another drink?"

"A small one, then."

"What's the matter? Can't you hold it?"

The remark had only a humour. That half glass of what had looked like neat whisky was mellowing her after the maudlin drinks of the afternoon. We had the same again.

"Funny," she suddenly said. "You came to ask about that old goat Baldlow. Pinky was here that morning he called."

"He came here?"

"What're you looking so surprised about?"

"I'm not really surprised. Why shouldn't he come and see you? After all, you were his niece by marriage. All I was think-ing was that he had some lung trouble and never went to town."

"Well, he came here," she said. "Last June it was. He rang me and asked and I told him why not. When he was here, who should come in but Pinky, so I had to introduce them. Pinky wanted me to give my husband his divorce and get back into the show business."

"What did Baldlow want?"

"He was snooping. Kept asking me about Charles—that's my husband as was. I didn't see what he was getting at."

"He wasn't trying to get you two together again?"

"Some hopes. As I told him when he kept asking about that yacht. That's what Charles has, down near Littleton. As I said, I didn't marry a man: what I married was a bloody yacht."

"You don't like the sea?"

"Can't stand it. I'm always sick. And there was his high-hat-ted friends. And that sister of his. A snooty bitch if ever there was one."

Her speech was slurred again. She leaned back with eyes closed for a moment or two. She blinked a bit, and the smile was maudlin.

"The trouble with me is I'm getting a bit tight. You getting tight?"

"A bit," I said. "I'd had one or two before I came here. What about making us some coffee?"

"Coffee?" She leered at me, or that's what the smile looked like. "Yes, coffee."

I took her by the arm as she got up and she made no protest. I guided her, and she me, to a kitchenette. She sat down on a cane-seated chair and told me what to do and where to find things. When I'd brewed the pot she told me to take it in. She was going to powder her nose. It took her ten minutes to do it. She looked as if she'd had a cold wash and had seen to hair and make-up, but her walk was still none too steady.

"My God, it's hot!"

She didn't know I'd put the pot back on the heater.

"Do us both good," I told her, and we got through a couple of cups of strong black.

"Feel better?"

"I'm all right," she said, and she was giving me a curious look. "I like you, you know. Come and sit here."

I poured out two more cups and came to the chesterfield.

"No, here."

I moved closer. Her arms went out and she had my face between her hands. There was a kiss. It took my breath away. I helped to make it good. It was all in the line of business. Then she snuggled against me. I gave her the coffee. One of my arms was round her and the other held my cup.

"Pinky," she said. "I like Pinky. He's straight, and there's no monkey-business."

"That's where you've got to be careful," I told her. "I wouldn't be surprised if your husband was having you watched. It's the only logical thing if you won't give him a divorce."

"Divorce?" she said. "I'm sitting pretty, ain't I? All this and an allowance." She gave another snort. "If he wants his divorce, then he's got to pay."

She finished her coffee. I put the two cups on the side table.

"What about a Benedictine? There's some still there."

I poured two and brought the small glasses over. She pulled me down to my corner again with her free hand. We were snug as a couple of newly-weds.

"You're going to make your husband pay, then?"

"And cheap at the price," she said. "What's a measly ten thousand—if he has it."

"And hasn't he?"

"I don't know," she said, "but he won't pay up."

"He'll have it now, though."

She wriggled clear, and sat up.

"What do you mean?"

I told her Baldlow had apparently died intestate. Charles would come in for his share of the estate. It ought to amount to far more than ten thousand.

"Don't get ideas," I told her. "He's not going to be such a fool as to part with ten thousand if he can catch you napping. You've got to watch your step. For all you know he may be having you watched by the staff here. One slip on your part and bang goes ten thousand."

"Don't worry about little Betty," she told me amusedly. "She could always take care of herself."

"That doesn't mean you've got to let up. Suppose some snooper with a master-key were suddenly to open that door."

"To hell with him," she said. "Can't I entertain a friend?"

But she got up, and reasonably steadily, and clipped a catch on the door. I was wondering where the evening would end, especially when my glasses got all steamed up with another kiss and we were snug in the chesterfield corner again. My face must have been a mess, what with lipstick and the stickiness of the Benedictine.

"Tell me about Baldlow." I tightened the pressure round her waist. "What else did he want that morning?"

"It was a scream," she said. She made as if to sit up, then changed her mind and snuggled back again. "You won't believe it but when he'd finished asking me about Charles, what do you think he did?"

"Don't know. Make a pass at you?"

"What him—the old goat! I'd have scratched his eyes out. No"—she gave a little giggle—"what he did was to ask me to pray with him!"

"Good lord, no!"

"It's God's truth," she said. "After he'd tried a bit of reconciliation stuff, that's what he did."

"He couldn't have been serious."

"You should have seen him. He was serious all right."

"And what'd you do?"

"Knelt down like he said. You don't think I'm a fool, do you? He had money, didn't he?"

"Remember what he said?"

"My God, no! I know it was all about Charles and me and divine guidance and hell knows what. I was having a hard job keeping my face straight. God, it was funny!"

"And all for nothing."

"Yes, blast him." I felt her give a little wriggle. "Except that I can put the screws on Charles when he gets his money."

There was a silence that for me was becoming a bit heavy. Then she did wriggle round.

"What about you staying for a bit?"

"Good Lord!" I said, and looked at my watch. I managed to get to my feet. "Do you know my man is waiting down there with my car? I ought to've been at Baker Street ten minutes ago."

"Wash it out. What d'you want to go to Baker Street for?"

"To meet my mother. I said I'd be there."

I was putting on my overcoat. I hadn't got it properly on when her arms were round my neck again.

"I like you." That was a whisper in my ear. "Like me?"

"Do I not."

The horn-rims got steamed up again.

"When can you come again?"

"You think it will be safe?"

"Of course it will." She gave a little gurgle. "Tell you what. You're a detective. Why shouldn't you be working for me?"

"A great idea. Soon as I'm free I'll give you a ring."

"Make it in the mornings," she said. "I don't often get up till about eleven. We'll have a long evening. You'll like that?"

"Don't give me ideas," I told her archly.

"Wait a minute."

She cleaned up my face a bit with a handkerchief. She peeped along the corridor both ways from the partly opened door. She blew me a kiss just as I went through.

Hallows had moved the car so that the entrance lamp fell on the evening paper he was reading. I got in behind the wheel.

"A pretty long session," I told him. "Well over an hour. But a mighty interesting hour."

I gave him an edited version. I asked if he had any ideas. He said he hadn't any, except that ten thousand pounds for a divorce was a capital motive for wanting Baldlow dead.

"If Tinley hadn't the money already," I said. "And if he knew there wasn't a will. Remember that the original will cut him off with a measly hundred pounds. That he might or might not have known. I think he didn't know it."

"Just one other thing," he said. "What she told you about him getting her on her knees seems to show the old boy had really got religion."

I said I'd been convinced of that for some time. I didn't say I had ways of proving it that I wasn't yet prepared to tell a soul. And I remembered I'd never told him about Morris and that Nordon report.

"That's something new," he said. "Sounds pretty interesting. Was she carrying on with that Morris?"

"She as good as swore she wasn't."

"But Baldlow didn't want him to come to Seahurst," he said, as if to himself. "She must have been using Morris. Was she trying to get money out of Baldlow? Or did he ask her to tell him anything about her husband that she might happen to remember, and Morris was the go-between?"

"Don't know," I said. "But this is what you'll do. I'm going down to that Littleton place in the morning and I'll take Nordon with me. You'll get Morris through any of the theatrical agencies. Billy Morris, known as Pinky. Try Holberg first and mention my name. Do your best to see if Morris has an alibi for Baldlow's murder. If it's humanly possible, find out why he rang Baldlow."

I dropped Hallows at the nearest Tube station. At the garage I rang Norris at his private address and told him I'd see him at half-past eight at the office next morning and that I'd be needing Nordon. Then I went home.

I'd had a bit of a facial at the garage but I thought it best to take Bernice into my confidence. I said I'd been involved, not too seriously, with a blonde in the way of business and there was more than a possibility she'd be ringing me.

"You're my secretary," I said. "Tell her I'm away for a day or two—anywhere you like—and that you'll give me her message the moment I get back. Her name's Elizabeth—Betty—Tinley. I may have to use her again. Between ourselves, it's that Baldlow murder case. She's a niece by marriage."

It's lucky I have a wife who knows that womanising isn't among my latter-day vices. Bernice seemed a bit thoughtful for the next hour or so, and no more. The blonde hairs, probably, that had been on my overcoat.

X

LITTLETON

WE DROVE to Littleton in Nordon's car, a journey of best part of three hours. During the journey I'd briefed him. What we had to do was locate Tinley's little yacht—at least I thought it was only a little one. My headquarters would be the Three Pigeons at Littleton. I'd have lunch there and he could report when something turned up. I had to keep out of things. Six-foot-three, horn-rims and a hatchet face make me someone who's remembered and I didn't want Tinley to know I'd been snooping round Littleton.

"I don't like to seem butting in too much, sir," Nordon said when I'd finished, "but is it in order to ask what's behind all this? I'm only suggesting it might help in whatever it is I have to do."

I didn't answer him for a minute. It's a nice point what to tell an operative and what to leave out. Hallows was a man to whom I'd tell anything, but I wasn't too sure of Nordon's discretion. He liked a drink and he might open his mouth just a bit too far at a pub or the hotel.

"I'll tell you when you've located the yacht," I said. "What comes after that is going to be pretty tricky."

I dropped him short of the village so that we shouldn't be connected. Then I had lunch at Littleton's hotel. It's a small resort, hardly more than a fishing village, but there're a couple of creeks rather more west that are handy for tying up a yacht. I didn't think Nordon would have much trouble in locating it. He didn't. He was back at one o'clock. After he'd had lunch we talked outside where we couldn't be seen.

He said it had been easy. He'd gone to a pub further along the road and had got into conversation with a couple of fishermen. He'd mentioned a little yacht he had at Dover and now he was thinking about bringing it round the coast, further west. From this and that emerged the locality of Tinley's yacht.

"You know that road we passed forking to the right just short of here, sir? Just beyond where you dropped me? That's the main road for the coast. This is a dead end because of the first creek. You go along that main road and a bridge goes round the creek. There's only about three hundred yards of it. You can take a path back along the creek to some cottages. Well, near the mouth and on this side is a little jetty and three big sheds, or whatever they are. They used to build boats there one time. Tinley's boat—the *Lady Clare*—is laid up for the winter in one of them. I had a good look at her."

He said he didn't know much about boats but she looked biggish, and not built for racing. She could have four small bunks, a little galley, and some sort of tiny lounge. On deck there'd be room for people to sit in deck chairs.

She was brought in at high tide though there was water enough through the creek at any tide, at least just to make the jetty steps, or so he'd been told.

"What's she used for?"

"Pleasure cruising," he said. "There's the little bay here that's partly sheltered and she can go where she likes in good weather. Tinley often had her away for a whole week-end."

"Any passengers?"

"Not often," he said. "There's a man named Grimble—a local fisherman—who looks after her and acts as crew. He's a red-headed chap of about fifty-five. Said to be pretty close-mouthed. They reckon Tinley pays him well."

"I see. Any other news?"

"Rawley, Tinley's manager at that Bond Street place, occasionally takes her out. He seems to have his own friends. Grimble is always there too."

You've watched a blackbird on a lawn, how it gives a prod or two with its beak and then cocks a head on one side as if listening? Nordon was rather like that while he was talking to me. He'd tell me something, then wait, as if he knew I was going to say something—or so he hoped.

"You stay here," I said. "I'll take the car round and have a look at the lie of the land. I might be gone some time."

I drove back to the fork and turned sharp left. In less than no time I was over the bridge that ran across the mere trickle that the creek had now become. I saw the three long, low sheds, and the little jetty and the path that led along the opposite side to the cottages. Then I pushed the car on, intending to go to Beach-bourne. But there was no need. At a four-cross way was an A.A. telephone-box and I had the key with me.

I looked up Customs and Excise at Beachbourne and rang them. A man's voice answered. I opened with plausible explanations about being sorry to trouble him and how I was a journalist just beginning a series of articles about smuggling on the south coast. Would he be so good as to give me a little information.

"Depends what sort," he said.

"Well, there's undoubtedly a lot of smuggling going on in this part of the world—"

"That isn't a question," he reminded me.

"Well, what steps do you take to combat it? I'm just starting the job, by the way. You have your Coast Preventive Men?"

"Yes."

"They patrol?"

"That's right. They join up with other men."

"And where do your tips come from?"

"Sorry," he said. "I can't tell you any more. You'd better refer to our chief office in London."

With that he rang off. I went back to Littleton and I wasn't much wiser than when I left. There'd been a possible confirmation, perhaps, of the fact I'd read somewhere lately, that a considerable deal of smuggling still went on, though not the kind that fought the Preventive Men and carried goods inland on ponies and pack-horses by secret paths. Smuggling would be streamlined nowadays, like everything else, and organised to perfection—or nearly so. One did hear occasionally about hauls from cars with secret compartments and that sort of thing, but I'd read nothing about smuggling purely by sea.

Nordon was in the bar lounge. I'd mentioned being away for some time and he looked surprised at seeing me so soon. An empty coffee cup was on the table and what looked like a sherry glass, almost empty.

"Brandy—the real stuff," he told me quietly. "You'd like one, sir?"

"Never suits me this time of day," I said. "And I think we ought to be getting along."

There'd been a tremendous surprise on his face when we passed the fork and were heading straight back to town. I thought I might open up a bit.

"Well, what do you think has been behind this little trip of ours?"

His smile looked a bit self-confident.

"Well, Tinley's in the jewellery business. That ought to include high-class watches, so why not use that boat of his for a bit of smuggling?"

"You're taking into account the fact that the Customs people must know all about Tinley?"

"There'd still be ways and means," he said.

"You tell me some. Suppose you're running the racket yourself."

"The least suspicion and that boat'd be searched as soon as she got inside the three-mile limit," he said. "I wouldn't be surprised if she'd been gone over for secret hiding places and so on, so what I'd do would be to drop overboard after dark something in a waterproof covering and attached to some sort of buoy. Grimble could pick it up in a row-boat. Or a small boat on the bigger boat could nip inshore and deposit or hand over whatever it was by arrangement, to pass to a waiting car. It'd only be a matter of eluding patrols in the pitch dark. It ought to be a piece of cake."

"Sounds as if we might be losing you shortly," I told him jocularly. "But let's suppose it's all true: that Tinley or Rawley, or both, have been smuggling. What's it got to do with Baldlow?"

I didn't think he'd have the answer to that one, and I was right.

"Can't say," he said. "There's no connecting link except that he's Baldlow's nephew. He might have killed the old man because he wanted money to finance this thing in a big way. There must be packets in it."

"Something in that," I said. "And what would you do about it?"

"That's a bit sudden, sir. I'd have to think."

It took him one cigarette to find a suggestion.

"What about this, sir? The old *agent provocateur*."

"You mustn't get a one-track mind," I told him. "You tried that recently and it happened to come off. But carry on. How's the scheme develop?"

"Well, I come back to Littleton looking a bit more like a wise boy. I get into touch with Grimble, flash a roll and ask him if he's the sort who'd like to make a packet himself. I say I've got the stuff on the other side and can get it near here, so what about the rest. I can quote French wholesalers and put up a front. It may take a day or two but either I'll know if he's already in a racket or if he isn't."

I told him it'd be something that needed very careful thought, though even at its best it'd be a round-about way of arriving at Baldlow's killer and an expensive one. But he didn't know then that already I'd made up my mind to try out some such scheme. And what he certainly also did not know was the dim pattern that was beginning to take shape in my mind about Baldlow and his death.

When we got back to the office I had Nordon wait in the operatives' room while I had a talk with Norris. He said he had a job for the next day for Nordon and I could have him from then on unless something important occurred. I said that would suit me fine, and pressed the buzzer for Nordon to come in. I told him Norris would be wanting him and there'd be a day therefore in which he could perfect details about that scheme he'd roughly outlined.

When I was leaving them, Norris remembered something. Hallows had been in and had left a letter for me. I ran a quick eye over it in Bertha's office.

It said that everything had been fine. He'd seen Holberg, who'd given Morris the best of characters. Morris had an office in Maryland Street at the back of Shaftesbury Avenue, so Hallows had gone there. The staff consisted of a secretary-typist and a junior typist.

"Morris's alibi is okay for that Saturday time," the chit went on. "He was in the office till well after one o'clock, so he couldn't have got down to Seahurst unless he flew there with his own wings. I was told he was now out on some business or other but would be back at about five. This is his private number. I'll be at home if wanted."

It was nearer six o'clock than five, so I got Bertha to ring the Maryland Street office. There was no reply. I tried the private number. Mrs. Morris answered. She expected her husband in at any minute. I gave her my name and said I'd call round inside half an hour on private business.

I had a cup of tea and set off. Morris lived at Peckham Road, Camberwell, and I was a bit late when I got there.

Mrs. Morris, a pleasant-faced woman of about fifty, said her husband was in. I was shown into a cold lounge-parlour. She switched on the electric fire and left me. In less than five minutes Morris came in.

He was a big man in every way: six feet of him and shoulders like the back of a barn. His face was florid and he had an old-fashioned handlebar moustache, just as in those photographs I'd seen at Mrs. Tinley's flat. His voice was surprisingly soft. "Mr. Travers? You want to see me, I believe."

Holberg had vouched for him and there was something about him that made me put my cards on the table. He'd read about the Baldlow murder. He made no bones about admitting that he'd once met the man.

"No names," he said, "but I was calling on an old friend whom I hoped to interest in a certain proposition and he happened to be there. Last June it was. I just had a word with this Baldlow out of politeness and made an excuse and left. I couldn't talk business when he was there and he looked like staying."

"You see how I'm placed," I said. "Everything, like this talk we're having, has to be in the strictest confidence. We had a man there, as I told you, and it might look as if he fell down on the job. That wouldn't do us any good."

"But where do I come in?"

"You don't," I said, "except to this extent."

I tried to be very apologetic but I had to admit having seen Betty Tinley and in the course of a talk about Baldlow it had been mentioned that Morris had called there when Baldlow had happened to be there too.

"I've got to explore every contact," I said. "I want to know everything I can about Baldlow's private life. It's the only hope of a clue to who killed him. Your name happened to crop up in the way I've just told you."

I don't think he cared a lot for it, but his voice didn't rise.

"Yes, sir, and I've told *you*. I was introduced to him and we had a word or two and that's about all. He did mention, I remember, that he lived at Seahurst. I saw Mrs. Tinley a day or two later and we didn't mention him. I also rang her when I read about the murder, just to be sure it was the same man. Simple curiosity, nothing more."

I got to my feet.

"He was little more than a name?"

"That's about it."

"You never saw him or spoke to him again?"

"Why should I? The man was no interest to me."

I held out my hand. I said I'd bothered him about nothing at all, as it'd happened, but I hoped he'd see my personal anxiety about the whole thing. As we parted at the door I mentioned that Holberg was a friend of mine in case he wished to check up.

So that was that, and mighty inexplicable it was. It was too much to think there'd be another Morris—or Maurice—who might have come into contact with Baldlow and who'd threatened for some reason or other to see Baldlow at The Croft. I could have sworn that my Pinky Morris wasn't a liar. He'd spoken quietly and unhesitatingly. There'd been no confusion and no turning the talk aside. All I could think of was that I couldn't be absolutely certain. Big things might have been involved. Morris might have expected to be questioned by someone sooner or later, and his answers had been ready. Holberg couldn't vouch for a man's private and unsuspected life.

But I wasn't happy. What I decided was that it was one of those things, like that enquiry into Jane Howell, that had got me nowhere and would have to be pigeon-holed till some other line of research cut clean across it, and then I'd be seeing it from another angle. So when I got home I rang Hallows and told him I'd seen Morris and he was a dead end.

"I'll be in the office at nine and we'll have a bit of a chat before the next step," I said. "Looks as if our next trip will be to Suffolk."

That ended a longish day, or so I thought. Everything started up again when I listened to the nine o'clock news.

*

It was a police message.

The police are anxious to interview Michael O'Brien—spelt e-n—late of Albert Road, Seahurst. . . .

There followed a description. O'Brien, it went on, was thought by the police to be in possession of information that might be of use in connection with the murder of Henry Baldlow. Any news of O'Brien to be telephoned to the Chief Constable, Seahurst—Seahurst 3113.

I waited for a few minutes, and then rang Seahurst. Grainger wasn't in but I did manage to get Padman after quite a time.

"Just heard your O'Brien message," I said. "What happened? Did he bolt?"

"You know as much as we," he told me. "Yesterday evening, it was. We'd had another word with him and the two women in the morning and got nothing out of 'em, and when we went again that evening as we'd said—the Chief had thought of a new angle—he was gone. The two women had been at the pictures that afternoon, and when they got back he'd packed and gone."

"And they didn't know where?"

"Lying like hell," he told me. "The yarn was all ready. Reckoned he'd been threatening to leave for some time. Said they'd suspected he'd got some other woman. Didn't know who or where. Just suspected."

"You ought to get him soon," I said. "Any other news?"

"No," he said. "We've been through all Baldlow's papers, and there's nothing. No sign of a will. We thought that might have been deposited at the bank in spite of what the lawyer said. One thing, though, Mrs. C. and her daughter were expecting a legacy."

"B. told them so?"

"He certainly did, or so they say, when he first let them know he was going to South Africa. Said he'd be making a new will and they'd be remembered."

"No reason why they should lie about that," I said. "The information wouldn't do O'B. any good. Has he a record, by the way?"

"No," he said. "We got his prints some days ago, though he didn't know it."

I thanked him and rang off. I wasn't depressed and I wasn't elated, and because I couldn't for the life of me fathom why O'Brien should have killed Baldlow. The business of thefts had never become in any way public, and in itself it wasn't a motive for murder. Nor was the matter of a possible legacy under a will about which O'Brien could have had no information whatever. Also the story the women had told might be true. Even if it weren't, there might be a good many other reasons for O'Brien to think it as well to get away from Seahurst.

That was as far as I'd got when the telephone went again. It was Norris, wanting to know if I'd heard that police message. I said I had and we'd go into the matter in the morning.

I thought that'd be the end of it, but it wasn't. Five minutes after I'd sat down again, the telephone went once more. I thought it might be Hallows, asking if there'd be new instructions, but it wasn't.

"You're through, caller." That was Exchange.

"Hallo," I said.

"That Mr. Travers?"

"Speaking."

"This is Tom Howell, Mr. Travers. You can hear me all right?"

"Perfectly."

His voice had been low but quite distinct.

"My wife's gone to bed with a nasty headache: that's why I'm able to ring. You heard that police message just now?"

"I did."

"You think this fellow they want is the right man?"

"Beyond me to say," I told him. "One thing you can rely on. As soon as I know the police are pretty sure—even if it's tomorrow—we shall close down on your case. We never spend a client's money unnecessarily."

"I wasn't thinking of the money."

"I know," I said. "I know just what you're thinking. But we've a reputation to maintain. As a matter of fact, up to the moment we're well inside our quotation."

"Anything to report yourselves?"

"Not yet. It's not an easy job we're doing. No further signs of worry on the part of a certain lady?"

"Glad to say no. This is just an ordinary headache. May be due to certain other things."

"That's something at least," I said. "Any developments arising out of tonight that I learn privately I'll pass on to you. But don't be too hopeful. There're things about which I have my own ideas. I can't say more."

"Very good of you. Good night—and many thanks."

The telephone was quiet from then on. Hallows at least wasn't panicking. Maybe it was that happy thought in a bleak evening that got me early to sleep.

I talked things over with Norris in the morning and gave him my views. As for that *agent provocateur* business at Littleton, he didn't like it in the least. He did have to admit that if we were forced to try that particular approach Nordon was the very man. He was a good mixer and his knowledge of French ought to be an asset.

"What's actually behind this enquiry into Tinley?" he asked me bluntly.

"Someone killed Baldlow," I said. "Baldlow mightn't have anticipated a lethal attack, but he did expect trouble, and after he'd seen those three people. And why? Because he was going to tell one of them he wasn't a fit and proper person to inherit any Baldlow money, and because of something he—Baldlow—had found out. It was what he'd found out that might put him in some danger, once he'd revealed that he knew it. Isn't that logical?"

"Well, yes—it is."

"I said *he*. You noticed that. We can't count Mrs. Howell in. She's the client. But about Baldlow. He was a shrimp of a man for all his cocksureness and blether. I think he was genuinely scared of what he considered it his duty to do: hence Nordon."

"You should know," he said. "But isn't there some other way of working on Tinley?"

I had to say I reluctantly thought there wasn't: not that I liked it any better than he. Finally he left it to me. I had all day in which to think and I'd see Nordon when he'd finished his day's assignment.

Hallows and I went out for a talk over an early cup of coffee. He agreed that O'Brien's bolting looked more than suspicious, and he was with me too on that absence of motive for Baldlow's murder.

"If you ask me," he said, "it isn't O'Brien who's the key figure there. It's that Mrs. Carver. If the police knew just why she went home that afternoon, they'd have the answer to O'Brien."

I agreed. But about ourselves. I shouldn't be free that day, so if Norris had no minor job for him, Hallows was to take the day off. In the morning he was to be at my flat at nine o'clock, and with his car. I didn't want the numbers traced on mine. I'd have rooms ready for us in Dunland.

"I don't know what we'll get to know about Lorde," I told him, "but what I'm hoping is that sooner or later something about one of those three relatives may cross the line of another. Even Morris, for all we know, might crop up somewhere. Or Betty Tinley. We've just got to keep digging away till it does."

It was six o'clock that evening when I saw Nordon. I told him I was agreeing reluctantly to that proposal of his about Tinley.

"These are instructions that are on no account to be modified," I said, and passed him a copy of what I'd written.

Firstly he was not to go near the hotel where he'd already been seen, or the pub. He was to go by train and bus, not by his car. He was to be a Frenchman who spoke very good English: only intonation was to show that he wasn't English in fact. He must have papers of some sort for the name he proposed to assume. He'd better have some elementary disguise, such as little side whiskers and glasses, and if he still had any clothes of distinctly French appearance, then he should wear them.

"You'll approach Grimble because you'll have learned he has charge of a yacht," I went on. "The approach is to be strictly an exploratory one so that you can sum him up and judge if it's necessary to resume negotiations. That all clear?"

He said it was.

"If I may say so, sir, this job's just up my alley. It's the kind of thing I did scores of times in Intelligence."

"That's fine," I said. "But don't slip up. I hope the job'll do both you and us some good. I'd be sorry if it didn't."

XI

DUNLAND

WE WENT by Epping, Hallows driving. There'd been a bit of a frost but the roads were good and we were in no great hurry. It's funny how a man can delude himself about his native heath. I could have sworn there was a difference in the air when we were out of Essex and into Suffolk. Soon we were within five miles of my old home and well-remembered names were on direction posts. It was grand—if it hadn't brought too closely the incredible passing of the years.

We were in Dunland by noon and it was market day: parking places chock-a-block and plenty of people in the streets. I just remembered the little town, and no more, for it must have been twenty years since I'd seen it. It was much nicer than I'd thought: some lovely old houses, a church that looked even up to the Suffolk standard, and magnificent pargetting on cottage plaster walls.

We went straight to the hotel and had lunch. Hallows's little car has no heating and we were both a bit cold. After the meal I looked up Lorde's business and private addresses in the telephone directory, and then Hallows and I went our various ways. His assignment was wide enough in scope—to find out all he could about Francis Lorde. My self-imposed assignment was the same, and we'd be comparing notes over a cup of tea at four-thirty.

A handyman who happened to be in the hotel garage yard told me the way to the Bury Road where Lorde lived. As soon as I'd got out of the narrowish, traffic-crowded streets, I was there. I let the car crawl and inside a minute I'd found the house.

There were really nice houses each side of that road and Lorde's looked as good as any. They were a mixture—most the usual Edwardian Tudor—with here and there a Gothic monstrosity and one or two Georgian. Lorde's was Georgian, though late. It was two storied with slated roof and the rooms would be large and lofty. It would be a fine house to live in provided it had been brought bang up to date.

It stood on a slight rise of ground and had a beautifully kept driveway. The lawns sloped up and were interspersed with flower beds. Nothing was cramped. The gardens would be at least two acres, and I could just discern past the opening between house and garage—built, by the way, in the same style as the house— the surround posts and wire of a tennis court. I liked the look of the whole place. It had an unpretentious dignity and a distinct charm of setting. It was the sort of place I'd have liked to live in myself. Expensive in upkeep, no doubt, but you can't take it with you.

I was just thinking of moving the car on when a man appeared in that opening between garage and house. He looked like a gardener and in the early thirties. He opened the garage doors and I saw there was a space for a couple of cars, though only one was in it. A minute and he was backing that car out. It was a nice little grey saloon. He backed it round, then drew it up before the front door—a nice period door with a good fanlight. He fussed inside the car for a minute, shook out a rug and replaced it, and then waited.

Almost at once the door opened and a woman came out. I guessed she was Mrs. Lorde: a tall, imperious-looking woman in a fur coat. I couldn't hear what she was saying to the man but the voice was a bit shrill and every now and again he gave a little nod of the head. Then he held the door for her and closed it when she wedged herself in. He touched his cap as she moved the car off.

She was driving in the direction of the town and I saw her plainly over the top of my newspaper as she passed me. She drove quite slowly, both hands on the wheel and elbows well out, as if the very driving had in it some grim purpose. Her complexion was high-coloured and she looked nearer sixty than fifty.

Once more I was about to drive on, but I saw a little notice board fixed to what was probably a tradesmen's entrance gate on the far side. I did drive on, reversed the car at a side turning and drew it up alongside that notice board. It was larger than I'd thought and a bill was tin-tacked to it. I couldn't read the smallest of its print but it was advertising a performance by the local dramatic society of *Laburnum Grove*. The interesting thing was that under the largish lettering of the dramatic society there appeared in smaller letters, but still readable—the name of its president—Mrs. Francis Lorde. I wondered if that slight flamboyance was really necessary, or was it that Mrs. Lorde was of such importance in the town that she had to be given her meed of publicity. And why the Mrs. *Francis* Lorde? Why not Mrs. F. Lorde, or merely Mrs. Lorde? Were there other Mrs. Lordes in the town?

I drove back to the hotel garage and then made for the church. It had a lovely interior with a magnificently carved roof. I had a look at the monuments. On one wall, below a copy of a late Italian head of Christ crowned with thorns, was a brass plate. It was the name that had attracted me—an Oswald French who for many years had been a churchwarden. He had died in 1935.

"You a stranger here?"

The voice startled me. I hadn't realised I was so near the vestry door and the feet had made no sound on the strip of red carpet.

"Yes," I said. "Just happened to be in the town. My name's Harrison."

"I'm Charters, the vicar here."

He was a lean, scholarly man of well into the sixties. He looked what I'd crudely call a good Christian—kindly, almost gentle in manner.

"I was looking at this tablet," I said. "It just happened to strike me how fortunate the church is to have its laymen—like this Mr. French—who're prepared to give years of good service. Or am I wrong?"

He smiled.

"My dear sir, you're quite right. French was a fine character. I knew him well."

"French," I said thoughtfully. "He wouldn't be a relation of General French of Saxmundham? His brother, for instance?"

"I think not," he said. "He was an only son. He had an only son too. A great tragedy. He was killed at Dunkirk."

"Tragic indeed," I said. "He was a solicitor like his father?"

"Yes," he said. "French, Son and Lorde. Francis Lorde—he and his family attend St. John's—is what you might call the sole survivor. You'd like me, by the way, to take you round?"

"Unhappily I have to be going," I told him. "Very good of you all the same."

"Some other time, then. You've seen our misereres? They're also called misericords or patiences, you know. Ours are very fine. Most rare, even for a thirteenth-century building like this."

We had a look at the misereres, the lower parts of the seats in the choir, with their grotesque carvings of mediaeval beasts and scriptural scenes. He said, and I could quite believe him, that some were as good as those at Exeter.

He walked with me to the door.

"I agree Dunland's a charming old town," I said. "I wish I could spend more time in it. And you seem very up-to-date. I noticed just now a bill advertising a performance by your dramatic society."

"Oh yes," he said. "We're not too far behind the times. But there again we have a certain continuity. It's a Mrs. Lorde who's such a keen president of that society. She does an enormous deal of work for the town. She had an O.B.E. for her work during the war."

We shook hands at the door and I promised to look him up if ever I happened to be again in the town. I'd covered myself by saying I was there on business, but I knew it best to get back to the hotel. I'd have liked to peer at any antique shops, but it wouldn't look so well if he saw me wandering loosely. And Lorde's office was just in a side-road off the main square, and he was the last man whom I wanted to meet.

In the hotel I had a word with the manager.

"Whom would you recommend in the town to do any simple legal business for you?"

"I've only been here about five years," he said, "but I know there's William Jagger and Howard in Cambridge Street."

"Isn't there a firm called Lorde, or something like that?"

"Of course," he said. "Just off the Square. They're a sort of family firm. Had a good connection with most of the old families."

I smiled.

"Why the *had*?"

"Well, you know how it is. They're the very ones who haven't any money. Taxed out of existence. It's the big farmers who've got the money, and the land. Mind you," he went on quickly, "I don't know anything about the affairs of the firm—French, Son and Lorde. I've just remembered the name. I have to listen to all sorts of talk and you can't believe half of it."

There was no point in pursuing things further and making an interest too prominent. I did a crossword in front of the fire in the residents' lounge till Hallows arrived. He'd got into conversation first thing with a blimp sort of retired colonel in the saloon bar of the other good hotel, and had learned quite a lot about Francis Lorde and his family.

There were two sons, described by the colonel—whether patronisingly or not—as very nice boys. Bernard, the younger, had not been in the war because of a game leg and was now studying medicine at Edinburgh. Godfrey, the elder, had risen to the rank of major in the war and had then resumed his job in his father's firm. Two years ago he had married a wealthy woman, slightly older than himself—a daughter of the late Hon. Frederick and Mrs. Vaughan-Pughe. They had a very nice place on the Cambridge Road, overlooking the golf course.

"What about the firm itself?"

"Hard to say," Hallows told me. "One of those dry-as-dust old firms with clients like themselves. Even their building looks like something out of Dickens."

"Financially they're probably good," I said. "Lorde's own house looks good. His wife has a car of her own and there's a gardener-chauffeur. Whether there's a maid or two I can't say. Now you tell me the son has money. Disappointing from our point of view. Where's the motive for murder?"

"About the wife," he said. "She has her nose into everything in town."

He glanced at his notebook.

"Yes," he said. "I learned this from the local paper and from the secretary of the local Women's Institute. She was of very good family when Lorde married her, but no money. A Quantrell, if that conveys anything to you. Said to be a very old name in these parts. I wasn't exactly told she poked her nose into everything. That's what I gathered from the way that Women's Institute secretary told it to me. Active in everything and a generous subscriber."

"Looks as if we might pack and go," I said. "Can you see even a vestige of motive for murder?"

"Can't say I do," he said. "Plenty of time yet, though."

There was nothing to be done till the pubs opened. Hallows went off like the quiet mole he was and I tried the saloon bar of the hotel. Before dinner I might as well have stayed in the lounge, for there was never a chance to get into conversation with a soul. After dinner, by about half-past eight, I did manage it with one of the local auctioneers. He was one of those men—I've known several in my time—who take a pride in their local dialect, even if their usual English is as good as that of most. I love the sound of it. It had warmed my heart that afternoon when I'd been passing a shop into which a couple of women were looking.

"Don't yew go and buy nothin' like that," one was saying to the other. "Do you'll repent it."

Just a few words but in them all that hopeless nostalgia for youth and the years that had gone. That was how it was in that saloon bar. This auctioneer, Tench by name, had come out with a bit of broad Suffolk to the barman. I introduced myself as a Suffolk man, and we had a drink together. He asked if I was retiring and coming to live in Dunland.

"Unfortunately no, but I'd like nothing better. I saw some very nice places when I was about in the town this afternoon. There were some in the Bury Road. One late Georgian one particularly took my fancy."

"On the right, about half-way down?"

That belonged to one of the town's solicitors, he said. Two or three years ago I could have bought it. They'd thought of selling.

"Didn't want a big place like that, really. Mind you, if you had bought it you'd have been sorry now. A couple of years ago it'd have cost you eight thousand, and what's it worth now—a little over six."

"You said a solicitor. I only know Jagger and Howard."

"This is Francis Lorde," he said. "A very old firm."

We had another drink. I kept the talk as close to the Lordes as I dared, but learned nothing more, except that the Hon. Mrs. Vaughan-Pughe had been an American—hence, one might say, the daughter's money. She and her husband had gone down with a torpedoed liner in 1942. The Godfrey Lorde wedding had been at the parish church—St. John's—and with all the trimmings. Honeymoon in Italy.

"Best part of a month too," Tench said. "Nice if you know how."

That was all I learned. One way and another I'd had enough to drink so I went back to the lounge. Three other guests were there: a business man and his wife, and a middle-aged parson. Before I'd had more than a few gossipy words with them, Hallows came in. We went up to my room as soon as I could say good night.

Hallows's night had been spent in grubbing deeper into the Lordes but he had nothing beyond what I'd learned myself, so we called it a day and turned in. But we'd decided to spend another morning in Dunland, and it was lucky that we did. What was luckier was the presence in the lounge the next morning of that parson whom I'd met the previous night. We exchanged the usual items of personal information and then read our papers and smoked our pipes. Naturally one of us would speak from time to time. It was a remark of his that made me prick my ears.

"Hello," he said, and looked up from his *Times*. "I see Lord Levenham's been identifying himself with the Oxford Movement." He smiled. "They don't call it that now—or did you know?"

I let my own paper drop to the floor. All that followed, by the way, may seem tedious, but let me assure you it had an importance.

"I know precious little but I'm most interested. I hope I'm not dropping a brick, but it's as a sceptic, not a believer."

"You've dropped no brick," he told me. "I had to fight them for years."

It was in a Far East country from which he'd come home after the withdrawal of the British. I was simply bubbling with questions: not about the Far East but the general set-up and activities of the Movement at home. And he seemed only too delighted to talk.

"Moral Re-armament," he said, was what they called themselves now. It was an immense organisation with headquarters at Caux in Switzerland. But let me make something clear. I'm telling you what I heard. I don't vouch for its accuracy, but I'd summed up that parson and he wasn't talking for talking's sake. He felt quite deeply about the whole thing. There was often a touch of irony or even bitterness in the way he spoke of things. Here are a few remarks of his.

"If you were a person of importance, Mr. Travers—you may be for all I know—and you showed an interest in Moral Re-armament, you'd have all their batteries on you at once. You'd be good publicity for one thing, and they'd try to get you identified in the closest possible manner. They'd like you as a subscriber to the funds. They'd like it still more if you left them something in your will."

I was able to bring in Baldlow.

"I've a friend—or he was a friend," I said, "who was roped in through his local vicar. He fell for everything, hook, line and sinker. He was leaving them money in his will. But tell me something, wouldn't his bishop drop down hard with both feet on a vicar who had a meeting in his church hall?"

"Heavens, no! I could quote you instances from my own experience. I wouldn't be staggered if someone told me the bishop himself had been at the meeting."

"What's the procedure, exactly, as a meeting? I know about the open confession business."

"That's been largely dropped," he said. "They used to call it sharing: sharing spiritual experiences, that is. Now they concentrate on big business and big labour. A speaker might talk about honesty in business or the way to improve relations between employer and employed."

"The meeting I had in mind was opened with a hymn and a prayer and so on. I can assure you that's true. And there were definitely open confessions."

"Perfectly understandable," he told me. "Their structure isn't rigid. Anyone can get up and talk if he feels an impulse to do so. But they've dropped the framework of Christian ritual, and I don't think there'd be hymns. They might be called that, but it'd be something out of their own song-book, as they call it. All very hearty. Mid-twentieth-century Moody and Sankeyism.

"The speaker at the meeting is picked according to the type of audience and the whole thing's rehearsed to the last details—however unrehearsed it will seem—even to questions that will be put to the speaker. That's especially so if it's a meeting designed to get converts."

"And would you say that a convert would then be a fanatical supporter?"

He smiled.

"I don't think, perhaps, fanatical's the right word. Everything's too suave for that. But, to use your own expression, he'd be in it, hook, line and sinker."

"Most interesting," I said. "But just one thing more. What good can you say for them?"

"Quite a lot," he said. "Just as one could for the sixteenth-century Jesuits. They're doing capital work in the fight against Communism, for instance. I can't say more but I know it for a certainty." His smile was even more dry. "As a matter of fact I spent a week at Caux. You could get an invitation too if you were interested and they thought you worth while."

That was about all, but for me it made a marvellous clarification of Baldlow's relationships with those three punctual visitors, and of the mind of the man himself. It lent a significance to that pattern of events which I'd begun some days ago to discern. But it didn't help in another thing—the reverse of the picture and what had been the relationships and the inward feelings of the three towards Baldlow himself. I still hadn't found out why they had come at the double when he had written them to come to The Croft. Unless it was something perfectly simple like a change of will.

I'm thinking of important modifications in my will before I leave, and as it is something that vitally concerns yourself, I suggest most urgently that you should see me on Saturday next. . . .

Would that fit the bill, I asked myself. Even if it did, it wouldn't explain why each of the three had lost or destroyed the letter. A coincidence, perhaps, but I didn't think so, and neither did Grainger. Nor did it explain the extreme perturbation of Jane Howell, or that strange visit of Baldlow to Betty Tinley's flat.

I did precious little else that morning, for the truth was I didn't know where to go for information. I did take a walk, and as I went by the offices of French, Son and Lorde I had my handkerchief to my face just in case Lorde himself might happen to pop out. The building was certainly an old one—half-timbering concealed by plaster—but it was in as good repair as its neighbours, and by its door was the usual brass plate. Inside it might be a warren of passages leading into small cluttered-up rooms, but so were a score of offices of country solicitors whom I'd known in my time.

Hallows was in when I got back to the hotel. He'd had a poor morning. Mrs. Godfrey Lorde had just had her first baby—a girl. Godfrey was nine years older than his brother: a sister in between had died young. Both boys had been expensively educated. That latter had been obvious. Lorde's boys would have had to be given the cachet of public school and university.

"Well, Dunland's been a blank," I said over our lunch. "We've learned nothing that makes even a semblance of contact with the Howells or the Tinleys. So where do we go from here—other than back to town?"

We talked it over and talked it over and nothing emerged. We packed and I paid the bill. It was after two o'clock when we left Dunland and we shouldn't be at the office before dark. Not that that mattered particularly. Slow driving gave us the chance for more, and still unproductive talk. Talk and interchange of ideas are the life-blood of a job like ours, and one always hopes.

We'd travelled across country avoiding the main arteries, and when we got to Great Dunmow I rang the office to give Norris an idea of when to expect me. It took me a good quarter of an hour before I had him on the line.

"I'm glad I got you," were his first words, cutting in on my own. "Tried to get you at Dunland but you'd just left. There's the devil to pay here, or there may be."

I cut in. Norris, ex-chief Inspector and hard to rattle at any time, must be faced with something damnably serious.

"Well, what is it?"

"Nordon," he said. "He's absolutely bitched up that job at Littleton. He's lucky not to be in jail. He may be yet."

"What'd he do?"

"Exceeded those instructions of yours. I can't go into it further. My own opinion is we ought to get rid of him. You'll know when you get here."

XII

WHAT'S IN A NAME?

"TAKE a seat, Nordon," Norris said. "I've been over this short report of yours with Mr. Travers and he'd like to check it with you."

Nordon was trying to conceal an uneasiness and making none too good a hand of it.

"I'll read the report back to you," I said. "If there's anything you'd like to modify or explain, then interrupt me. That clear?"

"As soon as Mr. Travers had briefed me I went home and thought things out. Then I called on a French friend and had a talk with him—his father's actually a whole-sale jeweller in Paris—and then I got busy on some faked papers. I also made a faked wad of notes wrapped in a fiver. I had to wait till the bank opened next morning to get the fiver. By the time I'd rigged up clothes and every-thing it was too late to get a train before the 1.30 p.m. . . . .

"This faked wad of notes," I said. "What was it for?"

"Well, to show him I had the cash if he'd do the job."

"But there was no mention of that in either your oral or writ-ten instructions?"

His shrug of the shoulders was almost a cringe.

"But surely something has to be left to initiative?"

"Think it out," I said. "You were on what might be called a probing patrol. You had to try to ascertain by means of hints whether or not Grimble was a likely person to be mixed up with smuggling. But he wouldn't be paid money."

He stared.

"The point would be to see if Grimble could dispose of the watches once they were landed. If he said he could, then clearly that would be a lead to Tinley. That was virtually all we needed. But let's go on.

"I made contact with Grimble just before he was knocking off for the day. It was getting too dark to see and he'd been doing some painting on the Lady Clare. I didn't find him so uncommunicative as I'd been told. He spotted me for a Frenchman, and I said my name was Pierre Costan, and I let him have a peep at my papers, but not too close. He said he knew the French coast, and we talked about that, and then I said I was in the jewellery business in France and had spent a week on the south coast trying to find someone who wanted to

earn some easy money. He said what sort of money. I flourished the roll and said that sort of money. He asked what I meant by easy, and I put up a choice of schemes like those I'd outlined roughly to Mr. Travers, only they were now better thought out. Then I boiled it down to one scheme. The boat would be mine and all he'd have to do would be to collect whatever it was and get it ashore. He wanted me to be a bit more explicit and finally I said it would be a big consignment of high-class watches. He didn't seem startled in any way. All he said was that money never did anyone any harm but he'd have to think it over. He'd have his tea and if I'd see him at half-past six we could go into actual details. His cottage is one of those on the far side of the creek, and at high tide he simply rows across in his own boat.

"It was then nearly five o'clock so I went to the hotel and had tea."

"Wasn't that absolutely contrary to instructions?"

"Not really," he said. "My own mother wouldn't have known me. I actually *was* a Frenchman. I had to use my head. You were afraid I'd be recognised at the hotel. I knew I shouldn't be, and I wasn't."

"Also," Norris put in dryly, "you had a nice tea in the warm, which was better than hanging about in the cold."

"I resent that," he told Norris hotly.

"Let's get on," I said. "We can always argue when we know where we stand.

"At just about the agreed time I went along the path from the bridge to Grimble's cottage. He's a widower, so we were alone in the house and we were to do our talking in his living-room which opens directly to the outside. He saw to the curtains and locked the door but the key was left in the lock. He offered me a drink and I had a bottle of beer. Then we got down to business. I had to go over everything again, and what it amounted to for quite half an hour was a rehearsing of that scheme I'd put to

him in the boat-shed. I gave him the name of my boat and where she was lying and how long it'd take us to be standing off Littleton. I even gave him the name of the crew, and I said we'd done business up till a few weeks ago with a man near Folkestone, but unfortunately he'd died. He wanted to know the name but I wouldn't give it. As I said, business had to depend on loyalty.

"He said he still ought to think it over a bit more, and he got up as if to stretch his legs. Then suddenly he was making for the outside door and hollering, 'Right!' If I hadn't been trained to act quickly I'd have been in the soup. He was just about to pocket the door-key when I got him with a ju-jitsu hold and threw him, and straight at the nearer of two men who'd evidently been listening to everything from the kitchen. I turned the key and I was out of that room like a bat out of hell. I heard hollering after me in the dark but I got away to the shore side of the cottage and the path that runs towards the second creek. I heard a car start up; then I carefully made my way towards the bridge. I struck out across open country."

"That's all that matters," I said. "You walked for what you describe as hours and finally got to a main road and thumbed a ride from a lorry. You were dropped the far side of London Bridge. You made your way home and dropped off to sleep."

"It was too early to catch either you or Mr. Norris here. I was pretty tired and I overslept. I'd had some pretty tough going across open country. When I woke up I jotted down some notes for a report and then came here."

"That's understandable," I told him. "No one can blame you for that. These two men that came from the kitchen were Preventive Men?"

"What else could they be?" he said. "Grimble must have been kidding me along. Soon as I left him at the boat-shed he got into touch and everything was rigged up. I was played for a sucker."

"To put it bluntly, that doesn't seem an understatement. But why in heaven's name did you exceed all instructions?"

"I was had," he said. "It could happen to anyone. I thought I was getting along fine. I was out to save the firm's time."

"Instead of which you've put us within the law," I told him. "What they're trying to do is trace that Pierre Costan. Someone at the hotel might remember you and me having lunch there or people might talk at that pub. Someone might have remembered the number of your car that day or that you were about the same build. What's to happen if you're traced to this office?"

"Impossible," he said.

"Let's hope it is. But that doesn't alter the fact that on your first big sole assignment—not counting the Baldlow one—you've broken instructions and caused us a great deal of anxiety."

"I want to resign."

"Resign?"

"Yes," he said. "I don't think I'm cut out for this job after all, sir, and that's telling the truth."

"Sulks are no good, neither is injured innocence," I told him tartly. "If you honestly and sincerely want to resign that's your business. My suggestion is this. We may still have a use for you. You'd soon be having a week's holiday due to you. Take it now and think things over. Report here a week from now. And see that we can get into touch if anything serious should crop up over this Littleton fiasco. And you may be wanted at Seahurst if the inquest's reopened on Baldlow."

Nordon left. I let out an exasperated breath.

"I think you've handled it just the right way," Norris said consolingly.

"Perhaps," I said. "But I got him here and he's my responsibility. I'm sick of the sight of him after this evening. And yet he's a fellow you can't help liking. But what about that chap Grimble? Why'd he get into touch with the Customs' people? Because he was honest, or because he wanted to ingratiate himself with them?"

"Might have been either," Norris said. "The latter, perhaps, if he has a racket of his own. But we'll never know now."

"We certainly shan't," I said. "We'll be lucky to hear no more about it."

I got up to go. The three evening papers had come in just before Nordon, and I picked one up and ran an eye over the front page. My eyes opened when I saw something in the Stop Press.

"Seen this, Norris?"

It is understood that the man Michael O'Brien, wanted for questioning by the Seahurst police in connection with the Baldlow murder, reported himself this morning.

"What's the idea?" he said. "If he reported voluntarily he must know he isn't guilty. Think you ought to ring Grainger?"

I didn't think so. What I did think was that I might do worse than see him in the morning when he knew just where he stood. If the O'Brien reporting had left him high and dry, he might welcome me.

I went home and had a service meal. My wife was away for the night. She usually takes advantage of my absence to see friends, and I don't blame her, but after the meal I felt at a loose end and I had enough worries of my own without having people ringing me up on the telephone, so I went along to my club to have a look at the current periodicals and to get a change of atmosphere generally. I was thinking of leaving when Arthur Nordon came into the reading-room. I couldn't have avoided him if I'd wanted to. At that latish hour we had the place to ourselves.

"I tried to get you," he said, "but you weren't in, so I thought I'd try you here. That nephew of mine has been to see me. He tells me he's made a mess of a job you gave him. Naturally he wouldn't say what."

"Uh-huh?"

"He owns up it was his fault entirely and he wants to resign. He told me what you'd arranged about him to think it over. I advised him the same. Most annoying after I thought he'd really settled down."

"Annoying for everybody," I told him non-committally.

"It's this modern generation," he said. "They can't get the restlessness out of their bones. He was talking, for instance, about a friend of his who's just going out to Australia. Thinks he'd like to try that. You never know where you are with them. Tomorrow, perhaps, he'll be all for getting back on the job with you."

"If we still want him."

"Yes," he said ruefully. "There *is* that, of course. But he's bound to see me again and I'll talk to him. I know he's had his pride shaken a bit by falling down on that job. You'll have a drink?"

I said I was just going when he'd come in. We agreed it was getting late. We walked together to the cloakroom and then to the street, and his taxi went one way and I walked the other. It had been a bad ending to what had been intended as a quiet hour or two, and the chance of getting a respite from the case had gone, and the only thing to do was to keep my thoughts fixed on O'Brien and what I might learn at Seahurst in the morning.

I left early and was in Seahurst soon after eleven. Grainger was in his room, but engaged. It was a goodish time before he was free.

"Thought I'd drop in on you," I said, "as I was going through. Glad you got O'Brien. He's confessed or anything?"

"Not to murder," he said. "He's a deserter from the army. We got on to him through the women."

A great light was suddenly shining.

"So that's why Mrs. Carver was scared at everyone being questioned by the police!"

"That's why. We managed to get a line on her. Her brother happened to die in that house where she lives now. She was living with her daughter at Lewisham. O'Brien—his real name's McShane—was on the run for a time. He knew his wife's house would be watched, and then everything happened to dove-tail in. He'd got some new ration books, and this brother died and Mrs. Carver got the house. So they came here with Mrs. Carver as her daughter and son-in-law, now the O'Briens. He'd been a garage hand originally so he got himself a job here."

"Where's he now?"

"The army authorities collected him early this morning. Mind you, he's still not in the clear. What if Baldlow had found out somehow and had had to be silenced?"

"At any rate you'll know where he is," I told him. "And what about the two women? They'll be for it too?"

"Yes, for harbouring O'Brien and other things. The trouble is I don't feel too happy about everything. Behind the scenes we've put in any God's amount of work. Cautious enquiries about those three callers; going through all Baldlow's papers, practically with a microscope."

"Those initials on the cheque stubs. Did you identify them?"

He opened a drawer and brought out a file and found a note. "All, except two—L.P. and W.F. And there's a funny thing about that. The corresponding cheque was for *cash*. Get me?"

"You mean he drew out money on cheques made out to cash and then paid the money, instead of giving a cheque to two people whose initials he put on the stubs."

"That's it. L.P. had seventy-eight pounds and W.F. had eighty-six. Secretive and suspicious. But what can we do about it? There wasn't anything among his papers to help an identification. Oh, and another thing. This was found. You needn't worry about handling it."

It was half a sheet of plain notepaper. On it was written a name—Lucilla Oliver.

"Identify her?"

"No," he said. "There isn't one in the town. I took a chance and questioned those three callers and Mrs. Carver, but none of them ever heard of her or Baldlow mention her."

I said the chances were that she had nothing whatever to do with the case.

"Any idea of your next move?"

"We'll have to throw our hand in," he said. "We just haven't the men or facilities for casting a net any further. I'm telling my Watch Committee about it in half an hour or so as a matter of courtesy. I'll be getting the Yard to send us someone down."

I said it was a pity, and it was. A man likes to handle his own crime and there's always a faint self-accusation and even the fear that something has been missed that should have been spotted.

"Just a final idea," I said. "Did you by any chance go along to that Oxford Movement—Moral Re-armament—meeting? The one that Baldlow had had specially arranged?"

"Believe it or not but we did," he said. "We thought for one thing someone who knew him in that connection might have been able to identify those two sets of initials. Might have been an anonymous subscription to the funds."

"Nothing particular happened there?"

"Not that I noticed. References to Baldlow, of course, and they'd a very good speaker who talked about cartels and monopolies and how they affect the working man. All very informal. No good to me, though."

That was all. I left a despondent Grainger and took a walk along the front in the company of an almost as despondent Travers. Then I had an early lunch and it was just after I'd paid the bill that I had an idea. I wondered why it hadn't occurred to Grainger.

I got Norris. I told him about that name.

"Go through all the telephone directories," I said, "and try to find a Lucilla Oliver. It may be Mrs. L. Oliver, or even Miss, but I've a hunch it'll be the full name. As a short cut begin with London, then Sussex and then Suffolk."

That short cut was a hope that Lucilla Oliver had been in some way connected after all with one of those three callers. The fact that each had denied knowledge of her was no matter, for any one of them might have something vital to conceal. That the whole thing was a shot in the dark I kept out of my mind as I drove back to town.

Nothing had happened when I got there except that the London directories had been gone through and Sussex was practically finished. Notes had been taken of L. Olivers. "This just came for you," Norris said.

It was a letter marked Personal—from Arthur Nordon.

... I saw Pat first thing this morning and I have an idea he'll be coming back to you if you still want him. He knows very well I can't finance any schemes for the Colonies. I'm generous enough as it is, and I have a son, as you know, and an unmarried daughter. I know he'd do anything to show he isn't such a fool as he made himself out to be. He has brains, you know. . . .

That letter wasn't so personal that I couldn't pass it to Norris.

"I don't like it," he said as he passed the letter back. "Nordon's just the sort of man who'd be badly hurt in his pride at having slipped up as he did. You don't think he'll go on doing things on his own?"

"He can't," I said. "He knows nothing: who we're working for or why. All he's been told is that Tinley may be involved in some way. And he can't do anything about that. He daren't show himself within miles of Littleton."

There was a knock at the door and Bertha came in. Usually she buzzes through first to see if it's necessary to come to the office.

"Think we've got it!" she was telling us excitedly. "A Mrs. Lucilla Oliver and another Mrs. Laura Oliver, so there shouldn't be any confusion."

"Yes, but where?"

"The second Suffolk directory we tried," she said. "That place Mr. Travers was at—Dunland!"

Norris had wondered if I might ring Dunland but to me it seemed that I had to go back there myself. I *had* to see the woman. There had to be a personal contact. It was true she might have a perfectly feasible explanation for her name's being found among Baldlow's papers—an explanation which would save a tiresome journey—but that wasn't all. There was another mystery. Grainger had enquired of Lorde if he knew of a Lucilla Oliver and Lorde had disclaimed all knowledge of one. Yet Dunland was the sort of place in which an inhabitant of Lorde's long residence must have known at least of the existence of a woman whose name appeared in the telephone directory of his town and district. Even if he didn't know her or even of her, he could easily have made simple enquiries, or consulted the directory himself. But he had said flatly that he didn't know her and he had not rung Grainger later to correct the mistake: a mistake which could easily have been discovered by a mere question to his wife—the woman whose finger was in every Dunland pie.

So five o'clock found me with Hallows in his car again and making for Dunland on a dark, overcast night. Rooms had been booked again, and when at last we got there I at once rang the Lucilla Oliver number. A vivacious voice was at the other end of the line.

"Lucilla Oliver."

"This is a Mr. Travers, Mrs. Oliver." She didn't correct it to Miss nor did she give me time to go on.

"Travers?" she said. "Do I know you?"

"You don't," I said, "but I hope I'm a very respectable person—"

"I'm sure you are."

"And I was a friend of the late Mr. Baldlow."

There was a moment or two of silence. Somehow I knew myself at some curious parting of the ways.

"Henry Baldlow!" There was both surprise and tragedy. "What a terrible thing! Whoever would want to harm such a charming man."

"It *was* terrible," I said. "I wonder if I might come and have a word or two with you about him? Only a few minutes. I have to get back to town tonight."

"But do!" she said. "You can come now? I'll have coffee kept back for us."

I told Hallows to have dinner and ordered something for myself an hour later, then I set off on foot for her home, which was in a turning off the Bury Road. A street lamp showed up a smallish, but quite nice detached house and there was a light outside the door. A rather thin woman of about sixty-five opened at my knock. I introduced myself and I was almost gushingly told to come in. We went into a beautifully warm drawing-room, so cluttered up with this and that that I guessed she'd been a widow for some years.

Lucilla Oliver was the fluttery sort, as her voice had practically warned me: all little gestures and movements of the head, and a tinkly kind of voice that wasn't altogether displeasing. Little bangles jingled on her arms when she poured the coffee. It had been easy to sheer away from Baldlow for she had brought the coffee in at once.

"You are a widow, Mrs. Oliver?"

"My poor husband was killed in a plane crash just before the war," she said. "But about poor Mr. Baldlow. How on earth did you know that we knew each other?"

I told her that her name had been found on a piece of paper in his desk. She took the address for granted.

"Such a charming little man," she said. "I happened to meet him one day with his step-brother—Mr. Lorde, you know—when I was in the town. He happened to mention he'd been in the jewellery business and I asked him to see some things of mine, and he did."

"When was that exactly?"

"About two years ago."

"Yes," I said. "He was staying here then. I happen to know that."

"He was a very clever man," she went on. "He seemed to know everything. I'm such a fool at business." A little laugh accompanied the confession. "I think some women are, don't you?"

"You mustn't libel yourself," I told her archly.

"But I am," she said. "I'm very fortunate, really, having Mr. Lorde to handle everything for me. But I was just a bit worried. It was about these Amalgamated Foundries."

"You mean some shares in Amalgamated Foundries?"

"Yes," she said. "A friend of mine had advised me to sell. They'd gone up, you know, but Mr. Lorde strongly advised against it. He advised me, if I wanted money, to sell something else. I forget the name now but it was something to which my husband had been very attached."

"I'm beginning to see it," I said. "Henry Baldlow called on you and saw your jewellery."

"Some old silver principally. And he seemed to know so much that I asked his opinion confidentially—about those Amalgamated Foundries, I mean. You won't mention a word of this to a soul?"

"Most certainly not."

She gave that thin trickle of a laugh.

"You see, I wouldn't want Mr. Lorde to think I'd ever gone behind his back. But it all turned out right in the end. The shares actually went higher and they were sold. I think it was about three months later, and I didn't really want the money so it was reinvested."

"How many shares did you hold?"

"Two thousand. I think they made almost two pounds ten shillings each."

"I hope you had a nice profit."

"I'm sure I did. I wrote a confidential letter of thanks to dear Mr. Baldlow."

"You think it was through him they were sold?"

"Well, yes. He said he'd speak to Mr. Lorde. I didn't see him again before he left but he rang me up and told me confidentially he thought everything would be all right."

"And you didn't worry Mr. Lorde again?"

"Well, no. You see both he and Mr. Baldlow must have been of the same opinion, and a woman like me just wouldn't dare to contradict—now would she?"

"You definitely took the right course," I assured her. "Mr. Lorde, by the way, was upset about his step-brother's death?"

She was suddenly going all mysterious. Her voice was lowered and the tone was most confidential.

"Between ourselves I don't think he wanted the connection to be known. He asked me not to mention it. I think he was right. After all, a step-brother is only a step-brother, and it isn't nice to be mixed up in a murder, if you know what I mean."

"Quite right," I said. "It would be what they call the wrong kind of publicity, and especially for what I suppose are an old-established firm."

"A very old firm."

I got to my feet.

"Well, you've been most helpful, Mrs. Oliver, and now I have to be getting back to town. I wish I'd had time to call on Mr. Lorde, but it just isn't possible. I broke my journey here especially to see you."

Then I cocked my head on one side and appeared to be thinking of something.

"I wonder if you'd do something for me?"

"But of course—if I can."

"Just tell Mr. Lorde that a Mr. Travers called on you—you needn't tell him why—and that if he's ever in town I'd like to see him. It might be as well to give me a little warning so that I'm certain to be at home. Here are a couple of cards, one for yourself. Perhaps you'll give him the other. Don't forget. If he'd like to see me at any time, just a few hours warning and I'll be sure to be at home."

I thanked her most warmly at the door and said what a pleasure it had been: tinctured, perhaps, with a little sadness. She said I really must come again if ever I was that way. There were so many things she had meant to ask me. I gave a last smile and a quick wave of the hand from the gate before she could think of them.

I wasn't too late for a hot meal at the hotel, and then I joined Hallows in the lounge. I peeped in first to see if my parson friend was there, but he wasn't. We had the room to ourselves.

"What's going to happen now?" he said, when I'd told him about my hour at Holmhurst.

I said I wasn't a betting man. If I were I'd give long odds on Francis Lorde's giving me a call within the next twenty-four hours.

XIII
FIRST DAWN

THE next day was a quiet one. Norris told me when we got back to town that Chief-Inspector Jewle and Sergeant Matthews—both very old friends of mine—had gone to Seahurst to assist in the Baldlow case. They already knew that the agency was indirectly concerned and, if Grainger couldn't supply them with everything they thought they might need, then Nordon might have to be re-interviewed.

I went home for a restful afternoon, though it wasn't quite that. My very last words to Mrs. Oliver had been that if Lorde wanted to be certain of catching me in, he was to ring at any time after six o'clock, and all the while that afternoon I was wondering if and when he'd ring me. As it turned out, he was absolutely on the dot. The telephone went at five minutes past. I recognised his precise voice at once. "Mr. Travers?"

"Speaking."

"This is Francis Lorde, Mr. Travers. We met, you remember, at Seahurst."

"Yes, I remember you very well, Mr. Lorde."

"Well, a Mrs. Oliver has told me you called on her yesterday in connection with Henry Baldlow's death and you expressed a wish to see me. I wondered if you might talk about whatever it is over the telephone."

"Afraid not," I said. "It's exceedingly confidential."

"Oh," he said and had a moment or two's thought. "You'd like to call on me here?"

"Again I'm afraid not," I said. "I think you should see me here. Believe me it's to your best interests. I'm speaking, by the way, strictly confidentially. I hope to keep it that way."

There was another short silence.

"This seems very mysterious. Can't you give me even a hint?"

"I'd have preferred not," I said. "But since you seem to think it necessary, we might have to discuss Amalgamated Foundries."

"I see." He said it heavily and I heard him let out a breath. "When will it suit you to see me?"

"First thing tomorrow morning. I shall be here till midday. I take it there's a train that will get you in well before that."

"Very well," he said, and now it was somewhat curtly. "I'll see you. I'll take a taxi from Liverpool Street."

Still striving desperately, I thought, to put up a front. But it eased my mind, even if I didn't ring Hallows to tell him the odds had been landed. I did see him in the morning when I made a quick call at the office, but ten o'clock found me at home. Lorde arrived earlier than I'd hoped. We went into my den which was snug enough for so frosty a morning, and Bernice brought us in some coffee. I could see that Lorde was rather uneasy at the friendliness of his reception. I knew, too, from the dark beneath his eyes, that he'd had a far from restful night.

"You run a private enquiry agency, don't you?" was the first thing he said when we were alone.

I told him about it. I said that clients of ours could depend, as in the case of all reputable agencies, on our absolute secrecy.

"But I'm not a client," he said, "even if I had anything to conceal."

"Permit me to be paradoxical," I told him. "I'm going to confer with you as if you *were* a prospective client, though I know you'll never be one. In other words, if you now tell me perfectly frankly whether or not it was you who killed Henry Baldlow, I shan't inform the police. It's something that begins and ends with you and me."

"But that's ridiculous. I don't mean . . ." He couldn't find the words and his hand waved impatiently. "I'd no reason to kill him."

"But you had."

He looked at me, mouth gaping slightly.

"You had a very good reason. But let me go on. I anticipated a certain difficulty in getting information from you, so do let me repeat that what's said in this room will go no further. You say you didn't kill him."

"I'd swear that if this was my death-bed."

"Then through you I must get information which might tell me who did kill him. For instance, would you mind telling me exactly what was in that letter you received from him? The letter that brought you to his house at a precise time that Saturday afternoon?"

"I've already told the police. I believe you were there."

"No more coffee?"

"Thank you, no more," he said. "Please thank your wife if I don't happen to see her."

"Then that's that," I said, and got to my feet. "Sorry you've had such a journey for so little. Let me help you on with that coat."

There was more than an uneasiness. He moistened his lips and he wasn't looking up at me.

"You mean you're perfectly satisfied?"

"That you refuse to talk—yes. What I'm now going to do, and inside five minutes, is talk to the police. Scotland Yard have been asked to help, by the way, and it's they who'll be questioning you from now on. You refuse to talk to me confidentially, so you'll have to talk to them openly, and after what it'll now be my duty to tell them."

"Tell them. What could you tell them?"

"You're putting up a good fight but it's hopeless," I told him. "I shall tell them about those Amalgamated Foundries shares and why they weren't sold when Mrs. Oliver wanted them sold. It's child-play to check the actual date of selling. There might be properties of other clients: if so, they'll soon find out."

It's shaming to see a man break down. As Lorde sat there, bowed head in his hands, the shame was for that unspoken claim of mine to a moral superiority that would now make him speak.

"Take your time," I told him. "I'm not blaming you. God knows I've no reason to act like God. What you did I might easily have done myself."

In a minute or two he began to talk, and it was a tale of accumulating financial worries. Five hundred a year for the two boys at public school in addition to their ordinary expense: a special operation to the leg of the younger boy which cost a lot of money but turned out to be worth it: decreasing income and a wife—he rather slurred over that—who'd got into the way of spending money lavishly. There was the need to keep up a front in view of the older boy's wedding, and of course, the standing of the firm. Nevertheless he'd tried to retrench—selling his house and taking a smaller one, for instance—but by then it was too late. Those Amalgamated Foundries were the only shares he'd sold.

Then had come the disaster of Henry Baldlow's visit. He couldn't ask for a loan from him and for the simple reason that that front had already been put up. There followed that unlucky meeting with Mrs. Oliver. Baldlow asked him about the shares and Lorde stalled by claiming inside information that the shares would rise much higher. Baldlow then apparently forgot the matter. But on his son's marriage, Lorde was able to borrow money from that son and so squared himself for the ostensible buying of shares with the proceeds of the Amalgamated Foundries. And now he had only the one son to support for a year or two, he was in a position to keep above water and after that to repay the loan from his elder boy.

"May I go on from there?" I said. "Henry Baldlow got religion a year or so ago. He was full of ideas about honesty in business and he spoke to me about regarding his money as a sacred trust. The bug had bitten him and he was going to leave some of that money to his local church and some to the Moral Re-armament Movement. It was the balance that was worrying him. Were his niece and nephew and yourself fit and proper people to have that balance? With regard to yourself he recalled that talk with Mrs. Oliver. He probably made confidential enquiries about the date of the sale by you of those shares, but whatever he did, he knew that you'd been fraudulently disposing of the property of a client, and that you'd had to resort to forgery to do so. If I'm right, then you can prove it. What was in that letter you received from him?"

"Roughly what you've guessed," he said. "He wanted to see me at his house at four-thirty precisely. To discuss a new will and the sale of certain Amalgamated Foundries shares. That was all but it was enough. I went through hell for a day or two."

"But you didn't kill him?"

"No," he said. "I swear to you I didn't go near the house till the time he stated."

"And that letter. You destroyed it?"

"Not till after I got home," he said. "It was too dangerous in view of what had happened."

"Well, everything's plain," I said. "What I'm going to add isn't a form of blackmail: it's for your own protection, and it's to be kept confidential. Would you care to draw up a contract whereby I look after your interests in the matter of the Baldlow murder in return for a sum not stated? The sum might be, say, half-a-crown."

We drew it up: a baldish statement on half a sheet of note-paper. A copy was made and we each signed.

"If I hadn't believed you, you wouldn't be pocketing that contract," I told him. "I hope that will ease your mind. But about the future. It's almost a certainty that you'll be re-questioned by the Yard. My advice is that you stick to your original story. You received an urgent letter which needed no answer if you were accepting the invitation. The letter was not important enough to be kept. Your idea was that the visit might have something to do with the making of a new will in view of his shortly leaving England. All of which is true. You didn't kill him and you've no idea who did. You'll find that the Yard won't bother you further."

He nodded: it was still hard to find words.

"Just one other thing. Let's assume that Jane Howell and Charles Tinley were called to Seahurst that Saturday because he'd also been prying into their affairs and had found something irregular. Have you the remotest idea what that something might be?"

He hadn't, so that was virtually all. When we were parting he gripped my hand so tightly that I felt it for long after he'd gone. But there'd been just a word or two before that.

"You didn't like him, did you?" I said.

"No," he said bluntly. "I always mistrusted him, even as a boy."

"I guessed as much. But remember I'm now in your employ. No one knows it but you and me. Don't give even a hint to the police. Let me know how you get on if the Yard questions you and for my part I'll keep you informed of any developments that might clear this whole thing up."

He was too near to me, even after he'd gone, for there to be self-congratulation. But that didn't alter the fact that a pattern, hitherto vague, was now clear. Baldlow had been in possession—or he'd thought he had—of information which those three people should be asked to explain, or with which they ought to be confronted. Each had been sent a letter and in that letter was some phrase or hint which showed the recipient what unsuspected secrets he possessed. In Lorde's case it had been the mention of Amalgamated Foundries.

Those timings were also explained. Baldlow had proposed to himself that three-quarters of an hour would be ample time needed for each caller. The caller would deny or confess: he or she would then be dismissed before the arrival of the next caller, after, perhaps, some pious homily on the part of Baldlow or even some kneeling in prayer. A sickening thought, but there it was.

Nordon too was explained. He would be necessary only after the events of that Saturday afternoon: from six o'clock onwards, which would be when Mrs. Carver left. In the matter of Lorde alone, one could see a justification of Baldlow's fears. Baldlow, and his possession of certain knowledge, alone stood between Lorde and exposure that would be utterly ruinous to himself and his family.

There then was the pattern: all that was necessary was to fill in the details by finding out just what had been the contents of those other two letters. In the case of Tinley, had Baldlow suspected smuggling? If so, that would mean an enquiry into Tinley's financial position. As for Jane Howell, all I knew was that that letter had caused her extreme perturbation, and that as I was employed—unknown to her—to protect her interests, she couldn't be driven into a corner whatever I might chance to discover, in the way that Lorde had been driven into a corner.

To sum it all up, there seemed no further avenue to explore, as the politicians have it, except that matter of Charles Tinley's financial position—that, and the highly nebulous connection of Pinky Morris with Baldlow's death. For Pinky had an alibi, and couldn't be personally involved. And people, at least in Britain, don't employ murder agents. Which left only Betty Tinley, and I couldn't envisage her in any Machiavellian scheme to arrange the killing of Baldlow so that her husband might inherit enough money to pay her the ten thousand pounds for a divorce.

So I did the one thing I could do—rang Hallows and told him to get to work on the financial position of C.T. Then I rang Betty Tinley.

"Why, hallo!" she said enthusiastically. "Where've you been? I rang and rang but couldn't get an answer."

"I've been away for some days," I said. "You likely to be in this afternoon—say at about three?"

She said she'd be there and I was to come straight up. Somehow I didn't feel so happy when I'd hung up. It was like ringing the dentist in a sudden access of courage and then hoping he wouldn't be able to see you, and in any case I'd rather have had an hour's drilling than an afternoon with a man-hungry woman like Betty Tinley. To make it worse, I hadn't been able to work out an approach. I couldn't very well ask her if her husband had done any smuggling—at least point-blank. The only question I could think of was why Tinley didn't pay the ten thousand, and even that might make it seem that she was someone he ought to be glad to be rid of, and at so stiff a price.

Even when I was ringing the bell of her flat I still had no idea what my approach would be. That was why, after the hat and coat business and the offer of a drink, I began to cast the net out generally. The atmosphere seemed propitious. It was daylight and a cold but sunny afternoon, and as yet she hadn't even resumed where we had left off, and embraced me. And if she'd had a drink, it wasn't more than one, or maybe two. And she'd made the very best of herself: the bulges not so evident and the hair-do and get-up something really smart.

"You're looking specially attractive this afternoon," I told her from a reasonably safe chair on my side of the electric fire. "Am I to flatter myself you had me in mind?"

She laughed, or was it leered?

"You men never kid yourselves, do you? You'll tell me I've got on a nice dress and all the time you know the kind of dress you'd like me in."

"Not a bit of it. There are times and times."

"Yes," she said, "and mostly times. You sure about a drink? It'll take the starchiness out of you."

"Too early for me," I said. "A cup of tea might be in order. Any more news about your ten thousand?"

"That," she said. "I've made enquiries. Might be months, so they tell me, before he gets that old goat's money."

"Why do you call him a goat? He didn't make a pass at you?"

She laughed.

"He looked like a goat. He even bleated like a goat."

"Maybe you're right," I said. "But that day he came here and started questioning you about your husband. What'd he want to know?"

"Well, he was asking about money. That's why I sort of led him on. I thought he might put me down for something good in his will. My God, if I'd known!"

"Well, you couldn't plead poverty in a place like this," I told her amusedly.

"That's all you know," she said. "I could put on an act, couldn't I? About soon being turned out into the cold, cold snow?"

"Wish I'd been here. It must have been good."

"It *was* good. A bit awkward, though, telling him about *Happy Holidays*."

She saw my puzzled look.

"You wouldn't know about that," she said. "It was when I was getting a bit restless and Charles thought he'd still like to keep me, so he put up the money for *Happy Holidays*. Supposed to be specially for me, though Margot Lane had the big part. I was all right, though. If we'd got as far as the West End I'd have had my big break."

"You didn't?"

"Even Brighton knew it for a flop." She was making for the drinks cabinet. "That was the end of getting me back into the show business. Charles lost a packet."

"What's a packet?"

"Ten or twelve thousand. You can't put on a musical for peanuts. Sure you won't have a drink?"

She brought her own towards my chair, perched on the arm and her hand went round to my shoulder. The bulge beneath her arms made a cushion for my head.

"Happy days. You're silly not to have a drink."

"Never start till sundown," I said. "And I suppose that was the end of you and Charles."

"As good as. I was getting fed up. Him and his snooty sister and his friends. We stayed with his sister for a week soon after she was married. Tom wasn't so bad: that's her husband— but *her*! You could just see what she was thinking. Just telling me in her own way she knew I was dirt."

She finished the drink, leaned sideways to put the glass on the carpet and pulled me that way with it. Now she had a free hand. It began fondling my hair.

"Even then I was decent to her," she was going on. "When she was having her baby I thought I'd see her, so I took the trouble to go all that way. Thought I'd show her I wasn't what she thought I was. And when I got there, what d'you think? She wasn't there. I'd taken it for granted she'd be having the baby in the house, or locally, but where do you think her ladyship was? Liverdale wasn't good enough for her. She had to go to some posh place in Buckinghamshire. Recommended by one of her posh friends, or old family doctor or something. God, was I mad!"

"You should have rung up beforehand."

"Well, who'd have thought? Besides, I wanted to surprise her."

"Know the name of that maternity hospital? A friend of mine was asking about one only today."

"Yes," she said. "I remembered it because I had a great friend once called Pickfield. Pickfield Hall, that was the name. It wasn't called a maternity home or anything. Just Pickfield Hall. And the baby had been born. Tom had been there and he told me. She was almost due to come home. And something else that made me blue, blazing mad. The old goat had been there, enquiring after his dear niece. If he'd been told about it, why not me? That about finished it. I had to be decent with Tom—he's really nice, and an absolute gentleman—but to hell with the Howells: that's what I told myself soon as I got in the train. And to hell with Charles."

"But not before you get the ten thousand."

"I'm not worrying," she told me. "I know more than you think. He's got a girl friend and he'll only get her after walking up the aisle, same as he had to get me."

Her cheek snuggled down against the top of my head.

"What about taking me out to dinner and doing a show? And coming back here for a drink?"

"Sounds pretty good to me," I said.

There was a kiss: one of those that you see sometimes on the screen. I thought my lungs would burst before she'd finished with me.

"How was that?"

"Almost a lovely death."

"You're funny," she told me. "Nice though. What time will you come for me? Or will I meet you somewhere?"

I told her I'd fix things and let her know.

I pulled up at the nearest telephone and rang the office. Norris was in.

"Anyone available to do a quick job?"

"Only Hallows," he said. "He wants to see you before he begins that job on Tinley."

"I'll see him later," I said. "Get him at the double down to Flat 21, Anstead Gardens, Kensington. The occupant is probably expecting a caller. I'd like him to find out who it is. He may be too late to see him enter but he might see him leave."

I drove straight back to Broad Street and I was hoping I'd been right. But I had to be right. Betty Tinley wouldn't have let me leave that flat so soon and so unscathed unless she had wanted temporarily to get rid of me. As for what I'd learned that afternoon, it had filled my head with all sorts of ideas and I couldn't quite see how to sort them out. It was like tidying up a mess. You look at it and wonder where to begin. Then you make a start, and, before you hardly know it, the mess is beginning to become something more like order. So that's what I did. I didn't like doing it, but I rang Tom Howell and took a chance.

An unknown voice—a woman's—answered me.

"May I speak to Mr. Howell?"

"What name, please?"

"Just tell him it's the agent—about that horse."

I held the line as told. A minute and I heard the sound of footsteps.

"Howell speaking."

"You guessed who this is?"

"I think so," he said, "but it's all right. My wife's having tea with some friends."

"Thought I'd let you know that things are beginning to get into shape. Can't say more at the moment but I really have hopes."

"That gardener chap?"

"Not necessarily. All I wanted to do, in lieu of a report, was to ease your mind. How's your wife, by the way?"

"In quite good fettle. Cheering up every day."

"Good," I said. "She having the baby at home?"

"This time—yes," he said, and I heard a little chuckle. "But, my dear fellow, that won't be for months yet."

"Of course," I said. "You must forgive me. I just don't happen to be a father."

"You may be yet," he said. "That money of mine running out?"

"Nothing like it, but thanks for asking. And sorry to have dragged you away from your tea."

"You must be a mind-reader," he told me. "Glad you did. Very good of you, and I appreciate it."

So much for that, but instead of helping it had made things more confused. I tried to look at things from Jane Howell's own angle. She'd naturally be nervous about that first baby, and if a friend strongly recommended a particular place for the birth she'd jump at it. Money was no object with the Howells, and especially at a time like that.

And then I thought of something else. *Phyllis Cavendall.* Could she have mentioned that maternity home? But she couldn't have. She hadn't seen Jane Howell for quite a time before even her marriage. Jane had dropped completely out of her life even before the end of the war. Why she had done so was a mystery both to Phyllis and her mother, Mrs. Habbord. Neither had even the faintest idea that Jane Tinley had married.

That made me think of something else. If there had been notices in *The Times* and or *The Daily Telegraph*, both must have seen it. Where then had the marriage taken place? That shouldn't be too difficult to find out, even if I'd have to wait till morning.

I asked Norris to ring me at the flat as soon as Hallows had anything to report. Bernice had just had tea when I got home but she made some for me. I thought I'd take her into my confidence—and mentioning no names. A woman's point of view might be just what was needed.

But first I got her to ring Betty Tinley, and in the role of my secretary. What she had to say was that I'd just arrived and found a very urgent message and had to leave at once for Edinburgh. I'd been very upset about breaking that evening's appointment but hoped to see her as soon as I got back.

I went out of the room while she rang. When she had hung up I came back.

"How'd she sound?"

"Not too pleased. In fact, distinctly annoyed. And, I think, a bit incredulous."

"Well, that's the end of her," I said. "I doubt if I'll need to see her again. If she should ring, then I'm still in Edinburgh."

Bernice looked at me with rather a puzzled air.

"How do you reconcile this telling of perfectly dreadful lies with your ordinary conduct?"

It was a nice point that took some explaining. I hadn't finished it satisfactorily when the telephone went. It was Hallows.

"I spotted that caller, Mr. Travers. You'd never guess who. It was Rawley, manager of that Bond Street shop."

XIV
ODDS AND ENDS

THAT rather amusing little discussion of the morals of a private detective had made me forget that problem I'd intended to put up to Bernice.

"That was Hallows," I said. "He'll be along in a few minutes, but there's something in connection with this case we're handling that I'd like to put up to you."

I told her as much as was necessary. She seemed to be taking it in her stride.

"I don't see any mystery," she said. "Naturally she'd be a bit nervous, and if there was a doctor at that maternity home whom she knew she'd consult him from time to time after arranging to have the baby there. As for having the second baby at home or near home, that's only reasonable. This time she won't be nervous, especially if there was no trouble over the first baby—the boy."

"What struck me," I said, "was being relatively so far away from her husband. Wouldn't she have liked him to be hanging around?"

"Probably the last thing she'd want," she told me with a little sniff. "But it's no real distance. A fast car could do the journey in a couple of hours."

"I know," I said. "Everything can be reasonably explained. But that's the trouble. I want you to believe me when I assure you that something simply *must* lie behind all this obvious or reasonable stuff. So will you do this for me, darling. Tell yourself that everything isn't what it seems. Try to work out any other reasons for having that baby at that Pickfield Hall place. If you think of anything, no matter how silly it seems, let me know."

That was how it was left. Hallows came in shortly afterwards and we adjourned to the den. I was bursting to hear about Rawley.

"Nothing to it," Hallows said. "I walked bold as brass up to the flat and hung around at the corridor angle. I saw one or two people but nobody challenged me and I hadn't been there more than five minutes before Rawley came along. He had his own key. He was there when I left. No point in following him since we know who he was."

"But why Rawley? What is he? Just an old friend? A go-between for husband and wife? Just a man when she feels that way inclined?"

I told him about my half-hour with her.

"I'd class him as an old friend," he said. "After all, she was putting in an evening with you later on, and having it end at the flat. Or so she thought."

We talked round it and nothing emerged. I had to smile rather grimly when Hallows had gone, at how—for all my clinging to marital chastity—I'd really been peeved at the idea that it was not for me she'd rigged herself up so admirably, but for Rawley.

"About the morning," I said. "Pay the usual fee and look up the marriage between Jane Tinley and Thomas Howell. About '47 or '48. Then consult the announcement columns of *The Times* for the appropriate dates and see if the wedding was actually announced. I think I'll run up to that Pickfield Hall place and cast an eye over it. We'll probably be able to compare notes at the office in the early afternoon."

Norris told me in the morning that nothing had so far happened about Nordon and that Littleton fiasco, and he thought we might start breathing normally. Just before ten o'clock I set off for Pickfield Hall. It was no great distance: an hour's trip, perhaps, according to the traffic.

Odds and ends—that was to be the story of the next thirty hours. That's how things go in our kind of job: digging down and digging around and never knowing till much later, or never even knowing at all, if the digging's been worth while. What I could never have foreseen was that when those thirty hours were over, the spade was to strike something good. Or, to change the metaphor, the smell of smoke and the signs of smouldering were suddenly to be a conflagration.

Pickfield Hall was just beyond Gerrard's Cross and to the north: a former spacious country house set in beechy woodlands. It had a long drive, and its rhododendrons must have been a glory of colour in the spring. As my car neared the long front I could see a sun loggia and women sitting there, and a nurse in a pale-blue uniform. Three cars were parked just beyond.

Swing doors had been installed and I went through to a large reception hall, and after the cold of the morning it was beautifully warm. There was no one at what looked like the bureau so I pushed the bell. An elderly woman, in dark-grey uniform and with some medal ribbons up, came through the door to my left. She gave me a very pleasant good-morning.

I told my tale. As I would be that way a friend of mine who would be having a baby in some six months' time had asked me to make enquiries.

"She would have to book almost at once," she said. "We're constantly having to turn cases away."

I said that could be done. But would it be necessary for her to see the Hall's doctor regularly beforehand? Or would a report from her own doctor be sufficient.

"Of course," she said. "If she lives a considerable distance away it would be foolish to report here."

I heard about fees—they almost took my breath away—and the qualifications of the personnel: in fact I heard everything. It was she who asked how the prospective mother had thought of the Hall.

"We always like to know. It's particularly gratifying when recommendations come from former mothers."

"That's just how this was," I said. "The recommendation was from a Mrs. Jane Howell. She was here just over three years ago. She was living then at Liverdale in Sussex. She had a boy."

I'd put in the *was* living because a letter might otherwise have reached Jane Howell, thanking her for the recommendation.

"I remember," she said. "A very charming woman. She and her husband were delighted with everything here. Now would you like me to show you round?"

I recoiled.

"Lord, no," I said. "What's a man know about such things?"

She laughed.

"I'll let my friends know I've been most favourably impressed," I said, "and then the prospective mother will almost certainly come here to see things for herself. I won't forget what you've said about booking early."

That was about all. Some name had to be given so I gave that of Hallows. I left to the warmest of smiles and well before midday I was back in town. What I'd learned at Pickfield Hall I frankly didn't know, unless it was that there'd been no need whatever for Jane Howell to put herself immediately after pregnancy into the hands of the doctor there. Her own doctor could have done what was necessary until within the usual time from the birth, and so have saved quite a lot of tedious journeys across country.

One other point did strike me. Surely the local doctor—the one who had attended her and her husband—must have been somewhat annoyed that he hadn't been consulted about the pregnancy. Had she now gone back to the local doctor? Had she explained things to him by saying an old friend of her family had been one of the doctors at Pickfield Hall? I didn't know. What I did know was that if Tom Howell hadn't been my client, I'd have tried to find out.

I parked my car and went along to Tom Holberg's office. Tom is under the impression that something I did for him once was of far more importance than I've ever thought it. He always has time for me, even if I have to wait, as I did that morning. He was most apologetic when at last I went into his office.

"About time I ceased being a deadhead and started paying you," I told him.

"Ah, no," he said, and passed me the cigarette box. "That would never be right by me."

"Well, this time I shan't keep you long—I hope. Know anything about a show called *Happy Holidays* that had a trial run at Brighton—"

He raised hands of horror.

"Don't tell me. Two, three of my clients were in that show. One of them, the best, I lost on account of it. What do they think I am? A crystal-gazer? How do I know what Brighton will do? Or London? I make contracts and I see they're honoured, and that goes for both sides. Me, I'm not a prophet."

"You're too modest, Tom. But what I'd like to know is this—in the strictest confidence. Wasn't the money put up for it by a man named Tinley?"

"Yes," he said. "His wife had a nice little part. She was good—that girl. A pity she's run to seed. A mutual friend told me as much."

He took it for granted I'd know he was referring to Pinky Morris.

"I don't know the theatrical jargon, Tom—begging your pardon—but did Tinley meet all his commitments?"

"He was lucky," he said. "There'd have been more commitments if the show'd reached town and flopped then."

"Well, that's about all I want to know," I said. "Suppose you can't tell me anything you happened to gather about his financial position?"

He gave a dry smile.

"That didn't concern me, beyond what I've told you. All I know is that he was a poorer man when he'd paid the last bill."

"To the tune of what?"

I like those Semitic gestures of his: the hunching of the shoulders and the spreading of the palms.

"Can't say. Eight thousand. Ten. I can't say."

"That's the lot then," I said, and got to my feet. "What about having lunch with me?"

He said if I gave him a quarter of an hour he could make it, so we had lunch at my club and talked about things theatrical—including Pinky Morris—and then as soon as he'd drank a cup of coffee he had to get back. So had I. I made it nicely before two o'clock and Hallows was there.

He had a copy of the wedding certificate. The ceremony had been at the Holborn Register Office.

"The witnesses look to me like the usual stock ones they always manage to get hold of," he told me, "judging by the addresses. A very quiet affair, apparently."

"Almost a hush-hush affair," I said.

"Some people are like that," he said. "Also she hadn't any mother to pester her into a church wedding with all the trimmings, or a father to pay for it."

"But that didn't prevent her brother's being a witness. Or did it? After all, that might have meant inviting Betty Tinley, and Baldlow, now I come to think of it. Neither was exactly *persona grata*. But what about *The Times*. Any announcement?"

"Nothing," he said. "Think I should go out to Colinton and look up the *Telegraph* files?"

"Not worth it. I think we should take it as read. But about the next move."

I gave him a letter to a certain man in a stockbroker's office.

"Perhaps you won't need any confidential information," I said. "But if you do, this should do the trick. They'll have the ordinary information about Tinley's Company, number of directors and fees and so on. You might be able to get how the fees are apportioned."

He wanted to know how the shares themselves stood. I'd looked that up at the club. Like all Commercial and Industrials they'd taken quite a knock in the last three years. As a luxury business their knock had been harder than most. Three years ago the £1 shares had stood at thirty-two shillings, and a dividend had then been paid of twelve and a half per cent, together with a bonus of two and a half. Now the shares stood at seventeen and six. Dividend had been paid the previous May at ten per cent—though the position didn't warrant it—with no bonus.

Hallows went off and I went home. It was about four o'clock when he reported to me there. What he'd got didn't look so good for Tinley. There'd been a bit of a squeal at the Annual General

Meeting and the directors had anticipated it by reducing their fees. Tinley, as director responsible for the London area, was down from three thousands pounds to two thousand.

"It's not bad," I said, "and it's not good. He's really a managing director for this area. But let's try to assess his expenses."

As we worked it out, two thousand wouldn't go near to covering them. Everything depended on what his income was from investments.

"I don't like it," I said. "It'd mean trying to find out what he got from his people's estate and what he's done with it since. Every step of the way means digging. There's how he acquired the directorate and whether he's got shares in the Company. There's the cost of that boat of his and the money lost on that musical comedy. He may have a Company car or have had to buy a new one of his own. It might take days to find it all out and I don't see how we can justify the expense, even if it's the client's money."

"Then where do we turn?"

I didn't know. I told him to go home and do some thinking and I'd do the same. Maybe we'd have some ideas by the morning.

Just as Bernice came in—she'd been doing a matinée with a friend—the telephone went. It was Jewle, ringing from the Yard. Would I do him the favour of coming along and having a chat about the Baldlow Case. It was nicely put, so I went. I like Jewle in any case.

"You've seen our man Nordon?" was the first question I asked him.

"It mightn't be necessary," he said. "I've seen his statements and had Grainger's side of things. I just wondered if you could fill in any gaps."

"What kind of gaps?"

"Well—gaps."

We laughed.

"You must have done a lot of private thinking," he went on. "You're involved to the extent of having had a man there. I just wondered if there's anything you'd like to pass on."

"Being involved very slightly is one thing but conducting an independent enquiry at one's own expense is quite another."

"Keep that for the customers," he told me amusedly. "You're not short of money, or afraid to spend it. I've known you in the old days, long before you bought that Agency, employ it out of your own pocket."

"Curious world you live in," I said. "Here's a fellow who's never heard of taxation and shortage of money."

"Shortage of money didn't stop you and your man Hallows going to Dunland. In fact you went twice."

"Fine," I said. "Glad you've got right down to the job. But the fact that I signed my own name in the hotel book is enough to clear me of underhandedness—if that's the term."

I filled my pipe. He waited patiently with the matches. "Look, sir," he said. "You and I know each other. For all I know, you might be working for a client. Why not tell me things—just between ourselves."

So I told him, even if it was the old, old story. Need to protect our good name: basic idea that the three callers had to be implicated, and therefore enquiries. Tactful enquiries and a survey of environments and backgrounds. Emphasis on need for money as a motive. Clean bill of health for the Howells. Lorde apparently doing well, and he had a wealthy son. Not so sure about Tinley, but he was spending money like a man who had it.

"And I'll end up with something else," I said. "I'm now at a loose end. I've gone so far and I can't get any farther. All I can now pray is that if you get your man, then our connection with the affair won't come out at the trial. Not that I shall ask for any favours."

"That'd be up to the D.P.P.," he said. "But we're the hell of a long way from that yet. I saw the Howells myself this morning and, frankly, they're not the killer type. And no motive. I'm seeing Charles Tinley at his flat some time in the morning. And I've seen Lorde. Again not the type. And no motive."

He lighted his own pipe and took his time over it.

"That question you put up to Grainger about the timings of those relations of Baldlow's. Any further ideas?"

I had to hedge.

"Don't they stand out a mile? He wanted to see each one separately and he didn't want one to see another."

"The way I see it," he said, "is that he wanted some information, not necessarily about themselves. The first two, that is. Lorde was to be seen last and because it would be as a result of that information that he'd frame his new will. Lorde would draw that new will up. That's why Baldlow sent out for a form."

"Maybe," I said, "but I doubt if a man like Baldlow would have employed an ordinary form."

"I know," he said. "He might have wanted to leave money in trust for the Howell or Lorde children and that'd have meant a pretty long document. And there was the money he was leaving to the church and that Moral Re-armament Movement. And to Mrs. Carver and her daughter. No," he said, "I think he wanted that form to jot down notes on for Lorde's benefit and according to what he'd hear from the first two callers."

"You're probably right," I said. "But about O'Brien or McShane or whatever he is. He's still on the list?"

"Very much so. He's no alibi. Baldlow might have wormed out something about him."

That was about all. We did go back over things but there was nothing new. He said he'd probably be in town till at least the following afternoon and I promised to pass on anything that happened to occur to me. But as I walked home I wasn't feeling happy. Jewle is such a good sort that it's a pleasure even to differ from him, but what I knew was that I was walking a tight-rope, and balanced precariously at that.

For one thing I was withholding evidence—a dangerous thing for a man in my position to do—and to claim that the police had the same chance as I to obtain it was mere sophistry.

Yet how could I tell what I'd begun to suspect? Had I told Jewle what I knew about Lorde, then Lorde would have been rubbed through a police sieve. If I had said that those three relations had been literally ordered to come to The Croft, then I should be making trouble for my client—or that client's wife—and it was her interests we were taking money to protect.

After the evening meal I realised that Bernice had not mentioned that Jane Howell problem I'd put up to her, so I told her about my visit to Pickfield Hall. I could point out that the plot, so to speak, had thickened. There had been no reason for her to keep travelling to Buckinghamshire for examination by the Pickfield Hall doctor.

"But didn't you say the doctor there was a family one? A kind of old friend."

"That's what she told her husband."

She frowned.

"But she needn't have kept travelling, as you put it. A healthy woman wouldn't need a lot of consultations."

"Mightn't Pickfield Hall insist on it? Because it would bring grist to their mill?"

"A reputable maternity home certainly wouldn't," she said. "But I've been thinking. I wonder if I might put things guardedly to someone at the hospital?"

She meant the hospital of whose original committee of management she was a member.

"Might be a good idea. It'd have to be kept purely hypothetical. And my name wouldn't have to be brought in."

"Surely you give me credit for a modicum of tact," she told me just the least bit frigidly.

I hastened to say that I always thought her about the most tactful person I knew. As for my own tactlessness, I hinted at the ticklish position in which I was beginning to find myself, and how it might be putting me rather on edge. So the evening proceeded peacefully, Bernice at her book and I at a crossword, and trying to keep my mind off the Baldlow case.

Daylight brought no new ideas. After breakfast I rang Hallows and he saw nothing for it but spending the client's money. I told him to take a day off. Something of a holiday would do both of us good.

It was by sheer luck that I happened to be in that afternoon. I had intended to see an Italian film that had been extravagantly praised, and then Bernice said she wanted to see it too and, though she had to go out, she could be back by four o'clock, so we might have tea and go to the cinema together. That was at about two o'clock, so I settled down in front of the fire intending to read a newspaper, and then somehow I dropped off to sleep. The ringing of the telephone bell woke me. How long it had been ringing I didn't know.

"Yes?" I said, a bit drowsily.

"That you, Mr. Travers?"

"Speaking."

"This is Jewle. Sorry to bother you, but could you come along to the Metropolitan Hotel?"

"In ten minutes. It's only five minutes' walk. But why the Metropolitan? You standing me a meal?"

"Something pretty bad," he said. "That man of yours— Nordon. Someone's shot him pretty badly. Right through the stomach."

XV

A MR. MYSTON

THE Metropolitan is a colossal place. Once, in my very callow youth, I spent a night there and was very impressed. All I know now is that the bedrooms are as good as in most hotels but the food unspeakable. Its present-day clientele is largely provincial business men and their wives, with a considerable admixture of foreigners and people who want somewhere absolutely central for just a night or two. It always seems crowded. There are queues for breakfast by half-past eight; queues at the reception desk trying to get in and queues at the cash desk trying to get away. Its gigantic foyer is fairly crowded too—people gossiping, people coming in and out or waiting for lifts.

So let's sum it up and say it's an ant-hill. I found all that out because I had to after that shooting of Nordon. I had to prove for myself that you could go to that reception desk and order a room and not be remembered afterwards, though it was not I who made the test but one of Jewle's men. We had to prove that you could walk in unchallenged and go up the stairs to where you liked. But you couldn't get into a room—unless you had had that room before and had made yourself a key.

One of Jewle's men who knew me was waiting at the hotel entrance. We went through the swing doors, dodged the people passing across the foyer, and up the main staircase to the second floor. He knew the way, or I'd have had to consult those hotel direction notices which direct you to various numbers. We went along a short corridor, turned into another, and there we were—at Room 229. Jewle was there and a couple of finger-print men were at work.

"A nasty business," he told me. "They had to rush him to hospital. He's probably having an operation at this very moment. If that door hadn't been left open by whoever shot him and a chambermaid hadn't seen it, he might have died here."

"How was he identified?"

"He had your Agency card on him. Luckily I was still at the Yard. Soon as I heard the name I got here at the double. Here's where he fell."

A chalk mark showed a body lying sideways, knees drawn up as if in agony. The head was towards the door in the comparatively clear space between the bed and the wardrobe.

"Looks as if he were going out with someone and that someone suddenly let him have it," Jewle said.

"But why here at all!"

"No idea," he said. "He came here for some very good reason. Both women came up from the reception desk and couldn't identify him. Here's a copy of the form filled in by whoever engaged the room."

The name was Harold Myston, said to have come from Bradford, and the room had been booked by telephone the previous night. Nothing could be gained, Jewle said, from the handwriting. Most of the form had to be in block capitals, and the signature was only a scrawl.

"Any hope of tracing the telephone call?"

"We shall try Bradford, just in case it's genuine. And try them for the name. Personally I haven't any hope. I think this thing was well planned."

"What's that?" I said. "Myston's bag?"

It was a fibre bag or case of medium size: no label and no hotel stickies. Jewle opened it with a grimace. All it held was packed newspaper to make it look full and two heavy pieces of rubble to give it weight.

"You see?" he said. "All carefully planned. At the reception desk he'd be automatically asked about luggage, so he'd just lift the bag and show it. He'd have people elbowing him this way and that way and the desk clerks would be rushed off their feet. Just before midday when he booked in. That's a busy time. People have to vacate their rooms by then. All those who've taken their time are making the getaway."

I asked who was on the job besides himself and he said Miller, the man who'd met me outside. I don't like things at second hand, though I didn't tell Jewle so. What I did ask was if I might see the manager.

"I'll come with you," he said. "We've got this hushed so far and he'd like it kept so. But what about these?"

I hadn't seen them because they'd been lying on the bed: a mask and a muffler. The mask was the papier maché kind of thing that children buy for Guy Fawkes Night—a night that was almost due. It had the flashy colouring somewhat exaggerated; little slits for the eyes, black eyebrows, and elastic that fastened it round the back of the head. It looked as if it would go upwards as far as the hair of the head and down nearly to the tip of the nose, and round as far as the ears. The elastic hung by one side only and the mask was torn at the side as if the elastic had been violently pulled out.

The muffler was brand-new: white or off-white artificial silk about a foot across, two and a half feet long and with a fringe at each end.

"Whose was the muffler?"

"How can we be sure?" Jewle said. "I'd say it was the other man's. Probably went across the lower part of his face at the desk as a sort of disguise."

"It and the mask were found like this, on the bed?"

"Now you're asking questions," he told me. "That hasn't been proved yet. Miller's on that now. But the sequence as far as I've learned is this. The chambermaid saw the door open and looked in. Nordon was on the floor. She didn't know he was shot—there wasn't a gun—so she thought he was ill. She phoned down to the manager. He came up and saw blood, so he got the local police. They later got the Yard and I came here as I said. Meanwhile a doctor had seen him, and he was out of here and round to the hospital at once. He'd passed out with the pain and the shock and I believe the doctor gave him an injection. So you see. All those people in here. Who moved the mask and muffler?"

"Any news about Nordon?"

"Far too early. We might ring the hospital from downstairs. But we haven't finished here yet."

He pointed to a spot or two on the carpet. There was no need to ask what they were.

"Either he struggled to where he collapsed," he said, "or else he was moved."

I looked round at the room. It was oblong, about fifteen feet by nine. The door was on the left of the room as one entered. To the immediate right was the wardrobe. On the right-hand wall was the basin and, just beyond it, a small recess for an electric fire. Under the one window was a table with a chair. As your eye went along to the left-hand wall, there was the bed and finally, just inside the door, the usual stand for luggage.

"How was Nordon dressed?"

"This is at second hand," he said, "but his hat was on the floor and he had on his overcoat."

"The hat fell off when he was shot," I said. "In other words, we can assume he'd either just come in or was just going out. But just a minute! Exactly why have *you* taken over? You think it's tied up with the Baldlow case?"

"It's something that's got to be taken into account," he told me evenly. "Nordon might have learned something at Seahurst—something he needn't necessarily be aware of—which Baldlow's killer knew to be dangerous. So he enticed Nordon here."

I saw that. But there was something else to be cleared out of the way.

"Apparently no one heard the shot."

"Bathroom on the right," he said, "and bedroom on the left. No one in either. It was the wrong time of day. In any case the killer had to take the risk. But I don't think there'd be all that noise with the door closed. Depends on the calibre of the gun. Just as Nordon's life depends on it."

I wondered if we could get a rough idea how it might have been done. The doors were automatically locking and so the door must have been left ajar. That was a certainty. If the killer—as it was convenient to call him—had opened the door and Nordon had seen a man wearing that mask, he'd have been alarmed, and if the killer had then shot, it would have had to be with the door open, and that would have meant a far greater noise.

In fact I thought it had been like this.

Nordon found the door ajar. The killer, sitting with his back to him at the window table and wearing his hat and the mask, would call—and without turning.

"That you, Mr. Nordon? Close the door, will you, and come in. I shan't be a moment."

Nordon came so far. The killer got up and whipped round and fired. Nordon collapsed. The killer lifted his body round and then bolted, and in such a hurry that he forgot his muffler and the mask which he'd necessarily had to take off. If he remembered them, what did it matter? He daren't go back, but what risk was there? He could turn up the collar of his overcoat and put a handkerchief to his mouth if he met anyone on the stairs, and all he had to do then was unhurriedly cross the foyer and go out through the swing doors. And he wasn't coming back. And the bag had been merely a blind in any case: something he was sure couldn't be traced.

There was a knock at the door. Jewle opened it and Miller came in.

"Nothing more to be learned downstairs, sir. Can't get a description of Myston. The room was taken up at about midday, but you know that already."

"What was the exact time when the chambermaid made the discovery?"

"About a quarter past two," he told me.

"I see, and no idea when he was actually shot?"

"The hospital will probably know," Jewle said. "Soon as the operation's over we can try to find out."

"Let's suppose," I said. "Would he have had a meal before he booked in? If not, mightn't he have brought some lunch with him?"

"No crumbs, if that's what you mean," Jewle said. "He wouldn't be worrying about anything so comparatively trivial as lunch. He deliberately took up the room at a busy time. He knew when Nordon was coming and he just had to wait."

Later we went along to the hospital, just a few hundred yards away. Nordon was off the operating table but not yet out of the anaesthetic. A man would be sitting by his bedside.

We saw the surgeon who'd performed the operation. Jewle wanted to know what chance Nordon had.

"A little more than an even chance," he was told. "His general condition is very much in his favour. Luckily, too, the bullet was small."

Jewle took it over. The Yard experts would know just what gun it had come from. Jewle thought it was a little automatic.

"Any idea, doctor, at what time he was shot?"

"Well," he said, "this isn't official, but I'd say about an hour before he arrived here. That's judging from the haemorrhage."

"Also unofficially," Jewle said, "that makes the time of shooting around two o'clock. But about his recovery, doctor. You wouldn't give him a better chance than just over evens?"

"One has to be conservative," the doctor told him dryly. "He'll have everything—blood transfusions, penicillin. The threat, in layman's language, is peritonitis. And shock."

"How long before he can talk?"

"What kind of talk? You mean coherent, logical talk?"

"Yes. Able to say what happened."

The doctor pursed his lips.

"Possibly in another eight hours' time. I'd prefer it much later."

"You're the arbiter," Jewle said. "But think of us, doctor. What if we miss a chance and he dies? Just a word or two from him and we get a murderer. No word, and a murderer goes free."

"What shall it profit a man?" Jewle was asked. He was a dry stick, that surgeon. "The mere questioning may mean a difference between life and death. Afraid you'll have to leave the decision to us."

"Not before the morning, then?"

"Certainly not before the morning. But no reason why you shouldn't keep in touch."

We went back to the hotel but we might just as well have gone to Margate. The early evening rush was on and we could think of no more questions. We went upstairs to that second floor. You knew the floors by the numbers. 329 would have been the third floor, and so on. Miller was in 229 and he had something to tell us about that. Myston had asked for the first floor but no room had been available, so he had to make do with what was.

"The first floor," Jewle said. "No need to take a lift. A liftman's on pretty close terms with his passengers. He might remember. A first floor for a quick getaway if the shot should have happened to be heard."

Miller had something else. Another chambermaid on the same floor, told about the supposed illness in 229 by the first one, had picked up the mask and muffler from the floor and put them on the bed. Her prints were on the mask, but no others.

Another half-hour and I left: there was nothing I could do and nothing else to ask. I'd already rung Norris and he was waiting for me at the office. All I could do was tell him what had happened.

"Nordon's uncle rang," he said. "A Mr. Arthur Nordon, apparently his only relative. He said you'd rung him and he'd been to the hospital. They wouldn't let him see Nordon."

"Keep him off my tail," I said. "I'm worried enough as it is without having Arthur Nordon round."

Hallows came in then. I'd rung him too and given a brief outline. The three of us went into conference, trying to think who could have shot Nordon. There weren't many to choose from. Tinley was the favourite. There could be no one else unless it was Lorde or McShane or Pinky Morris. Bertha was still in and she got Lorde's private number for me.

I had a good excuse for ringing him—to tell him confidentially he'd been given a clean bill of health by the police.

"You sound tired," I said. "Had a trying day?"

"I suppose I did," he said. "Attending an inquest most of the morning and one of those rather tiresome clients most of the afternoon."

So Lorde was definitely out. Next we got Grainger. He said he'd just been rung by Jewle, and about McShane. The army authorities were being rung on another line and he'd ring me back.

Next I tried Pinky Morris. His wife answered. Her husband was away, she said, and had been since early morning and he wouldn't be back till the following day. He was up north—at Blackpool—talent-spotting.

"That seems to let him out," I said. "Better ring Jewle and put him on to Tinley, if he hasn't got on to him already."

Jewle had been to the Yard and gone again—but not back to Seahurst. There was nothing to do but wait. Grainger rang first. McShane was okay, he said. Half an hour later Jewle rang. He'd just seen Tinley and Tinley had an alibi of sorts. There was a gap of only a few minutes—between the time he left the restaurant where he had lunch and the time he'd got back to his office. He'd said he'd walked as it was a fine, cold afternoon.

"I'll keep in close touch with you about Nordon," Jewle went on. "If he's okay in the morning and we can get a statement, I'll let you have it at once."

I said I'd be in the office from eight o'clock onwards, and that was that.

"There we are then," Norris said. "Everybody's got an alibi. Only one answer to that. Someone's faked one. Whoever was clever enough to do that hotel shooting would know he'd have to have an alibi."

I said we'd done our best and we'd leave things to the morning. The Yard in any case would probe those alibis: they'd have to be more than water-tight to be passed.

So I went home, to a wife who'd found my note and had gone to the cinema alone, and to a belated evening meal. She was very upset about Nordon, even if she knew nothing of the circumstances, because she had seen him once and had liked him. She had even been a bit superior about it—wondering why he wasn't at some better job. I had had to ask mildly if what was good enough for me wasn't good enough for him, though I didn't say it as directly as that.

I didn't know when I'd felt so dog-tired. I went to bed early and I was asleep at once. I hardly knew I'd been asleep at all when the alarm clock woke me half an hour short of my usual seven. Eight o'clock found me at the office.

The night operative was still on duty and he gave me a message received at seven o'clock about Nordon. He had had as good a night as could be expected, but he was still on the danger list. But he was alive. Whether he would be able to do any talking was quite another thing.

Norris arrived and the day might have seemed just another day. But everyone knew it wasn't. Nordon was our man: still on our payroll. Even the Yard was recognising that we were not only interested in the man who'd shot him but that if that man weren't found, then we'd still go on trying. Every one of us was interested: that was why I'd put a copy of that latest bulletin in the operatives' room. Every one, as far as I could gather, had liked Nordon, even if the older hands had regarded him—as old hands will—with a certain condescension. There had been even a rumour, I was to learn, that on account of his social status he was being groomed for a directorate.

I didn't want to get in Norris's way, so I adjourned to Bertha Munney's room and read a paper or two and began pottering about with a crossword. Even Bertha was on edge, and I was just thinking of getting out from under her feet and having a cup of coffee when the call came from Jewle.

"That you, Mr. Travers?"

"Speaking."

"Can you get here at the double? Nordon can talk, but not for long. But he won't talk to anyone but you."

"Right," I said. "I'll be with you as soon as my car'll get me there."

Nordon would speak only to me. I wondered why. It had to be something to do with his job: some peculiar loyalty which he wanted to put into words. But it was no use to guess and I had traffic to watch. The lights were mostly with me and I made it pretty fast. So into the hospital; the same old smell and it might have been the same people; Miller waiting for me and the two of us going up in the lift. Along a short corridor to a private ward. Jewle was waiting outside the door.

"We isolated him in here," he told me. "Thought it might be better."

"How is he?"

"About the same. Take it easy with him."

A young doctor was there, hovering in range of the door, and trying to look as if he'd dropped in by chance. I went over to the bed. Nordon's face was very white. His lips shaped to a wan smile as I gently patted his head.

"How're you feeling, son?"

I don't quite know why I called him that, unless it was the pallor and the utter helplessness, and it had been the way my father had almost invariably addressed myself.

"Not too bad. Guess I'm shot full of dope."

The voice was very quiet. The lips barely moved.

"Tell me about yesterday. Take it easy. Don't waste words."

"Guess it was my own fault," he said, and I had to bend over him to hear the words. "I thought I'd be clever and show you I wasn't such a fool—well, you know. A man rang me and asked if I was the one who'd been at Seahurst living with Baldlow. I said I was and he said he had some important news for me and would I meet him at Room 229 at the Metropolitan Hotel that afternoon at two o'clock. I thought I'd be clever and get the credit. That's why I didn't ring the office."

His eyes closed. The doctor had contrived to be just behind me. He was just about to speak when Nordon himself began speaking again, eyes still closed.

"I went there. I found the door ajar and a man was sitting at the table at the window. He said to come in and shut the door. Then when I turned round he was showing me a gun and he had a mask on. I put my hands up and I knew it was some sort of frame-up, so before he could speak I tried to rush him. I guess I thought the gun wasn't loaded. I remember I did get my hands on that mask but he'd got me just before that and then I fell. That's about all."

"You recognised him?"

"Never saw him before in my life."

"Description?"

"Can't think," he said slowly. "Not big. Dark hat and overcoat." The eyes seemed to be screwing up in the effort to remember. "Only saw his face for a flash as that mask came away."

"It'll come to you later," I told him.

And then the eyes opened. The head turned towards me.

"Put your head down, sir."

It was a question that he wanted to whisper.

"What chance do they give me?"

"Far more than an even one," I whispered back. "You're going to be fine."

"Good," he said. "I'll find that bastard who got me if it takes me the rest of my life."

The doctor was tapping me on the shoulder and making signs at his watch.

"Don't worry, son," I told Nordon. "By the time you're on your feet again we'll have him for you."

The doctor was fussing us out of the room. Miller stayed by the door, but Jewle and I went along to the lift. I told him what I'd learned and he got me to write it down while I remembered it. I had to explain that bit about Nordon's being too clever, but

I didn't say it was anything to do with the Baldlow case on which he'd fallen down.

I had no further news of Nordon that day. Jewle had in any case said he would ring me only if there was a crisis. It was a strange sort of day: the sort one spends rather blankly and bleakly when some long expected event has been suddenly postponed. As far as the Baldlow case was concerned, there was nothing that could be done. Both Jewle and I had relied on at least some adequate recognition by Nordon of his assailant, but there had been none except the almost useless mention of someone not big. That much seemed in keeping. The not-bigness would have given Nordon just that much sense of ascendancy to make his own attack something more than a chance. Not that that helped. All we could do was hope that in, say, another twenty-four hours Nordon would have gained more strength and would have been able to remember just that little more that might make all the difference.

Nothing happened the rest of that day, as I said, but the morning brought a letter from Tom Howell.

Dear Mr. Travers,

I am writing to you personally because of your special knowledge about my wife and because of the way I have come to regard you, by which I mean that I'm sure you'll understand.

The fact is that my wife is now so very much better in every way that I no longer see any point in protecting her interests. So will you be so good as to render me an account that will be absolutely up to date, including any commitments, and you shall have my cheque by return.

What I cannot pay you for is the tact you have shown in whatever enquiries you have been making, which has acted as a kind of buffer, if you understand me, between my own feelings and my wife's. I'm not too good a hand at letter-writing outside sheer business. Perhaps we may have the pleasure of seeing you here when all this business is finally over.

Yours sincerely,

T. HOWELL.

That letter had been sent to my flat. I gave it later to Norris to file, and then we had to have a consultation about another job that had come in. It was about half-past ten when I left the office—Nordon, by the way, was alive but *incommunicado*—intending to have a coffee at the usual place. Then I changed my mind: one of those casual things that happen and which lead to what we mistakenly cite as coincidences. For I'd walked on and was getting an all-round tonic from that bright, bracing air of earliest November when whom should I run into, not far from the Mansion House, but Laurie Peters of Private Enquiries, Ltd.

XVI
ONE ANSWER

PRIVATE Enquiries are an old-established firm who, like ourselves, are retained by various private companies. I'd known Lawrence Peters for years. He was the managing director, and from time to time we'd helped each other out. He's a man of about sixty, an ex-superintendent from a provincial police force and about as decent and reliable as they come. The Norris type, in fact.

There were the fancy-meeting-you's and all that, and the suggestion of a drink. Beer's my usual tipple, as I told him, but that morning was a bit too cold and I suggested coffee. We went into a handy café and sat yarning over the hot cups and biscuits. We discussed business generally and taxation and the shortage of money and how we were lucky to be keeping our heads above water.

"Let me see," he said. "You rang me about Luke Layman and whether we'd had a job for him just before he had that accident.

I was sorry about Luke. He lifted his elbow occasionally but he was a nice chap. Good at his job."

"That's right," I said. "We did ring you. We felt a certain responsibility since we'd given him the very last job he ever did. When did you employ him last?"

He hesitated; frowned. He leaned across the table and his voice lowered.

"For God's sake keep this under your hat, but you knew that chap Baldlow who was murdered at Seahurst? Well, we were doing a job for him. One of those ticklish jobs where you have to use two or three men and none of them must know enough to get the whole background. Luke was one of them and he knew more of the picture. We were a bit short-handed at the time."

Something came to me. I daren't let voice or face show it.

"Any rumour ever reach you about us working for him too?"

"There *was* something," he said. "I wasn't interested. I didn't want to get involved myself. A client's a client, even when he's dead."

He was right. Even with Laurie Peters I'd never have discussed a client's affairs; and though they might have helped us out with a man, he'd never have discussed a case with me. That's the basis of the absolute confidence that must exist between client and agency. And naturally he didn't want to be involved with the law. If, mark you, he'd been absolutely sure after Baldlow's death that he had private information that would very definitely find his murderer and that murderer wasn't his client, then he might have imparted that information gratuitously and in the very strictest confidence. I'd have done the same. What I therefore knew was that Peters had no such information.

But while I was thinking all that, a something else was at the back of my mind. Suddenly it came into the open.

"A funny bird—Baldlow," I said. "Strictly between ourselves, did he insist on paying cash to you personally, the same as he did with me?"

"As a matter of fact he did," he said. "Not that I worried. Cash is cash. Sometimes a cheque isn't."

I sheered away from Baldlow and about ten minutes later we parted. He was making some enquiries in the City and I said I was going Cannon Street way. What I did was take the Underground and eventually it landed me at Holborn. I walked from there to the offices of City Detection Ltd., another reputable firm with whom from time to time we'd had dealings. Bill Fraser owned it and him also I knew quite well. He happened to be in. He was a short, plump man with a cherubic face: a latter-day Pickwick with a really good brain.

"What brings you this way?" he asked me as he held out a hand across his desk.

"Just happened to be passing and thought I'd be friendly. How're things with you, Bill?"

"Slow," he said. "Just one of those times."

He passed me his tobacco pouch and I passed him mine. We got our pipes going.

"Good stuff, this of yours," he said. "Things must be looking up."

So to the same old talk: taxation, shortage of money and even the atom bomb.

"Talking of sudden death," I said, "it was bad about Luke Layman. We rang you, if you remember, about a job you might have given him the very day of his death."

"That's right," he said. "Poor old Luke. A nice chap. Quiet and reliable. Had his faults, but who of us hasn't."

I had to use the same approach I'd tried with Peters. Did he know we'd had a man working for the late Henry Baldlow? He didn't, but I could see he was interested.

"Funny thing is," he said, "but we did a job for Baldlow this spring."

You can guess the rest for yourself, for it again followed the very lines of the confidential talk between Peters and myself. I'd known the information was there: all I had wondered was if I could bring it into the open. After it I had to sheer away from Baldlow. We discussed a hypothetical problem of his and then I rose to go.

"Mind if I use your telephone?" I said. "I really ought to be going back to the office but I feel damn lazy this morning. Think I'll go home instead."

I rang Norris and said I'd be at home and anything urgent could be passed on to me. He said nothing further had come in about our friend. So I hopped a bus and went home. It was about time for lunch and Bernice and I had a service meal. Then I went into the den and switched on the electric fire.

A miracle had happened but I was just quietly confident. All I knew at that moment was that what I'd guessed about those three relations was proved beyond doubt. Three detective agencies who all advertised in the best-class papers. More than three, of course, but meeting Peters had led me to the two that mattered. Baldlow had seen the advertisements and had employed both Peters and Fraser. Once Peters had told me he'd worked for Baldlow, the rest followed.

Those initials that had been found on the cheque stubs, they were the clue. Laurie Peters was the L.P.—that couldn't have been coincidence, after Baldlow's using us. All I had to do then was cast my mind over other agencies for the W.F., and there it was in William *alias* Bill Fraser.

But there was another problem. Only two agencies had been employed; if not, then there'd have been another set of initials. And therefore only two of the relatives had been enquired into. That seemed logical. Baldlow was secretive. He wouldn't have given one agency two jobs. Therefore he had enquired into two of the relatives because he already knew something about the remaining one. If one was unfit to be left money, then why not the other two? That had been his argument. How could I tell which one?

Lorde seemed the likeliest, after Baldlow's visit to Dunland and his call on Mrs. Oliver. After he got religion he might have remembered that, and had his suspicions, and it would be an easy job to find out when those Amalgamated Foundries had actually been sold. Let that be granted, I told myself. So Baldlow had had enquiries made about Tinley and his sister, Jane Howell. And then I remembered something—that look of sheer panic on the face of Phyllis Cavendall when I had said that I myself was a private detective.

Phyllis Cavendall had been questioned by a private detective. That seemed a certainty, and that that detective had been one of Peters' men or Fraser's men. It might even have been Luke Layman! Not that I saw that much falling into place. What I did see was that there must have been an enquiry into Tinley. That, it now seemed, was why Grimble had thrown Nordon to the Preventive Men. Grimble had also been questioned before and had wanted to put himself in the clear.

But in spite of the fact that we had found out nothing about either Jane Howell or Charles Tinley, the fact remained that Baldlow must have found out something about them. Other agencies had been more successful than ours because they hadn't started from scratch. Baldlow had begun with certain clues and had therefore directed them along certain lines. And why shouldn't something have been found out about them? There are skeletons in most cupboards. If anyone had seen fit to delve down deep enough into the starry-eyed and callow young manhood of Ludovic Travers he might have unearthed an affair with a married woman: an affair that makes me go hot and cold at a distance of almost thirty years and about which I've never breathed a word to Bernice.

But to the general pattern. It was what I'd always seen it, if only vaguely. Those three people were going to be startled by Baldlow by some such revelation about the past. A hint had been given in the letters, and he knew each would come at the time stated. Would he have gloated? I didn't think so. He'd have spoken more in sorrow than anger. And would he have ended by telling each that he or she was disinherited?

Again I didn't think so. What I was compelled to think was something utterly nauseating: something that almost made me on the side of the one who'd killed him.

Maybe you won't agree, but take that Moral Re-armament meeting that Baldlow had had specially arranged. What Canon Orifice had told me frankly wasn't satisfying enough. Baldlow didn't want that meeting as a kind of farewell to England.

He wanted it as a stool of repentance for those three relatives. If they were prepared to attend that meeting and make open confession and show what he considered genuine repentance, then he'd be prepared to see that it was recognised in his will. Too repulsive, you say. I don't know. I do know that Baldlow was a repulsive man. Remember too how he knelt and prayed in Betty Tinley's flat.

I began to think back to all I knew or had learned about him, and the more I remembered, the more sure I was. And then suddenly, right out of the blue, something hit me clean in the wind. It was something now so obvious that only a fool wouldn't have thought of it before. Everything fitted. Everything dovetailed perfectly. What I knew, in fact, was this. *I knew who had killed Baldlow, who had shot Nordon and who had been responsible for the death of Luke Layman.*

And how could I prove it? Easily enough if only Nordon was well enough to be closely questioned. Or perhaps there might be some short cut, and at once I was worrying my wits to find one. What I didn't know was that in a minute or two I was to be handed it on a gold platter.

I heard Bernice come in. I drew up my long legs from the fire as I heard her at the door of the den.

"How beautifully snug," she said. "If you let out the tobacco smoke we might have tea here. Oh, and I got this from young Dr. Lacey."

"Lacey?"

"Of course," she said. "He'd be after your time. He's the assistant gynaecologist. A great detective-novel reader."

Though I'd taken the envelope I hadn't realised that she was talking about that problem I'd set her.

"I made it all very hypothetical," she said. "To be perfectly frank I wasn't exactly truthful. I said it was to be an idea for a detective story a friend was writing. I'll get tea and you can see what he says."

Lacey was certainly a fan. He had it all nicely set out.

THE CASE OF THE CAREFUL MOTHER

Let W be the woman. The problem is why she had her first baby far from her home when local first-class facilities were available. The fact that she knew one of the doctors at the distant nursing home not being taken into account, or being considered as a definite untruth.

A very feasible solution of the problem is this, and it should be accepted that this solution is realty feasible in every way. It could in some ways have happened to myself. It hinges on the fact that the woman had been delivered of a baby before she married and therefore wished at all costs to conceal the fact from her husband.

Now W might have managed to conceal at marriage the fact that she wasn't a virgin. That wouldn't have been too difficult. Also the husband wouldn't have noticed critically the deepening colour of the nipples—a tendency from pink to brown. There needn't have been any striae (stretch marks of abdomen) to give her away, but those things would have been noticed by the doctor and nurse present at the second delivery.

I suggest then that W found a nursing home in one of the glossy magazines and decided to use it. She *could* have asked to be originally seen—immediately after she was aware of pregnancy—by the actual doctor who would be present at birth. She could have confided in him and gained his sympathy and co-operation and his silence by quoting certain circumstances. He, in his turn, might have arranged for a not too experienced nurse to assist at the delivery. The nursing home would be expensive and he'd like to accommodate a patient in a perfectly ethical way.

What were those circumstances? I suggest the events should be antedated so that W spent a week-end with a man who was at once leaving for France. If W has to be a good character, then it could be said there was no time for a marriage, and that the man was killed fairly soon, even before W knew she was pregnant. W, through the co-operation of her mother or some relative, could have had her baby at some place where she wasn't known. Also, making things happen in war-time lends feasibility. She could always be a wife whose husband was far afield. The country was full of them.

H.L.

If this helps I shall want an autographed copy of the book!

So there it was: out of the mouths of wives and doctors. Maybe I'd seen some of it but looked clean over it. And two things still remained. Why the panic of Phyllis Cavendall? How did Baldlow become aware of the truth?

Bernice brought in the tea tray. I told her she and Lacey had done a fine job: given me, in fact, just what I wanted. Loose ends to tidy up, of course, but that didn't for the moment matter. But after tea I got my pipe going and began trying to answer those two questions. As soon as I put myself in Jane Howell's shoes, I found a good enough answer to the first.

It had to depend on the fact that McLeod must have been killed before or immediately after pregnancy. What would Jane do? She'd go to Phyllis. She'd suggest, even plead for, an illegal operation. Phyllis had got scared and had begun to hedge, and she could have quoted reasons why she daren't try the operation herself. That was why the two had parted. Jane had probably gone to her commanding officer—if that's what they called her in the Wrens—and told the truth about the pregnancy and obtained leave of absence. The fact that Jane had no parents and that there were extenuating circumstances might have helped. So Jane had her baby. Maybe it was still-born. And she had plenty of money to pay for secrecy.

The Baldlow business worried me far more. It took me quite a time to arrive at anything satisfying, and I was never to know if it were true. As I saw it, or indeed knew, Baldlow was always in touch with his niece and nephew, though on different terms with their parents. To explain the few months' absence on special leave, Jane could have told him she was being sent temporarily abroad, and on something very hush-hush.

There came the marriage to Howell and the birth of their boy. Betty Tinley had told me that Baldlow had been to Pickfield Hall to see Jane. Why not something like this:

Baldlow: What sort of time did she have?
Nurse: No trouble at all. Besides, it wasn't as if it was the first—Oh, I'm sorry, I was thinking of someone else.

Two things, then, that might come to Baldlow's mind when he began thinking of his money and his heirs. But the great thing was that whether the deductions were true or not, I now had enough to finish the case.

So I tried to get Jewle. The Yard ran him to earth at the hospital. I asked him if he would wait the ten minutes till I could get there.

He was waiting for me in the reception hall.

"How's Nordon?" I asked him.

"Asleep at the moment," he said. "They think he'll pull through."

"You questioned him today?"

"Just after lunch. He couldn't remember anything else that helped."

I drew him over to a corner.

"I'd like to make a bargain with you. You let me ask Nordon just one question absolutely privately. Give me, say, two minutes with him, and then I'll hand you Baldlow's murderer."

"If I didn't know you," he said, "I'd think this was a trick."

"Everything's above-board," I told him. "There's only one string attached. I'm not to be asked what I say to Nordon. You keep your side of the bargain and I'll keep mine."

He frowned, he looked sideways, he rubbed his chin.

"Won't it come out at the trial if Nordon gives evidence?"

"Not if the murderer pleads guilty," I said. "But you've got to trust me. I can only do it my way."

He threw in his hand.

"Right. What're you going to do? Stay here till he wakes up? Or see if they'll wake him?"

I left it to Jewle. He went upstairs, and when he came down, and that was quite a time later, he said I'd be talking to Nordon in a very few minutes. We both went upstairs to wait.

It was about ten minutes later that I was being shown in. Nordon looked just as ill to me, but now he was under artificial light. He turned his head slowly and when he spotted me he gave me that wan smile. I drew a chair up. I leaned over and began very quietly to talk.

It was just under the two minutes when I came out. I couldn't even look at Jewle for a moment.

"Well?" he said.

"Not here," I told him. "Let's get outside. It's only five minutes to my place."

We walked along to the flat. Crowds were thronging the pavements and the coloured lights came off and on and twinkled and I was hardly aware of them. Then we left them behind and cut through the short way. We took the lift up. We went through to the den and I switched on the fire. I went out and got two bottles of beer and glasses.

"Good of you not to pester me," I told Jewle. "I was pretty sure I had the answer before I went into that room, but all the same it was a nasty shock. Nordon's your man. He killed Baldlow."

XVII
SPOKEN AND UNSPOKEN

JEWLE stared.

"Nordon! But he didn't shoot himself!"

"He didn't," I said, "but that's another story. All I know is that he killed Baldlow."

It was a story that took some telling. In that walk from the hospital I'd had time to think things over, and I was hoping I'd know just what to leave out.

I told him about Nordon's background: a mother's darling, used to extravagancies and the good things of life: the man who'd taken a pretty short time to run through his inheritance. Then the other two sides of him: the Commando and the Intelligence man.

"Even my wife thought him far too good for just an operative," I said. "He was eminently likeable, perfectly mannered, and public school written all over him. He was simply filling in time with us, hoping his uncle would find him something well paid and not too onerous. And he had a friend who was going to Australia. You might get the facts of that from his uncle. All I know is that he'd need money.

"We sent him down to Seahurst, as you know. He was a good mixer and he had that ingratiating manner, but he also had brains. Baldlow was a gabber. I'm prepared to swear he gave Nordon a rough idea of why he wanted to see those three people that Saturday. Baldlow liked Nordon. He wrote specially and told us so. But Nordon wanted to know more.

"I'm giving it to you in a sketchy way because everything can be worked out later. But remember this, or, if you don't know it, hear it for the first time. Nordon brought up from the kitchen both after-lunch tea and before-bed cocoa. There were sleeping tablets available and he could easily have bought some for himself. What he wanted to know was the full story, and what was in Baldlow's safe. Both were easy. When Baldlow was doped and asleep he could help himself to the keys.

"I'd say that in that safe was an envelope on which was written—'To be handed to the police in the event of my death from other than natural causes.' I'd say the envelope wasn't sealed, and because as a result of what was to transpire on the Saturday, there might be more to add. But what it did contain were things that each of those three would have given the devil of a lot not to be known. If it becomes strictly necessary I'll tell you only one of them which I happened to discover, but it'd have to be in the strictest confidence.

"Now do you see? Nordon had a young fortune in his possession. He'd been working previously on a blackmail case of ours where a woman had extorted quite a lot of money. He now had a safe way of making quite a lot for himself. What he intended was to take a stiff sum from each, assuring each it would be a final payment, and so finance himself for that shift to Australia. I don't say that if he hadn't succeeded there he'd have come home and put the screws on again.

"So to the murder. Hardly a murder, really, from his point of view. Baldlow asleep on that Saturday and not to be disturbed by anyone, certainly not by Mrs. Carver. What more simple and less messy than to press a cushion or a pillow over his face, and then to open the safe, take the envelope and secrete it, or post it to his flat when he went out. That would be after Mrs. Carver had gone home to change. He then opened that dining-room window or rejoiced to see that Mrs. Carver had forgotten to shut it. Then he went out to get a Last Will and Testament Form which Baldlow had never wanted. But it made a good excuse. It fitted in with what would be known about the visits of the callers, especially Lorde who is a solicitor.

"Mrs. Carver was expected back at half-past two, and it would be for her to discover the body. It was sheer luck that I happened to be there, as you know. And, luckily for Nordon, none of the three relatives had a sound alibi. Even if one or all had had one, it might have been faked, and in any case the whole thing would have been confused. And Nordon himself was safe. Where was his motive? And he had an alibi. Mrs. Carver had seen him go out. She didn't know he'd slipped back again. Remember, too, that house wasn't overlooked from across the way.

"Grainger came and the usual enquiry began. Nordon made a full statement, with our complete sanction, of why he'd been at The Croft and what he'd observed. All his later reports to us must have been cooked so as to prepare the way for the actual killing of Baldlow, but we took them as genuine and so did Grainger. He'd gone through the safe and taken only what he actually needed and so burglary couldn't be entertained, and I gather nothing was missing from the house itself. So suspicion fell on the three relatives. Then O'Brien-McShane became a suspect through the curious movements of his mother-in-law, and Grainger went off at a tangent. Every day would make Nordon safer in his own

188 | CHRISTOPHER BUSH

mind—not that he'd ever been suspected. But it gave him the assurance he wanted for beginning to blackmail.

"And that's about all," I said. "It's given you enough to work on. Or hasn't it?"

"Well," he said, "I see him as the chief suspect. I might go further if you'd tell me how you got on to him. The way you've told it, you might be a ruddy thought-reader."

"How I got on to him," I said slowly, and knew I hadn't better mention Luke. "There're all the things I've already told you—his suitability and so on. I also asked myself who was left but Nordon after the relatives and McShane had gone. Would anyone but Nordon have known that Baldlow was sleeping at two o'clock—anyone likely to kill him, that is? And once I'd got that idea of secret information in Baldlow's mind, I had to ask who could have got at the safe? And who wouldn't have been suspected if seen coming out of the house? Dozens of things like that, floating about and then coalescing.

"But something else."

I told him about Pinky Morris: a man whom I'd considered quite incapable of even complicity in murder: the man for whom Tom Holberg had twice vouched. I told him about that report of Nordon's: how he'd heard Baldlow telling Morris almost frantic-ally that he wasn't to come to Seahurst.

"That was a red-herring, skilfully drawn across by Nordon," I said. "But I had to ask myself, once I was convinced that Morris couldn't have been in any way concerned, how Nordon got hold of the name. He could only have got it from that envelope in the safe. I'd say that when Baldlow wrote down what he knew or suspected about Tinley, he mentioned certain information he'd extracted from Tinley's wife at her flat and how that a man named Morris had called while he was there."

"Well, I still don't quite see how it's all going to be proved," Jewle said dubiously. "Mind you, I believe every word of it. You say you know it's true and that's good enough for me. But how can we prove it?"

"You won't have to," I said. "Nordon, when charged ultim-ately, will plead guilty to Baldlow's death."

"You sure?"

"I have his word for it. I think he has that much decency left. All you have to do is keep a man at his bedside so he doesn't change his mind and bolt when he gets stronger. I don't think he will. I also don't think he'll speak. He'll say he killed Baldlow and at the trial he'll plead guilty."

Jewle's jaws clamped tight and he gave a slow shake of the head as if it was something beyond all experience—which it probably was. Then he thought of something.

"What about the shooting? Who did that?"

"Do yourself and me a favour at the same time," I told him. "Nordon's not going to bring any charge against the one who shot him." I checked his question. "No, don't ask me about it. Follow the course I've suggested. What more do you want? Nordon'll plead guilty. Do you want to drag all sorts of people's names through the mud?"

"No," he said slowly. "Maybe I don't. All the same I'd like to know a whole lot more."

"You shall," I told him. "When the time's ripe you *shall* know a whole lot more."

Jewle left. I wondered what he'd have said if I'd told him about Luke Layman. But Luke was dead and a jury had given its verdict. Keeping quiet about Luke, and certain other things, was the price I'd had to pay for Nordon's confession. But Nordon had certainly killed Luke. There wasn't a doubt about it.

The vital clue was why Luke had taken with him that diary book when he'd set off for Maverton. Look at what had gone before and judge from that what had to come after.

Luke and Nordon had been working together on a blackmail case. It was one that had to be handled slowly and carefully, with a building up of confidence. Luke and Nordon would have spent quite a lot of time together. Luke wouldn't be so close-mouthed when under the influence of more than a few drinks. Nordon, as a beginner, would have got him to relate his experiences, and Jane Howell—I thought she must be the one—had been mentioned. Also Nordon must have seen that diary book and have known what was in it.

So when that Baldlow scheme took shape in Nordon's mind, Luke was a danger. Nordon rang him with an assumed voice to make sure Luke would be in later. Then he told him something. What? Frankly I don't know, but probably that we wanted help, but very much on the quiet, and Luke was to come at once to Maverton and Nordon would meet him there and have a conference. It had to be all very hush-hush. So Nordon drove his own car to some lonely spot near where the side road met the Maverton Road. He'd probably taken the car out earlier and left it parked somewhere. He had with him a doped flask of whisky. It'd be cold in either car and Luke would like a good nip. After that there was only to drive the car on and send it and Luke over the cliff. Nordon would have known from the weather forecast that there would be fog. An empty quartern bottle was left in Luke's car. Nordon then had ample time to get back before seven o'clock, fog or no fog, to Seahurst.

So Nordon would hang for Baldlow and not for both Baldlow and Luke. But what did it matter? It'd be the same drop on an early morning.

But there was something else I hadn't told Jewle, and because it seemed unnecessary—just what it was that I'd said to Nordon. But you'll hear about that later. All I will say is that the following morning Jewle rang me to say he'd decided to act upon the lines I'd suggested. After that I'd only to wait. Each day the reports on Nordon's condition were better, and I still couldn't help wondering why he hadn't tried to do away with himself. But maybe Jewle's men at his bedside were attending to that.

Then the day came when Jewle told me that I had been right. Nordon had been charged and had said he was pleading guilty to killing Baldlow. Every effort would doubtless be made—as it always was—to make him change his mind before the trial.

"I'm sure he won't," Jewle said. "I'd like to know what it was you told him that evening. It's certainly clammed down those jaws of his pretty tight."

That was all I wanted to know. I rang Charles Tinley first, if only as a matter of curiosity.

"Can you spare me a few minutes if I slip along at once?" I asked him.

"Sorry, I'm really busy," he told me just a bit abruptly.

"This afternoon?"

"Sorry—not this afternoon."

"Not too busy to discuss the contents of a certain letter?"

That shook him.

"What d'you mean?"

"You know," I said. "I'll be round inside half an hour."

I wasn't kept waiting more than a very few moments and that was only for show. He didn't look too pleased when I was shown in. He half rose as a matter of perfunctory courtesy and then sank back again in the swivel chair, finger-tips pressed tightly together.

"Isn't all this rather high-handed?"

"Not a bit of it," I said. "I'm bringing you good news. It's strictly confidential, but the police know your uncle's murderer."

"Really?" He actually smiled. He pushed the silver cigarette box towards me. "Not that I was worrying. I told you I knew nothing about it."

"At any rate you ought to be glad you won't be bothered any more," I said. "All that's left is that letter you got from your uncle. Like to tell me about it? In the strictest confidence."

"My God, you've got a nerve!" he said. "I told you what was in the letter."

"But only part," I said. "I'd hate to go to the police with what I know. They'd only start digging down into things again. Believe me, by the time they'd finished they'd even know your daily rate of diapers when you were a baby."

"And what *do* you know?"

"You tell me," I said. "I repeat, in the strictest confidence."

"You're to be trusted," he said. "I've made enquiries about you—but not so far as that." He smiled, but it was to himself. "Someone got the idea I'd been smuggling. A clumsy bit of work."

"News to me," I said. "But hadn't you?"

"I certainly hadn't. It's a mug's game. Financial and social suicide if you're caught."

"Yes," I said. "And you couldn't have been dodging income tax? Keeping two sets of books."

"Don't make me laugh. I'd rather be grilled by the Customs and Excise people than those fellows."

"What about switching export licences?"

It was the last bluff I could put up and I'd tried to make my look searching. I knew I'd rung a bell. He got to his feet. He pretended to flick some ash from his coat and trousers.

"If you think that, then you'll think anything," he told me. "Sorry, but nothing doing. What passed between me and the late uncle—if anything—is our business."

And that was all I was ever to know. That it was something to do with a switching of export stuff to the home market seemed most likely, and Baldlow might have got hold of it through another director. But, as I said, for once I had to let curiosity continue to gnaw.

Just before midday I managed to get hold of Tom Howell. I told him I wanted to see him on a matter of urgent business. It was Tinley all over again. He was very busy and hadn't we concluded all business? We'd received his cheque, and he'd had a receipt.

"I still want to see you," I said. "Believe me it's for your own good and the good of your wife."

"What d'you mean?"

"You know and I know," I said. "I shall be at that halfway private hotel where we met before. We'll say three o'clock."

"Don't know what you're getting at," he said, "but I'll try to make it."

He made it. It was just after three so I ordered tea for both of us. It was an excuse for using the hotel and for waiting till we were alone and in an atmosphere conducive to talk. I wouldn't say a word about my business till the tea had come and the waiter had gone.

"Now," I said. "You tell me just why you shot Nordon."

"Nordon! Who the devil's Nordon?"

"I'm telling you," I told him patiently. "You never saw him in your life and he'd never seen you. He wasn't at The Croft that afternoon when you came there. He was with the police making a statement: a false statement if you like. It was he, as you've probably guessed, who killed Baldlow. The police have him but he'll plead guilty. Your name won't come out. But you can thank your stars he didn't die."

"Well, that's good hearing," he told me grudgingly. "But you mentioned shooting."

"I won't get up and leave you to stew in your own juice," I had to tell him. "I like you, Howell. I might have acted as you did. I'm regarding you as still a client of mine. No single word you tell me will ever go outside this room."

It was like drawing an elephant's tooth with a pair of sugar-tongs, but I broke him down at last, and only because I could show him that there was little about himself and his wife that I didn't know.

"This was how it was," he said. "My wife's offhand about money matters. She likes everything invested and sometimes she's overdrawn. I know managers are supposed to keep clients' business inviolate but our manager has a confidential arrange-ment with me. He gives me the tip when Jane's account—mind if I call her that?—is getting low and then I sweeten it. My money or hers—what's it matter. Well, to cut a long story short, he let me in on something peculiar. She wanted a thousand pounds in small, used notes, and in a hurry, and he was to sell some stock. It was good stock, splendidly invested, and he thought I ought to know about it on the quiet.

"That was only part of it. I knew from various signs that something was in the wind. Then she said she had to do some shopping in town. I drove her, deliberately early, to the station, and she told me not to wait. I didn't. I drove off and nipped back and got on that train without her seeing me. I followed her when she got out at Charing Cross. She was evidently early for her appointment and she did some window-shopping. At half-past one or soon after she went into the Metropolitan. I was behind her. I saw her go into a certain room which was opened for her. I went into the bathroom next door and tried to listen with my ear against the wall. I heard voices and no more, but I could tell my wife was very distressed.

"It was not till just before two that she came out and I saw her through a slit in the door. Her handbag was very much thinner. I'd brought my little automatic with me, and I went to the door she'd come out of and tapped at it. A voice said, 'Who's that?' I put on a falsetto and said the chambermaid. I was told to wait a moment, then the door was just opened. I hurled my weight against it and I had the little gun in my hand.

"I shut the door and backed him across the room. He had a kind of mask thing in his hand and I ripped it out. On the bed was the money my wife had brought, covered with a scarf. As I uncovered it he sprang at me and I let him have it. It was me or him. I pocketed the money, heaved him round to face the door, peeped out to see if the coast was clear and then walked off down the stairs. I took a train to Tonbridge and a private car from there and was home when Jane got there."

"And she told you about—things?"

"Yes." He hesitated for a moment. "I had to ask her to."

"And it'll make no difference to you?"

His eyes narrowed.

"Good God, what sort of a swine do you think I am?"

"Not that sort," I said.

"No," he said, and nodded slowly to himself. "Poor little devil. Keeping that to herself all these years."

"Tell me just one thing," I said. "Was that first baby still-born?"

"Thank God it was."

After that we talked on, but easily, like two old friends who have shared a common danger. It was almost five o'clock when I started back.

I must have been very quiet that night as I sat ostensibly over a book. Bernice was knitting and reading assiduously at the same time, so maybe she just hadn't time for me too. But my mind was full of the tragedy of young Nordon: the waste of all that might have been so fine. Maybe it was his mother who should have been hanged.

And I was thinking of those two minutes I'd spent with him alone. My fear had been that he'd brazen things out when he began to realise that the police were really on to him. He'd deny the murder, in fact, and own up to attempted blackmail, for though he'd never seen Tom Howell he'd have guessed who he was. Mind you, I wasn't sure of the attitude of Jane Howell and her husband when I walked into that private ward for my two minutes, and so I had to put up a bluff. You might give it a far worse name, but is there any trick so dirty that it ought to be banned for the trapping of murderers?

I've heard that a sports' commentator in full blast can get three hundred words on the air per minute. I didn't talk that fast. What I did was to sit by his bed the way his head was facing, and then just say nothing at all. Very soon that look was on his face: the wonder if I'd been sent to break the news that he wasn't going to recover after all. Then I talked with my month at his ear.

"I've got you myself, Nordon, for Luke Layman's murder. On the way to Maverton he remembered that another firm had sounded him about a job, so he rang them and said he was just going to Maverton to do what'd be probably a temporary job for us. That ties you in.

"But I'm not going to throw you to the police for that," I went on, "because they've got you for Baldlow's murder. O'Brien's a witness, for one thing. He saw his mother-in-law go out that Saturday because he was sneaking into the tool-shed to borrow a special tool he wanted, and then he saw you nip back and open that window. And the police know how you got hold of Morris's name. And the two Howells are giving evidence; even the husband who shot you."

I let that sink in. The fear on his face wasn't for death in that bed but already he was looking ahead to the early morning walk and the long drop.

"Do a decent thing for once in your life," I told him. "I'll keep Luke out of things if you do. No need to drag his name in, or the Howells. Plead guilty to Baldlow's murder. Take what's coming to you. Is that a bargain?"

His lips finally moved but I couldn't see that they shaped a yes. But I thought I saw the answer in his eyes.

"I'm trusting you for that much," I told him as I rose. "Don't forget there'll be a man at this bedside from now on."

I left him there, deathly white and eyes still wrinkling with the fear that was still on him. As I went out of the door and Jewle's man came in, I took a last look at him, and, for the life of me, all I could feel was an enormous pity. You see, I'd liked him. Perhaps something in him had brought back my own vanished young manhood.

Now as I sat looking into that fire—knowing as I did that he was prepared to plead guilty to Baldlow's murder—I couldn't help seeing that other side of him: not the smile and the charm but the shallowness and the self-interest. I wondered if he'd been still romanticising himself by doing that final and decent thing. Or perhaps he was never intending to take that last morning walk and feel a rope round his neck. In him, and in spite of Jewle's man or men, there'd still be a confidence that even if it were by suicide he could still cheat the gallows.

That made me think about Jewle, and I winced as I wondered if he had thought I was putting on an act of omniscience when I had told him all about Nordon. Perhaps he hadn't. I didn't know. I only know that I sat there, staring at that fire and seeing in it the faces of this one and that who'd been a part of that tragedy, while somewhere in the far background was the faintest clicking of knitting-needles.

THE END

Printed in Great Britain
by Amazon